HOODWINK

HOODWINK

BILL PRONZINI

PaperJacks LTD.

TORONTO   NEW YORK

PaperJacks

HOODWINK

PaperJacks LTD.

330 STEELCASE RD. E., MARKHAM, ONT. L3R 2M1
210 FIFTH AVE., NEW YORK, N.Y. 10010

PaperJacks edition published March 1987
2nd printing April 1987

This is a work of fiction in its entirety. Any resemblance to actual people, places or events is purely coincidental.

ISBN 0-7701-0549-1
Printed in U.S.A.

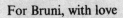

For Bruni, with love

ONE

I was sitting tilted back in my office chair, reading one of Russell Dancer's private eye stories in a 1948 *Midnight Detective,* when the door opened and Russell Dancer walked in.

Coincidences happen now and then; I knew that as well as anybody after the Carding/Nichols case I had been involved in a few months ago. But they still jar you a little every time. I opened my mouth, closed it again, blinked a couple of times, and then got on my feet as he shut the door.

"Hey there, shamus," he said. He came through the rail divider, gave the scattered cardboard packing boxes a curious glance, and plopped the briefcase he was carrying down on the visitor's chair. "Remember me?"

"Remember you? Hell, I was just reading one of your old pulp stories."

"You kidding?"

"Not a bit." I held the magazine out for him to look at. "One of the Rex Hannigan novelettes."

Dancer glanced at the title above the interior illustration, and his sardonic mouth got even more sardonic. " 'There'll be a Hot Crime in the Old Tomb Tonight!' Frigging editors loved pun titles in those days—the worse the better."

I said, "Bad title, maybe, but a good story," as we shook hands.

"If you say so. I wouldn't recognize a word of it after all these years."

"Don't you ever reread your early work?"

"I don't reread what I wrote six days ago," he said. "Besides, all my pulps went up in the fire, remember?"

I remembered. It had been almost seven years ago, down the coast a hundred miles or so at a village called Cypress Bay. A woman named Judith Paige had hired me to follow her husband because he kept disappearing on weekends and she suspected he was seeing another woman. Paige led me to Cypress Bay—and straight into a nasty triple murder that revolved around tangled relationships out of the past and a twenty-year-old paperback mystery written by Dancer. The novel, through no fault of his own, had almost cost him his life—no doubt would have if he'd been home at his beach shack, instead of celebrating the completion of his latest Western with a bottle and a woman, the night it was deliberately set ablaze.

"You didn't replace any of the books and magazines you lost?" I asked him.

"No."

"How come?"

"Too much trouble," he said. "I used to keep file copies of most of my published shit, but I kind of lost interest after the fire." He shrugged. "Guy who wrote all that early stuff is dead and gone anyway."

Still the same old Dancer, I thought. Bitter, cynical, full of self-mockery and something that approached self-loathing. He had cared once; you could tell that, and how much talent and promise he'd had by reading the pre-1950 Hannigan stories. But that had been a long time ago, a lifetime ago, before a combination of things only he could understand had soured and blighted him.

If he cared for anything now, it was probably money and liquor. He was sober enough at the moment, but there was the faint smell of bourbon on his breath that said he had drunk his lunch and maybe his late-afternoon snack as well. And he had all the physical signs: ruptured blood vessels in his nose and cheeks; the grayish dissipated appearance of his skin; the washed-out blue-gray pupils and bloodshot whites of his eyes. He was at least fifteen pounds thinner than I recalled, and starting to lose some of his dust-colored hair.

He had to be about sixty now, and he looked every year of it—every hard, unhappy year.

Some of what I was thinking must have shown in my face. Dancer grinned at me in a lopsided way, without humor. "Pretty sorry specimen, right?" he said.

"Did I say that?"

"You didn't have to." He shrugged again. "All writers are drunks, you know. Would-be, borderline, confirmed, sodden, reformed; one stage or another. All drunks, every damned one of us."

I had no comment to make on that. Instead I said, "Things been that tough for you lately?"

"They couldn't get much tougher. I haven't made a dime in five months or written much of anything in four. Not because I can't write any more; because I can't sell any more."

"Why is that?"

"Market's tightened up. Competition is stiff from top to bottom, so most of the old-line hacks like me have been squeezed out. Lots of hackwork being published, but it's either big, specialized crap on assignment or through packagers, or it's genre stuff done by stable hacks. Not much chance of me getting into one of the stables today; paperback editors are all twenty-five-year-old English Lit majors who never read a goddamn word of paperback fiction before they were hired. They build up their own stables; they only use upward-mobile hacks. My agent's trying to work out a deal with one of them now—a series of heavy-breathing adult Westerns at three grand a crack. Pun intended. But it'll never happen."

"So how are you getting by?"

"Scraping, brother. I gave up my apartment three months ago and moved in with a lady friend."

"In Cypress Bay?"

"Near there. In Jamesburg. But she's not too well off either. She'll throw me out sooner or later if I don't bring some bread into the house."

I didn't say anything.

He lit a cigarette, threw the match in my wastebasket, and glanced around the office. "Doesn't look like you're exactly in the chips yourself," he said.

"Well, I'm not starving."

"Then how come the packing boxes?"

"I'm moving next week, not being evicted."

"Better digs?"

"A little better, yeah."

"Glad to hear it," he said. "This place is like something out of a forties pulp, you know that? One of the Hannigan stories, maybe. Private eye in a shabby office with stains all over the walls, sitting around waiting for clients to walk in. You wouldn't happen to have an office bottle, would you?"

"No," I said.

"Too bad."

"Sure." I had begun to feel a little uncomfortable, and I guess that showed in my face, too. Dancer gave me another of his sardonic grins.

"Don't worry, I didn't come all the way up here to put the bite on you," he said. "I'm not that desperate. Not yet, anyhow."

"Just to say hello, huh?"

"Nope. I'm in town for the convention."

"What convention is that?"

"The pulp convention, what else?"

"Oh?"

"You mean you don't know about it? As into pulps as you are?"

"I've been pretty involved the past couple of weeks," I said. "Fill me in; it sounds interesting."

"Not much to it. Bunch of pulp collectors and fans got together and decided to put on a convention. Going to be an annual event if they don't lose too much money on this first one. You know the kind of thing: panel discussions, speeches, dealers selling old pulps and books, kids running around asking you for autographs. Guy I know dragged me to a science fiction con about ten years ago. Bored the hell out of me, but I guess some people get off on them."

"Why go to this one, then?"

"Because I'm getting paid for it," Dancer said. "Not much—what they call an honorarium—but it's enough to bring me up here for three days. Besides, it's kind of a re-union."

"Reunion?"

"You ever hear of the Pulpeteers?"

"No. What's that?"

"A private writers' club back in New York in the forties. Only those of us who wrote or worked on the pulps could join; more of an excuse to get together once or twice a month and booze it up than anything else. We had maybe a dozen members at one time or another. Some of them are dead now—only eight of us left."

"And all eight are coming to this pulp convention?"

"Right," Dancer said. "Don't ask me how Lloyd Under-wood—he's the head of the convention committee—managed to dig up all of us, but he did it."

"Anyone else whose name I'd know?"

"Probably. Bert Praxas, Waldo Ramsey, Jim Bohannon, Ivan and Cybil Wade, Frank Colodny."

I recognized all of those names. It was a pretty impressive list; the first five were a kind of Who's Who of pulp writers in the forties, and the sixth, Frank Colodny, had been a well-known editor of the Action House line of pulps.

I said, "All of them don't live in California now, do they?"

"No. Convention people flew Bohannon in from Denver, Praxas from New York, and Colodny from Arizona. Most of us arrived last night."

"When does the convention start?"

"Officially, it starts tomorrow. But there's a get-acquainted party tonight at the hotel, for the Pulpeteers and some of the convention people. I can get you in if you're interested."

"I'm interested. Which hotel?"

"The Continental."

"Is that where you're staying?"

"Right. Room six-seventeen."

"How many days does it run?"

"Until Sunday." Dancer fumbled inside the rumpled sports jacket he was wearing and came out with an ocher-colored brochure printed, appropriately, on pulp paper. "Here's the program they sent me. It'll tell you when the panels are scheduled, what they'll be about."

"Thanks. I'll read it later."

He jabbed out his cigarette in the ashtray I keep on the desk for clients and promptly lit another one. I watched him without a trace of envy. It had been almost two years since I'd quit smoking because of a lesion on one lung that had turned out to be benign—this time. I seldom even thought about cigarettes any more.

There were a dozen or so seconds of silence. Then Dancer waved his hand in a deprecating way, as if he were annoyed with himself, and said, "Ah hell, I'm jerking you around here. I didn't just drop by because of the convention. There's something else."

"Uh-huh," I said.

"You figured I was after something."

"I figured."

"Not much gets by you, right?"

"Me and Hannigan," I said.

That got me a rumbly laugh. "Okay. I don't want much; just a favor."

"What kind of favor?"

"Do a little snooping for me."

"What kind of snooping?"

"There's something screwy going on and I want to find out what it is. I can't pay you anything, you know that. But you're going to be there anyway, and I can introduce you around, give you a chance to rap about pulps with me and the other old farts."

"Tell me what's going on that's screwy."

"I can do better than that," he said. "I'll show you."

He hoisted the briefcase onto my desk, unlatched it, and took out a nine-by-twelve manila envelope. "This came in the mail three days ago. Take a look."

I opened the envelope and withdrew its contents—the photocopy of an old forty-page manuscript carbon. You could tell it had been copied from an old carbon from the dog-ears, tears, and faded and smeared typeface. In the middle of the topmost sheet was a one-word title: "Hoodwink." No author's name or address appeared in the upper left-hand corner of that sheet nor any of the others.

"It's a novelette," Dancer said. "Set in England in the Victorian era. Psychological suspense, not too bad. You remember a big-budget Hollywood flick came out in 1952, called *Evil by Gaslight?*"

"Vaguely."

"Well, the movie was written by somebody named Rose Tyler Crawford. Supposed to be an original screenplay, not adapted from any other medium. But the plot of the movie and the plot of this story are identical. Only difference is the title and the names of the characters."

"Plagiarism?"

"So it would seem." Dancer took something else out of the briefcase—a plain piece of white paper this time—and handed it over to me. "This came with the manuscript," he said.

It was a letter, typed in business format, on a different typewriter from the manuscript, and addressed to Dancer. It said:

> Enclosed is a copy of an original manuscript entitled "Hoodwink" which I have in my possession. Also in my possession is proof that you are the one who plagiarized it and sold it to Hollywood under the name Rose Tyler Crawford and the title *Evil by Gaslight.*
>
> Bring five thousand dollars ($5,000) with you to the pulp convention in San Francisco. In cash, small bills only. I will contact you there. If you do not bring the money, I will notify your agent and all your publishers that you are a plagiarist. I will also notify the film company which produced *Evil by Gaslight,* and turn over all material in my possession to the newspapers.

There was no signature written or typed.

When I looked up Dancer said, "Well?"

"That's my line," I said. "*Are* you Rose Tyler Crawford?"

He made a snorting sound. "Christ, no. I wish I had been, though. Whoever she is or was, she probably made a potful."

"Then what's the point of trying to extort money·from you?"

"You tell me. That's why I want you to snoop around."

"Maybe it's not extortion," I said. "Maybe it's somebody's idea of a practical joke."

"I doubt that; I don't know anybody clever enough or smartass enough. It might be a publicity stunt for the convention, too—but I talked to Lloyd Underwood and a couple of others this morning, and they say they don't know anything about it. I don't see that they'd lie if they did know."

"Why did you think it might be a publicity stunt? There'd be no guarantee you'd make it public. And besides, one incident like this wouldn't be enough to attract attention to a pulp convention."

"How about *five* incidents like this?"

"What?"

"I talked to the rest of the Pulpeteers, too," Dancer said. "Seems I'm just one of a crowd. Each of them also got photocopies of 'Hoodwink' and extortion letters identical to mine."

TWO

We spent another fifteen minutes kicking it around. It was
screwy, all right. Why would anybody accuse six different
writers of plagiarizing the same manuscript and then try to
extort money from each one? And why wait thirty years after
the alleged plagiarism took place to make the accusations
and the demands? It could be some sort of mass extortion
ploy; but the only way one of those can work is if each of the
potential victims thinks, first, that the extortionist really does
have something incriminating against him, and second, that
he's the only one being victimized. All six of the Pulpeteers
could hardly be plagiarists. And the extortionist had to
know—at least he did if he was sane—that one of the six
would be sure to mention it to another, and pretty soon
everybody would know everybody else had been approached. Nobody was going to pay off under those circumstances.

So what was the point of it all?

According to Dancer, none of the others had any more of
an idea than he did. All of the envelopes, as far as he'd been
able to determine, had been mailed in San Francisco, which
meant that any one of several million people, including the
convention organizers and a few dozen friends, relatives, and
casual acquaintances of the six writers, might be guilty. The
"Hoodwink" novelette had been unfamiliar to everyone, although they all remembered *Evil by Gaslight*; the movie still
ran pretty often on TV. The author's style had also been
unfamiliar—probably that of a beginner, they all agreed,
rather than an established professional.

9

Most of the Pulpeteers were inclined to shrug the whole thing off as the work of a crank, but at the same time they were curious and maybe just a little uneasy. Unusual or abnormal behavior, particularly by a party or parties unknown, always tends to make people nervous. So when Dancer had mentioned my name to them, the consensus was that it might not be a bad idea to have somebody around who was both a detective by profession and a knowledgeable pulp collector by avocation.

"Whoever's behind this might not even be at the convention, you know," I said. "Chances are it's all some sort of hoax and you'll never hear from 'Hoodwink' again."

Dancer said, "But suppose one of us does hear from him?"

"Well, that's a bridge to cross if we come to it."

"Then you'll snoop for us?"

"Sure, I'll do what I can. You've got me curious too, now. Just don't expect too much of me wandering around the convention. If I can do anything at all, it'll probably be through channels."

"What channels?"

"I know a guy down in Hollywood," I said, "who knows some people in the movie industry. He might be able to dig up something on the background of *Evil by Gaslight*—something on Rose Tyler Crawford—that'll tie in with this extortion business."

Dancer liked that approach and said so. Then he looked at his watch, wetting his lips the way a man does when he's thirsty. "Hey, almost five o'clock," he said. "I've got to be moving."

I nodded. "Okay if I hang onto the manuscript? I'd like to read it so I know what I'm dealing with."

"Sure, go ahead."

I asked him about the party tonight, and he told me it started at eight o'clock in Suite M on the fifteenth floor of the Continental. Another handshake, and off he went to do something about his thirst. When he was gone I went and did something about mine too: poured myself a fresh cup of coffee from the hotplate I keep on the file cabinet.

The hotplate was brand new; the old one, the one I'd bought when I first rented this office twenty years ago, had been badly damaged during that Carding/Nichols case a few months back. The whole office had been badly damaged—torn apart, raped, by a paranoid psychotic who thought my investigative efforts were part of a complex and nonexistent persecution plot. So to go along with the new hotplate, I also had a new desk and chair from a secondhand office-supply company, my old desk and armchair having been scarred and slashed beyond repair. I even had a new poster of my favorite *Black Mask* cover to replace the one that had been ripped off the wall and shredded out of its frame.

It was the same office I had worked in for two decades and yet it wasn't.

The new furniture did not look or feel right. The walls and floors still bore the stains of splashed coffee and spilled white glue—the stains Dancer had mentioned earlier. They were a reminder of the rape, and a reminder, too, of Taylor Street and the deteriorating Tenderloin that lay outside. No, it wasn't the same anymore and hadn't been for months. Hadn't been, maybe, for some time before the violation.

And that was why I had finally decided it was time for a change. Time to find a new office in a safer building in a neighborhood that would inspire rather than diminish confidence in potential clients. Time to take a step up in the world, or at least a step sideways into a better environment. Time to put on the front of a higher class private detective, as befitted what some local yellow journalist had called "the last of the lone-wolf private eyes."

My new offices were on Drumm Street not far from the waterfront. The building had been renovated a couple of years ago, and I would have two large, cheery rooms instead of this dreary one-and-an-alcove. The location, in an area more or less surrounded by the financial district, the waterfront docks and warehouses, Embarcadero Center, and the Ferry Building, was attractive and easy to get to. And the best part was, the rent amounted to only forty dollars a month more than I was paying here after the latest increase.

I was all set to move in any time after next Monday, which was the last day of the month. A two-year lease had been signed, and I had given notice to the landlord here; all I had to do was pack up everything that belonged to me and then make arrangements with one of the smaller moving companies to transfer boxes and furniture.

And yet I kept putting off the packing job. I had brought the boxes in three days ago, and I'd had plenty of free time since then, most of which I had spent, as usual, reading pulp stories by Russ Dancer and his peers. Maybe I was just lazy. But more likely it was psychological: giving up a place where you've spent a substantial part of your life, a place full of memories more pleasant than unpleasant, is something that does not come easy to somebody with my temperament.

I would have to do it before next Tuesday, but now I had an excuse not to do it at all this week. For the next three days, I would be rubbing elbows with pulp writers at the Hotel Continental. I would not really be working, because I wasn't getting paid, but that was all right. Next week I could pack boxes and finally get out of here and into my new offices; next week I could worry about building an image as a better-class private eye and also start making lots of money—enough, maybe, to get myself some fancy electronic surveillance equipment, not to mention a sexy secretary.

Right, Mr. Marlowe?

You bet, Mr. Spade.

I carried the coffee back to my desk and sat down with it and the copy of "Hoodwink." The style in which the manuscript was written was not my cup of tea: florid descriptive passages, some of them a little stilted; arch dialogue and not much in the way of action. But for all that, there was power in the words—a kind of brooding and atmospheric sense of evil that hooked you and kept you hooked from the opening paragraph—

> The hansom cab drifted spectrally out of the fog-enwrapped London night, its horse's hooves clattering upon the cobblestones, the crack of its driver's whip not

unlike the snapping of a condemned man's neck on the gallows at Newgate Prison. When it drew to a halt before the entrance to No. 7 Kingswood Crescent, the silence which settled around it seemed to possess a sudden sinister breathlessness. The tall man who alighted drew his cloak about him, stood peering up at the great house through its garlands of clinging mist. In that moment of silent motionlessness, man and hansom had the aspect of two-dimensional shadows newly sketched on night's dark canvas, with ink still wet and glistening.

to the final paragraph—

The identity of that caped figure sent her reeling away toward the open window and the darkness beyond. The stationary objects in the room seemed to swirl past her, shading into distorted and colorless images much like those in a surrealist composition. The darkness reached out for her, yet she was no longer afraid of it. Fearful darkness? No! Merciful darkness. Darkness, her last lover. And when it embraced her in that first instant of weightless descent toward the black waters far below, she cried out not in terror but in ecstasy at the fulfillment of the dark promise which now, at long last, would be hers.

The plot was solid and cleverly worked out: a psychological study of two women and a man, one of whom was a murderer, living in the London of 1895, and of a mysterious fourth person—a caped figure—who wasn't identified until the last page. That final revelation was surprising in print, but cinematically it had been stunning—the main reason why *Evil by Gaslight* had been such a box-office success in its time.

I hadn't seen the movie for a while, and then in an edited version for TV, but its plot and that of "Hoodwink" struck me, as they had Dancer and the other Pulpeteers, as being identical. So did some of the more memorable passages of dialogue. Which started me wondering if maybe the novelette had been written *after* the film instead of before it—if "Hoodwink" was the plagiarism, copied as a prose work for the purpose of extortion. But even if that were the case, the mechanics of the scheme still escaped me. How could you collect extortion money by accusing six different writers of a thirty-year-old act of plagiarism none of them could have committed?

I studied the extortion letter again, but it didn't tell me anything more than it had the first time. So much for research. I put letter and manuscript back into the envelope, pulled the phone and my address file over in front of me, and called Ben Chadwick down in Hollywood.

Chadwick, like me, was a private investigator. Unlike me, he specialized in work for the major film companies—investigating property-room and backlot thefts, insurance claims against the studios, missing actors or actors' relatives, things like that. I had met him a few years ago on a routine case, and he had looked me up once when he was in San Francisco; we were friendly enough for me to ask a favor and him to do it if he was free.

He was in, free, and willing. When I explained the situation, he said that offhand he couldn't remember any sort of scandal connected with *Evil by Gaslight* or even anything memorable from behind-the-scenes. Sounded like a nut thing to him, he said, but he'd see what he could come up with by the first of next week.

After we'd rung off, I picked up the convention brochure Dancer had given me. They had quite a program mapped out for the three-day con. There were two panel discussions on Friday, two on Saturday, and one on Sunday morning; there were cocktail parties on Friday evening and Saturday evening, a banquet Saturday night, and a Sunday luncheon; and there was a pulp art show, a screening of the old *Shadow* film serial with Victor Jory and another of *The Maltese Falcon*, and a special auction of more than fifty rare and valuable pulps.

The first of Friday's panels was called "Weird Tales and the Shudder Pulps" and would be chaired by Ivan Wade, whose specialty during the late thirties and throughout the forties had been some of the grisliest horror fiction ever set down on paper. He was also something of an authority on occult themes and stage magic, the brochure said. Bert Praxas would head the second panel that day, about "The Super Heroes," a topic on which he was well qualified. He had written some 130 full-length novels between 1939 and 1951 about a crimefighter called The Spectre, one of the era's rivals to The Shadow, Doc Savage, and Operator #5.

Saturday's panels were "The Western and Adventure Pulps," chaired by Jim Bohannon, one of the most prolific writers in each of those categories; and "The Pulp Editor Versus the Pulp Writer," headed by Frank Colodny. The final, Sunday morning, panel was the one that most interested me: "The Hard-boiled Private Eyes," with co-chairpersons Russ Dancer, Waldo Ramsey, and Cybil Wade, Ivan's wife. Dancer's qualifications were obvious, as were Ramsey's —I recognized his name as a semiregular contributor to *Midnight Detective*, one of Colodny's Action House pulps, and others such as *Black Mask* and *New Detective*; he had also become a successful suspense novelist in recent years. But I didn't know what Cybil Wade was doing there until I read her list of credits and discovered, with some amazement, that she was Samuel Leatherman.

If I had been asked to name the best writer of pulp private-eye fiction after Hammett and Chandler, I would have said Samuel Leatherman without having to think twice. The Leatherman stories, all of which featured a tough, uncompromising detective named Max Ruffe, had run in *Black Mask, Dime Detective*, and occasionally *Midnight Detective* throughout the forties. They were lyrical studies in violence, poetic in the same way Hammett and Chandler were poetic, with more characterization and insight than any five average pulp stories. But they were *male* stories from beginning to end; the style was masculine, the appeal was masculine, even the insights were masculine. The fact that they had been written by a woman was more than a little remarkable. And it made me want to meet Cybil Wade even more than any of the others—to find out what sort of woman she was and also to find out why she had never taken Max Ruffe into book-length novels, why she had let him die along with Dancer's Rex Hannigan and so many others.

I could feel myself getting excited about the next three days, the prospect of talking with half a dozen old pulp writers—a feeling that may or may not have been childish for somebody my age, but what the hell. As Dancer had said, I was into pulps and had been for more than thirty years. I had more than six thousand of them, nearly all mystery and detective issues, in my Pacific Heights flat, and I read them with a great deal of pleasure. Psychologically, in fact, they were the reason why I had become, first, a cop and later, a private detective. Emulation: you grow up worshipping a certain kind of hero and if you can, you want to become the same sort of hero yourself. Life-imitating-art in its purest form. So here I was, living out some, if not all, of my youthful fantasies. Erika Coates, a woman I had almost married nine years ago, had been the first to point out to me that I was trying to *be* a pulp private eye—in an age when the hero was no longer fashionable, in a city that already had Sam Spade. She thought it was unhealthy and counterproductive, and maybe she was right.

But trying to be a pulp private eye made me happy; reading pulps and talking to old pulp writers made me happy. And wasn't being happy what life was all about?

Damn right it is, Mr. Marlowe.

Let's go meet some pulp writers, Mr. Spade.

THREE

The Continental was an old Victorian hotel not far from Union Square, in the heart of the city. It had been built around 1890, at no small expense, which meant that it had a pillared and frescoed and English tile-floored lobby, and ornamental Queen Anne fireplaces in every room. Although it was too small to compete with the St. Francis, the Fairmont, and the other fancy hotels, it catered to the same type of well-to-do clientele. More or less, anyway. In recent years the management had been forced to relax its standards somewhat, as a result of increased operating costs, and to allow people and events in its hallowed halls which might not otherwise have measured up. If you had suggested twenty years ago that a pulp magazine convention be held there, they would have thrown you out on your ear.

I got there a few minutes before eight, all spruced up and chewing a Clorets mint to conceal the pepperoni pizza I had had for supper, and took one of the mirror-walled elevators up to the fifteenth floor. Suite M was at the southern end; there was a table to one side of the entrance with a banner hanging from it that read: *Western Pulp Con—Private Reception.* A balding, fortyish guy in a turtleneck sweater and sports jacket was sitting behind the table, making notations on a mimeographed list. When I told him my name, he smiled broadly, letting me see an uneven set of dentures, and pumped my hand as if the two words were a hot tip on an Italian horse.

"Pleasure," he said. "Pleasure. I'm Lloyd Underwood, convention chairman. From Hayward."

"How are you, Mr. Underwood?"

"Call me Lloyd. Glad you could come. I've heard about you—before Russ Dancer mentioned you'd be coming, I mean. Spotted your name in the papers a few times. Like to see your collection one of these days. Got any good duplicates for trade?"

"Well . . ."

"Let me know if you need any pre-1930 *Black Masks*. I'm selling off part of my collection. I've got two from '27 and one from '24 with a Hammett story; all three near mint, white pages, no cover defects. I'll give you a complete list later."

"Uh, sure . . ."

"We'll have plenty of time to talk," Underwood said. "Come early tomorrow if you can. Registration starts at noon, but I'll be setting up at ten-thirty and the huckster room will be open then. You might as well have your name tag now, though."

"Name tag?"

"Have to wear one so you can attend all the events. This must be your first con." He wrote my name on a gummed label and handed it to me. "There you go. Bar's to your left as you go in. But if you like beer, there isn't any. I asked room service to send some up, but they haven't got here yet."

I nodded without saying anything, because antic types like him tend to make me inarticulate, and entered the suite through the half-open doors. It was one big room about the size of a cocktail lounge, divided into three sections by two pairs of circular pillars. Rococo chandeliers hung from the ceiling, and there were two Queen Anne fireplaces, one at each side wall; the whole of the end wall facing the entrance was windows, some of them open to let in the mellow summery air San Francisco gets in late May. Heavy Victorian furniture was placed at strategic locations so you could sit and admire the view. And it was some view, too, particularly on a night like this: Twin Peaks to the west, the glistening black of the Bay, and the mosaic of city lights in between.

There were about twenty people standing or sitting together in small groups, making party noises and bending party elbows. None of them paid much attention to me as I wandered through, although I did get a somewhat lengthy glance from a tall, good-looking woman with coppery hair. But that was probably because I almost bumped into her and knocked her down, which is what happens to clumsy people who try to walk, peel the paper backing off a name tag, and look for a familiar face all at the same time.

I found Dancer holding up one of the pillars, talking to a scrawny guy about sixty with turkey wattles and the kind of suntan you don't get on a three-week vacation. Dancer was saying something about Norbert Davis being the only pulp writer who could be funny and hard-boiled at once, but the scrawny guy did not seem to be listening. He wore a worried and preoccupied expression, and he kept patting the half-dozen hairs combed grid-fashion over the top of his skull—as if what he worried about was that they would fall off or disappear.

When Dancer saw me he said, "Hey, there he is, the shamus," and reached out to smack me on the shoulder. The scrawny guy swiveled his head like a startled bird and peered at me. Then he patted the six hairs again. The ice in the glass clamped in his other hand made nervous tinkling sounds.

"This is the pulp-collecting dick I told you about, Frank," Dancer said to the scrawny guy. Then to me: "Meet Frank Colodny. Meanest damn editor the pulps ever saw. Twice as mean as Leo Margulies in his heyday, and not half as decent underneath. Right, Frank baby?"

Colodny had nothing to say to that. I gave him my hand and told him it was an honor to meet him. He had been something of a scourge in his time, all right—a tough-minded, hell-raising boy wonder who had taken over a floundering *Midnight Detective* in 1942, when he was twenty-three years old and a 4-F asthmatic, and kept it—and more than a dozen other detective, Western, love, and air-war pulps—alive during the war and for nearly a decade afterward. You wouldn't guess it to look at him, but he had also had a reputation as a high-living, hard-drinking roué. Well, maybe this was what happened to high-living, hard-drinking roués: they turned into scrawny guys with turkey wattles and suntans and six hairs on their scalps. Low-living, light-drinking, near-celibate types like me might like to think so, anyway.

Colodny did not think it was an honor to meet me; he grunted something, let go of my hand the way you let go of things you don't like the feel of, and knocked back half of his drink. He still looked worried, and he still looked preoccupied.

Dancer said to me, "You know what he did when Action House collapsed in '50? Goddamnedest thing you ever heard. I still can't get over it. Tell him, Frank."

"You talk too much," Colodny said, and pushed past me and headed for the bar.

"Friendly sort, isn't he?" I said.

Dancer's mood seemed to shift from good humor to sudden anger, the way a drunk's will. And he was drunk, all right, or close to it; his eyes told you that. "He's a lousy son of a bitch."

"Why do you say that?"

"Screwed me out of a thousand bucks in the late forties, that's why. Screwed a lot of other writers, too."

"How did he do that?"

"He had ways." Dancer's hands clenched and he glared over at where Colodny was at the bar. "Lousy son of a bitch."

"Take it easy," I said. "The time to start trouble was thirty years ago, when it happened." *If* it happened, I thought. "What did Colodny do when the pulps collapsed in 1950? You started to tell me but you didn't finish it."

Mercurially, Dancer's mood shifted back to the previous good humor; the sardonic smile quirked his mouth. "Bought himself a town."

"How was that again?"

"Bought himself a town. Moved out to Arizona and bought a run-down old ghost town up in the hills some-where. Can you beat that? Isn't that the goddamnedest thing you ever heard?"

"What did he do with this ghost town?"

"Didn't do anything with it. Said he always wanted to own a town, and now he does. Named it after himself too, by God. Colodnyville. Isn't that the goddamnedest thing you ever heard?"

"He's been living in a ghost town all these years?"

"Off and on, he says. Most people have a cabin in the woods; Colodny's got a frigging ghost town in the hills. Isn't that the—"

"Yeah," I said. I was still fiddling with the name tag; the paper didn't want to come off the gummed backing. The hell with it, I thought. I did not like name tags in the first place, and besides, Dancer wasn't wearing one. I put the thing into the handkerchief pocket of my jacket, where I would be sure to forget about it.

Dancer said, "Aren't you drinking?"

"No. Lloyd Underwood told me there's no beer."

"Beer? *Booze* is free tonight, you know."

"I only drink beer."

"No kidding, huh? How come?"

A big elderly guy in a Western shirt and a string tie saved me from having to explain my drinking habits. He wandered through the crowd and between Dancer and me, presumably on his way to the bathroom; but Dancer reached out and caught hold of his forearm and stopped him.

"Jimbo," he said, "rein up a second. Want you to meet the shamus I was telling you about."

"Well," the big guy said, and a smile creased his leathery features. He was about seventy, but he stood tall and straight, with his shoulders back and his head high; you got the impression that he was a proud man. And an active one, too, who hadn't been slowed down much by age. He gave me his hand, saying, "I'm Jim Bohannon. Glad to know you."

"Same here."

"Jimbo was heir to Heinie Faust back in the forties," Dancer said. "The new Max Brand—king of the oaters."

"Horse manure." Bohannon said.

"Sure you were. Wrote a lead novel just about every month for Leo Margulies at *Thrilling* or Rog Terrill at *Popular*. How many pulp pieces you do altogether, Jimbo?"

"Oh, maybe a thousand."

"Prolific as hell. Still does a novel once in a while. Must have ground out a hundred books by now, huh, Jimbo?"

Bohannon frowned at him—but tolerantly, the way a father might at a noisy, abrasive, but still likable son. Then he looked at me again, and the easygoing grin came back. "Hell," he said, "you're not much interested in the Bohannon statistics. I understand your pulp collection is mostly mystery and detective: you've probably never read a word of mine."

"I'm interested, all right," I said, and meant it. "And I *have* read some of your work."

"Oh?"

"Sure. The series you used to do for *Adventure*, about the Alaskan peace officer in the twenties. And the series about the railroad detectives, Kincaid and Buckmaster, in *Short Stories*. Pure detective fiction, and some terrific writing."

Bohannon's grin widened. "I don't know if that's grease or not," he said, "but I like it anyhow."

"It's not grease."

"Well, thanks. It's nice to have your work remembered."

"Maybe you think so, Jimbo," Dancer said, "but not me. Who the hell really cares if you've published twenty million words and I've published maybe ten? Who cares about all the lousy stories and books we've written? They're all just so much garbage rotting away in basements and secondhand stores."

Bohannon sighed. It was obvious he'd heard that particular line, or a variation of it, before and that he'd learned the only way to deal with it was to ignore it. So it seemed like a good idea for me to help him out by changing the subject.

"About the manuscript and letter you and the others received, Mr. Bohannon," I said. "Do you think it's a serious extortion plot of some kind?"

"Oh, I doubt it. Somebody's idea of a joke, probably."

"Did the novelette ring any bells?"

"None, I'm afraid."

"Was the style at all familiar?"

"Nope," Bohannon said. He grinned. "I don't know much about Victorian melodramas; horse operas are what I like."

"Another twenty years," Dancer said, "there won't *be* any more horse operas for anybody to like. Not even any of the adult porno crap that's all over the place right now. Nothing. *Nada.*"

"Maybe not, Russ. But I'll tell you one thing there'll still be plenty of twenty years from now."

"What's that?"

"Horses' asses," Bohannon said.

It was a pretty good exit line, and Bohannon knew it; he nodded to me, showed me his grin one more time, and moved off. Dancer stared after him, but there was no anger in his expression; maybe it was only Frank Colodny who made him feel belligerent when he was tight. Then he shrugged, lifted his glass, saw it was empty, and scowled at it.

"I need another drink," he said, as if he were surprised at himself for overlooking the fact until just now.

"It's early yet, Russ."

"Damn right it is," he said, misinterpreting my meaning. "Come on, we'll get a couple of belts, and I'll introduce you to the rest of the Pulpeteers."

He turned toward the bar, walking steadily enough, and I followed and watched him tell the young guy who was tending it to pour a double Wild Turkey on the rocks. There was still no beer, it turned out. Dancer started to make a fuss about that, but I told him it didn't matter, I wasn't thirsty anyway. And prodded him aside.

But I did the prodding a little too forcefully, because he turned straight into a heavy mahogany coffee table and stumbled against its leg. Some of the liquor spilled out of his glass onto the table. The two women sitting behind it on the plush Victorian settee hopped up to keep from getting splashed; then the older of the two reached down just in time to prevent her purse, which was perched on one corner of the table, from toppling off.

Dancer recovered his balance, smiled in a wolfish way, and said, "Sorry, ladies. A slight accident."

"There's always a slight accident when you're around, Russ," the older woman said.

"Now, Sweeteyes, don't be nasty."

The woman said something to that in an undertone, but I was looking at the younger one and I didn't hear it. She was the tall, good-looking redhead I had almost run down earlier, and she was even nicer to look at up close. Not pretty in any classic sense, but still striking: animated face etched with humor lines; generous mouth, sleek jawline, dark eyes that had no makeup to accentuate them and didn't need any; slim long-fingered hands; stylish shoulder-length hairdo; willowy figure in a dark green suit. She might have been thirty-five or forty, not that it mattered.

She gazed back at me without conceit, offense, or false modesty—just a frank steady look that said she liked to be appreciated. Not eye-raped, but appreciated. "Let me guess," she said. Sexy voice too, like Lauren Bacall. "You're the private eye."

"That's me. And you're—?"

"Kerry Wade," Dancer said. "And this is Cybil Wade. Two-thirds of the Wade family. Old Ivan's around somewhere." He leered at the older woman. "Old Ivan's *always* been around somewhere, hasn't he, Sweeteyes?"

"Don't call me that, Russ," Cybil Wade said.

"Why not? Fits you."

He was right about that. Her eyes were huge, tawny-colored, guileless—sweet. Combined with dimples, the same coppery hair and willowy figure as her daughter, and a radiant smile, they gave her a kind of ingenuousness that even six decades or so of living had failed to erase. Kerry Wade was attractive, yes, but Cybil Wade was beautiful. Had been beautiful when she was young and was still beautiful right now—a sixty-year-old knockout in a white satin dress.

I touched hands with her and with her daughter, and we all said how pleased we were to meet each other. It seemed to me that Kerry's hand lingered in mine, but maybe that was just wishful thinking. And the one thing about Cybil that did not fit the sweet, wholesome image she presented was her voice: it was even sexier than Kerry's.

"Hard to believe this little doll wrote the Max Ruffe private eye stuff, isn't it?" Dancer said. "Never could get over it. Wrote just like a man—all hard-edged blood, guts, and sex."

"Not only like a man," I said. "Better than just about all of them."

Kerry's gaze was still on me, and it seemed to have some speculative interest in it. "Have you read a lot of Cybil's pulp stories?"

"Enough to put her in the same league with Chandler and Hammett. I can even quote a line from one."

"Really?" Cybil asked.

"Really. I read it five or six years ago and I've never forgotten it. 'He had a face like a graveyard at night—cold, empty, a little frightening—and when he opened his mouth, you could see stumps of teeth sticking up here and there like headstones.' "

She rolled her eyes. "My God," she said, "are you sure I wrote that?" But she sounded pleased just the same.

"Positive. I forget the title of the story, but the author was Samuel Leatherman."

Dancer said, "You always were good with the brooding metaphor, Sweeteyes. Wrote just like a man, all right. One thing, though, that you never wrote as well as a hack like me."

"What would that be, Russ?"

"A kick in the balls," Dancer said. "Only a man can do justice to a kick in the balls."

He seemed to expect some kind of reaction to that but not the one he got. Kerry and I just looked at him the way you do at somebody who makes a boorish remark at a party; but an expression of ironic amusement crossed Cybil's face, and she reached out and patted Dancer's arm like somebody patting a dog on the head.

"I'm not so sure about that. Russ." she said. "Would you like me to kick you in the balls so we can find out?"

Dancer didn't much like that; he glared at her for a long moment. I took a step toward him in case he got nasty. But then his facial muscles relaxed, and he shook his head and began to laugh.

"Any time, Sweeteyes," he said. "It might even be fun." And he laughed so hard that he banged into the coffee table again and spilled a little more of his drink. He also dislodged Cybil's purse this time, sent it off onto the floor before she could grab it. It popped open when it hit, and some things spilled out.

She bent down to it, saying, "Damn you. Russ." I started to help her, but she shook her head and did the scooping up herself.

"Sorry about that." Dancer said. "Another slight accident."

Cybil straightened up, ignoring him, and tucked the purse under her arm. "I'm going to the powder room." she said to Kerry, nodded to me, and headed toward the entrance doors.

Kerry gave me a faint smile that might have meant anything or nothing at all; then she moved to the bar. I watched the way she walked—smooth and flowing, almost catlike—but only part of my mind noted and registered it. The other part was working on something else: one of the things that had fallen out of Cybil Wade's purse, that I had glimpsed before she could shove it back inside.

What was a nice, sweet-faced lady like her doing at a party with a .38 snub-nosed revolver?

FOUR

I was still puzzling about Cybil Wade's gun when Dancer called my name. But not from close by; from across the room, where he had wandered and joined a group of three other men. He was making beckoning gestures, so I went over there before he could shout again or do something else to make a horse's ass out of himself.

"Want you to meet the last three Pulpeteers," he said when I got to him. Then he blinked a couple of times, with alcoholic surprise at what he took to be his own cleverness. "Hah! The Three Pulpeteers, by God. How about that?"

I didn't say anything. Neither did any of the three men. They were all around sixty-five, but physically, at least, age was about all they had in common. The guy on Dancer's left was tall, gray-maned, and vaguely cadaverous-looking, dressed in a dark suit and a blue tie with yellow ovals on it that looked like eyes. The guy in the middle was a head shorter, pudgy, with a Friar Tuck fringe of reddish hair, wearing a loose green turtleneck sweater and a pair of Levi's. And the guy on my right was of average height, handsome in an athletic sort of way, brown-haired and sporting a neat black mustache; he wore casual but expensive sports clothes.

Dancer performed the introductions in his mildly insulting way and managed not to spill the rest of his drink on anybody while he was doing it. If I had had to guess which was which beforehand, based on their pulp writing and on subsequent endeavors, I would have said the tall one was Ivan Wade, the pudgy one Bert Praxas, and the well-dressed one

Waldo Ramsey. And I would have been wrong three out of three.

The somewhat cadaverous guy turned out to be Praxas—an even more prolific writer than Jim Bohannon in his day, although he had been retired for close to twenty years. In addition to his novels about The Spectre, written under the house pseudonym of Robert M. Barclay, he'd done several hundred mystery and detective stories and half as many air-war adventures for *Sky Fighters* and the other aviation magazines. But The Spectre novels were far and away what he was best known and most remembered for; the brochure Dancer had given me said he'd become something of a cult figure among collectors and aficionados and often appeared at conventions of this type.

The pudgy, red-haired guy, it developed, was Waldo Ramsey. He had been something of a minor pulp writer, in the same sense that Dancer had been minor—a competent storyteller whose work for *Midnight Detective* and others was sometimes dazzling but more often careless and indifferent. But where Dancer had slid steadily downhill into hackdom, Ramsey had found himself, nurtured his talent over the years, and climbed upward into respectability and success. He had been writing suspense novels since the mid-fifties, and in the past few years had hit it semibig with a pair of ambitious espionage books that he had sold and adapted to film. Which probably explained why he was dressed as sloppily as he was: it's the people with money who can afford to dress at public functions as if they *haven't* got money.

And the athletic, mustachioed man was Ivan Wade, Cybil's husband and Kerry's father. He had a quiet, reserved sort of face, with all the features grouped in close to the center, and gentle eyes. According to the convention brochure, he had started out writing for *Weird Tales, Dime Mystery,* and other fantasy/horror pulps, and gone on from there to radio scripting, the slick magazines, some TV work, and finally to novels and nonfiction books on occult and magic themes. The things he wrote about, and the things Cybil had written about, made me wonder what it had been like for Kerry growing up. It was an irrelevant thought, but I wondered just the same.

When the introductions were over and I had finished shaking hands with the three of them, Ramsey said good-naturedly, "A pulp-collecting private eye. I never thought I'd live to see the day."

"I guess it is a little unusual," I said.

"You can say that again."

Praxas asked me, "What do you think of our little mystery? I assume Russ has filled you in on the details by now."

"Damn right I have," Dancer said.

I said, "I don't know what to think. Not yet."

"If whoever it is is serious," Ramsey said, "he's also crazy. He'd have to be to think any or all of us are plagiarists."

"Well, I suppose we'll be contacted in any case," Praxas said. He had a sepulchral voice, like John Carradine or Karloff without the lisp, that sharpened his cadaverous image; the more you looked at and listened to him, the more it seemed he ought to be the one who wrote horror fiction. He would have made a beautiful stereotype. "Should we tell you when that happens?"

"If you like," I said. "I don't know what Dancer told you, but there's really not much I can do except keep my eyes and ears open and offer advice if the need arises."

"Told them you were the best damn private eye in the business," Dancer said. "Told them you'd get to the bottom of it whether you were getting paid or not."

He was beginning to irk me. The drunker he got, the harder it was to keep on liking him. "Yeah, well, I'm not the best, and I'm not likely to get to the bottom of anything. The fact is, I'm here mostly as just another pulp fan."

"Sure you are. Best damn private eye in the business."

Ramsey said, "You're a pain in the ass, Russ, you know that?"

"Damn right I am. Best damn ass pain in the business."

Ramsey shook his head and watched Dancer knock back

what was left in his glass. Then he asked me. "You been a detective long?"

"About thirty years, public and private."

"How long collecting pulps?"

"Same."

"You go to conventions regularly?"

"No. This is my first."

"Mine too. Bert here thrives on them, you know."

"I wouldn't put it quite that way," Praxas said. "I go to conventions for the same reason I give talks at colleges and universities: I enjoy meeting fans and it helps keep my work alive. But I hardly thrive on them."

Dancer said, "Good for the old ego, huh, Bertie?"

"Yes. What's wrong with that?"

"Nothing. How about the money?"

"Money?"

"Sure. The old honorarium."

"I don't know what you mean."

"How many cons you go to in a year?"

"A half-dozen or so. Why?"

"All of them on the pulps?"

"No. Most are science fiction- or comic-oriented."

"Pay better or worse than this one?"

"About the same."

"What about the college lectures? They pay good?"

"I suppose so."

"How much per? Five hundred?"

"In most cases, yes . . ."

"Plus expenses," Dancer said. "A half-dozen cons, a half-dozen lectures, that's six grand a year. Plus expenses. By God, Bertie, it's not a bad scam. Beats hell out of beating a typewriter. Maybe I'll try it myself."

"I doubt if you could, Russ," Ivan Wade said.

"Oh, is that so? Why not?"

"Because you're an obnoxious drunk."

"Hah?"

"Convention organizers aren't interested in drunks. Neither are college faculties. And neither are the fans; they don't care to watch sodden hacks stumbling around making fools of themselves."

It got quiet among the five of us. Wade had spoken softly, evenly, but each of the words was like an arrow coated with venom. Dancer opened his mouth, closed it again as if he were still casting around inside his head for a suitable comeback. He had absorbed abusive remarks from Bohannon and Cybil Wade and Ramsey, but they had each had a bantering quality; he could deal with a few harmless insults among old cronies. But he didn't seem to know how to handle the real thing—a combination of dislike and disgust.

Ten seconds went away. And finally Dancer found words, so inadequate after all that silence that they were an anticlimax: "So I'm a drunk and a hack, Ivan, so what?"

"So nothing," Wade said. "So you're a drunk and a hack, that's all."

Dancer did not get angry, or laugh, or shrug it off. Wade's words seemed to have cut deep inside him, sliced into a nerve somewhere. Pain showed on his face, but it was not self-pity this time—it was hurt just as genuine as Wade's disgust, a reflection of the festering spiritual anguish that had made him a drunk in the first place.

His eyes shifted away from Wade, flicked over Ramsey and Praxas to me, and then focused downward on the empty glass in his hand. Without saying anything, he turned from us and went to the bar.

Ramsey said, "You put it into him kind of deep, didn't you, Ivan?"

"Did I?" Wade said. He shrugged, his face impassive. "If you'll all excuse me . . ." And he went away too, over toward the windows.

"What was that all about?" I asked Ramsey and Praxas. "Something between the two of them?"

"You could say that," Ramsey answered.

"Mind if I ask what it is?"

"It's a long story," Praxas said. "And ancient history."

Which meant that he didn't want to discuss it. Neither did Ramsey, judging from his expression. So I let it drop; it was none of my business, really. Unless it had a bearing on the extortion business, and that seemed doubtful.

Dancer came back from the bar with a fresh drink. But he didn't rejoin the three of us; he plopped himself down in a chair not far away and stared out at the mosaic of city lights. Then, almost at once, he began to sing. Not in the loud boisterous way of most drunks at a party; in a subdued and dolorous voice that barely carried to where we were standing. I could just make out the words—the same four-line, mostly Spanish verse over and over, not so much a song as a chant. Or a lament.

> "*No tengo tabaco,*
> "*No tengo papel,*
> "*No tengo dinero—*
> "*Goddammit to hell . . .*"

While the three of us were listening to that, not saying anything, Jim Bohannon came wandering over. He stopped beside me, cocked his head in Dancer's direction, and said to Praxas, "Some things don't change much in thirty years, I reckon."

"Apparently not."

Ramsey saw me looking puzzled. "Russ used to recite that verse at Pulpeteer meetings," he said, "every time he dived into the sauce. Drunker he got, the more he'd feel sorry for himself; and the sorrier he felt, the more he'd recite. Used to drive us crazy."

"Well, at least he's learned to be quiet about it," Bohannon said.

I asked, "Did he make it up himself?"

"No. It's an old cowboy lament, from down along the Mexican border—"

There was a sudden commotion behind us, in the center of the room: loud voices and the sound of glass shattering. Bohannon and I both spun around; all the party noises seemed to stop at once, including Dancer's singing. Twenty feet away two men stood facing each other, a broken high-ball glass and a streak of wetness and melting ice cubes like a dividing line on the carpet between them. One of the men was the scrawny ex-editor, Frank Colodny. The other one I didn't know; he was a dusty, sixtyish guy wearing horn-rimmed glasses and an ancient sports jacket with elbow patches.

Colodny had his right hand up, forefinger extended and shaking within an inch of the other guy's chin. His face was congested and his eyes had bright, hot little lights in them. "Stay the hell away from me, Meeker. I'm warning you."

"Say that a little louder," the man named Meeker said. He looked just the opposite of Colodny—calm and coldly deliberate. "Let everybody hear it."

"You crazy bastard—"

"Louder, Frank. Louder."

Colodny seemed to have a belated awareness of his audience; he lowered his arm, licked his lips, and backed off a step. Then he clamped his lips together, made them disappear into a thin white slash. And swung around and stalked out of the suite, brushing past a startled-looking Lloyd Underwood who had hurried in and was half blocking the entrance.

The other man, Meeker, watched him go with a faint, humorless smile plucking at the corners of his mouth. When Colodny had disappeared, Meeker sat on his heels and began to pick up the broken shards of glass. And as if that was a cue for the rest of us, the frozen tableau dissolved and people began moving around and talking again, letting the mood of the party regenerate like new skin over a minor wound.

"No tengo tabaco,
"No tengo papel . . ."

Bohannon said, "Now what the devil is Frank so heated up about?"

"That's a good question," Praxas said. "He seemed jittery and upset when he got here."

I asked, "Who's the fellow named Meeker?"

"Ozzie Meeker. An oldtimer like us."

"A writer? I don't recognize the name."

"No. An artist."

"He worked with Frank at Action House in the forties," Ramsey said. "Did most of the detective and Western covers, and some of the interior black-and-whites."

"His name wasn't in the convention brochure, was it?"

Praxas shook his head. "I understand Lloyd Underwood wasn't able to locate him until after the brochures were printed. But he's exhibiting some of his work in the Art Room."

"Nostalgia got to him, same as it got to us," Bohannon said. "He was one of us for a while, you know."

"The Pulpeteers, you mean?" I asked.

"Right. He started coming to meetings in the late forties, after he went to work for Action House. He and Colodny were always friendly back then. Wonder what set them off now, after all these years?"

Nobody seemed to know.

"No tengo dinero—
"Goddammit to hell . . ."

The little group we made began to break up one by one. Ramsey drifted off to the bar for another drink; Bohannon's wife, a pleasant gray-haired lady, came over and got him and took him away to meet someone; and one of the convention organizers, or maybe just a fan, collared Praxas and began asking him questions about The Spectre's sex life. Which left me standing by myself, listening to Dancer sing his monotonous little lament. And wondering about things like the .38 in Cybil Wade's purse, Dancer's dislike for Colodny, the sudden tension between Colodny and Meeker, the deeper-seated tension between Dancer and Ivan Wade.

Not that there was much point in my worrying about any

of it. I had no particular desire to involve myself in a lot of private, thirty-year-old interrelationships among ex-pulp writers. Despite what Dancer had gone around telling people, the old lone wolf was here to enjoy himself more than he was here to work at detection.

And one of the ways I might like to enjoy myself started toward me just then, smiling in her frank, attractive way.

Kerry Wade.

FIVE

She had a small snifter of brandy in her left hand and a bottle of Löwenbräu in her right. So when she stopped in front of me, I said with spontaneous and devastating cleverness, "Two-fisted drinker, are you, Miss Wade?"

Which probably made me seem like a half-wit. Made me feel like one, anyway, when she extended the bottle, saying, "The bartender told me you'd asked for a beer earlier. Room Service finally decided to deliver some, so I thought I'd play waitress."

I said, "Oh. Um, thanks." And thought: God, you're sharp tonight, just full of urbane remarks and sparkling repartee. No wonder you're such a hot number with the ladies—you klutz, you.

Kerry seemed faintly amused: maybe klutzes appealed to her sense of humor. "It's not Miss Wade, by the way. It's Mrs. Dunston."

"Oh," I said again.

"But I don't use the Dunston anymore. Not since my divorce two years ago."

I started to say "Oh" a third time, caught myself, and said, "So you're a divorced lady," which was even dumber.

"Mm-hmm. How about you?"

"No."

"No what? No, you're not divorced?"

"No. I mean, I'm not married."

"Never been?"

"Never been."

"A bachelor private eye," she said. "Do you carry a gun in

36

your shoulder holster and have a beautiful secretary and keep a bottle in your desk drawer?"

"No to all three."

"How come?"

"I don't like guns much, secretaries are too expensive, especially beautiful ones, and I drink only beer."

"That's better," she said.

"Better?"

"You were all flustered there for a minute. I was afraid you were one of these men who don't know how to talk to a woman. Either that, or you were gay. You're not, are you?"

"Me? God, no."

"Good."

"I wasn't flustered, either," I lied.

Her smile broadened; I was not fooling her at all.

"Are you also a writer, Miss Wade? Or should I call you Mrs. Dunston?"

"Neither one. Try Kerry. No, I'm not a writer. I had aspirations once, and maybe a little inherited talent, but my parents did everything they could to discourage me. It's probably a good thing they did."

"Why is that?"

"Being a writer isn't all people think it is."

"It's been a good business for them, hasn't it?"

"For my dad it has. At least most of the time."

"But not for your mother?"

"No. She hasn't written a word in twenty-five years."

"I didn't know that. How come?"

"She isn't able to write any more," Kerry said. Some of the lightness had gone from her voice. "She wants to, but she just can't. It's hell for her. But then, if she *was* writing that would probably be hell for her, too. It was when she was doing her pulp stories."

"I'm not sure I follow that."

"It's the nature of the business. Professional writing isn't glamorous or exciting; it's a lot of hard work, for not all that much money and no real security, and on top of that it's the loneliest profession in the world. 'Always having to live inside your own head,' is the way my father puts it. Plus it's one of the most stressful professions. That's why the percentage of alcoholics and suicides among writers is double or triple that of just about every other business."

"I didn't know that, either," I said.

"Most laypersons don't."

"Laypersons?"

"Well, nonwriters. Are you a chauvinist, by any chance?"

"Not me."

"Fictional private eyes usually are," she said, and a sort of bawdy gleam came into her eyes. "In fact, most of them seem to be obsessed with male-dominant sex. The gun they all carry is a phallic symbol, you know; every time they shoot somebody with it, it's like having an orgasm."

"Uh," I said.

She laughed. It was a nice laugh, a little bawdy to match the gleam, and it did things to what was left of my shriveled libido. No wonder she made me feel flustered; I had not slept with a woman in months, and I was not used to outspoken, attractive, horny-eyed ladies coming on to me in the first place. And Kerry Wade *was* coming on to me, no doubt about that.

Wasn't she?

I thought it might be a good idea to change the subject; otherwise I was liable to tuck my foot into my cheek in place of my tongue. "You didn't answer the question I asked a little while ago," I said. "About what you do. For a living, I mean."

Her eyes laughed at me this time. I would have given anything to know what was going on behind them, what she was thinking about me. "I'm an advertising copywriter for Bates and Carpenter."

"That's a San Francisco firm."

"One of the largest."

"Then you live in the Bay Area?"

"Here in the city. On Twin Peaks."

That surprised me a little. The convention brochure said that Ivan and Cybil Wade lived in North Hollywood, and so

I had automatically assumed Kerry was also from Southern California. There were notions in my head already, but the fact that she lived in San Francisco gave me a few more. If she really *was* coming on to me . . .

"Well," I said in my sophisticated way, "how about that?"

"Mmm. Where do you live?"

"Pacific Heights."

She raised an eyebrow. "That's a nice neighborhood."

"Yep. But it's an old building, and I've had my flat and the same benevolent landlord for more than twenty years. Otherwise I couldn't afford it."

"Do you really own twenty thousand pulp magazines?"

"Is that what Russ Dancer told you?"

"It is. Not true?"

"Not true. More like sixty-five hundred."

Mention of Dancer made me aware that he was no longer singing his little lament. I glanced over at the chair he'd been sitting in, but it was empty now; the party crowd seemed to have thinned out somewhat, and I didn't see him anywhere else in the room either. Gone to the john, maybe. Or to his own room to sleep it off. *No tengo* Dancer, in any case, and that was probably just as well.

"Looking for somebody?" Kerry asked.

"I was just wondering what had happened to Dancer."

"Don't worry about him. He'll be drunk the whole weekend, now that he's seen Cybil again, but he won't bother anybody. He seems to stop just short of being obnoxious."

"Why would seeing your mother send him on a four-day binge?"

"You mean you couldn't tell?"

"Tell what?"

"He's in love with her. He has been for thirty-five years."

"So that's it."

"He had it so bad, Cybil says, that he even tried once to talk her into divorcing my father and marrying him. That was back around 1950, just before he left New York and moved out here."

"Your father knew about this?"

"Sure. He and Cybil never had any secrets from each other."

"Well, that explains why he doesn't like Dancer," I said.

"You noticed that much, at least. Dad hates him, I think; he didn't even want to come here when he found out Dancer would be on the program. But Cybil talked him into it. It's all water under the bridge as far as she's concerned."

"Then she'd hardly be afraid of Dancer, would she?"

"Afraid of him? Lord, no. She's not afraid of anybody. She's as tough as Max Ruffe used to be in her stories."

Yeah, she is, I thought. And she's packing a rod just like Ruffe did, too. How come? I wanted to ask Kerry, but this did not seem to be the time or place to spring that kind of question. Besides which, as I kept telling myself, it was none of my business. Not unless Cybil intended to take potshots at somebody. And I doubted that.

Kerry finished what was left of her brandy, and I asked her if she'd like another. She said, "I don't think so. Two drinks are my limit on an empty stomach."

"No dinner tonight?"

"Nope. I had to work late."

"You must be pretty hungry, then."

"Getting that way. Want to buy me a sandwich?"

"Sure."

"Is that a serious offer?"

"Italians are always serious when it comes to food," I said, which was the first semiwitty line I had managed in her presence so far. "There's a coffee shop down in the lobby. Or we could go over to Rosebud's on Geary."

"Rosebud's sounds good," she said. "We'll have to stop by my folks' room first, though; I left my coat there. Just let me get the key."

I watched her move away to where Cybil and Ivan were talking to another couple, and I thought: So maybe she really is coming on to me—how about that? I felt pretty chipper. My somewhat bruised male ego had taken a much-needed stroking in the past few minutes—and never mind what it was she saw or thought she saw in me. Never mind the erotic fantasies, either, that were starting to simmer in the back of my dirty old brain. It was just nice to find an attractive woman who found me attractive in turn, even if it never led to anything more than a late-night supper at Rosebud's English pub. She made me feel awkward and comfortable at the same time, which is a stimulating way to feel, and I liked her frankness and her sense of humor and the way her coppery hair seemed to ripple with reflections of light. In fact I liked everything about her so far.

She came back after a couple of minutes, and I finished the last of my beer and we went out. On the way to the elevators I asked her, "What would you say if I told you I became a private detective because I wanted to be like the private eyes I read about in the pulps?"

"You mean tough and hard-boiled?"

"No. Just a private eye—doing a job, helping people in trouble."

"In other words, being a hero."

"Well . . . in a way, yes."

"Then I'd say you made a good choice. I'm partial to heroes myself, all kinds, even if it's not fashionable any more. The world would be a much better place if there were more heroes and fewer antiheroes. Not to mention fewer politicians."

I liked that too.

We took a down elevator and got off on the tenth floor. The Wades' room was 1017, just down the left-hand hallway—a suite, judging from the juxtaposition of numbered doors on that side. Kerry got out the key her mother had given her, scraped it into the latch, unlocked the door, and pushed it open. She reached inside for the light switch, but when she flipped it nothing happened.

"Damn," she said. "Now the chandelier doesn't work."

"Maybe there's a short."

"Well, I'd better put on a lamp for the folks. My coat's on the sofa."

She moved inside, feeling her way in the darkness. I took a step through the doorway after her and stepped to one side, so I wouldn't block the light from the hall. On the left I could make out a pale grayish oblong—part of the window over which the drapes had been half drawn. Enough reflected light from outside filtered in through there to outline the bulky shapes of furniture, to turn Kerry into a fading silhouette like a shadow image moving behind a screen—

But we weren't alone in the room.

I sensed it abruptly; there was no sound, no movement, just the sudden feeling of occupied space and another presence nearby. The realization sent a cold slithering along my spine, bunched the muscles in my arms and across my shoulders and back. I held my breath, listening. Silence except for the slide of Kerry's shoes on the thick carpet. I took another step forward, acting on reflex to get to where she was before she put on the lamp; there wasn't anything else I could do. Trying to locate whoever it was in the dark was no good, and neither was calling out a warning to Kerry.

Something made a low thumping sound. Then she said "Damn" again in an exasperated tone. "Now where's that bloody lamp—"

A stirring off to my left.

And the silhouette of a man loomed up between me and the window, head down and rushing toward me or the open door behind me.

I turned to meet him, trying to set myself, but he was there, an indistinct male shape, before I could get my feet planted; I smelled the sharp sour odor of whiskey just before he hit me with an outthrust shoulder. The force of the blow spun me half around and threw me into something, a table, and I went over it ass-sideways and down in a backward sprawl. My chin cracked against something else and for an explosive instant there were pinwheels of light behind my eyes, a ringing in my ears. Then the light and the ringing faded, and I could hear Kerry shouting my name in a stunned way, the thud of a body hitting the wall beside the door and then skidding through into the hall. I was already rolling over onto my knees; when I righted myself I had my head up and my eyes open and half focused through a haze of pain. But by then the doorway was empty and so was the corridor beyond.

The table I had fallen over was on my left; I used it as a fulcrum to shove up onto my feet. Kerry was close by, reaching toward me in the darkness, saying "My God, are you all right?" But I went away from her, struggling with my balance, still fighting off the effects of the blow to my chin, and said, "Stay here, wait inside," just before I lurched out through the door.

The hallway was empty in both directions, but he hadn't gone back the short way to the elevators. I could hear the faint echoes of somebody running down where a cross-hall intersected with this one, over in the east wing. I lumbered off that way, making snuffling and snorting sounds like an old bull until I got my breathing under control. When I got to where I could see eastward along the cross-hall, there was nothing to see: he had disappeared. But I could still hear faint running echoes, hollow-sounding now. And underneath a green exit sign, the door to a set of fire stairs was just closing on its pneumatic tube.

I knew it was no good, I'd never catch him, even before I got down there and hauled the door open. The running steps were louder in the stairwell, magnified by its narrow depth, but still fading. He was two or three floors below me already. And he could duck out on any floor he cared to, or go all the way down to the lobby or the basement parking garage, before I could get anywhere near him. There just wasn't any point in putting my paunchy fifty-three-year-old body through any more wind sprints, particularly down several flights of stairs.

I slapped the door open again, went back into the hall, and leaned against the wall to mop sweat off my face with my handkerchief. Sweat, at least, was the only wetness that came off the cloth: no blood from where I had cracked my throbbing chin.

Damn sneak thief, I thought. Sneak thieves were a problem in hotels these days. Hundreds of rooms were broken into each year in San Francisco alone, and small fortunes in cash, jewelry, clothing, and other hockable personal possessions were stolen. And security at the Continental, I had heard from one of my cop friends, was not all it could have been. Sure—a sneak thief.

Except that sneak thieves are a sober lot, at least while they're working. They need a steady hand to pick door locks and suitcase and jewelry case locks, a clear head to stay alert for returning guests or hotel employees. So how come this one had a breath like the inside of a whiskey keg? And how come he took the time to gimmick the chandelier so the lights wouldn't come on? Sneak thieves like to get into a room and out of it again with their booty in short order; they don't linger to take precautions that could backfire on them.

If not a sneak thief, then who? Rapist? Not likely. Somebody after something that belonged to the Wades, that was among their belongings? Possible. And also possible that it was somebody waiting to do harm to either or both of them, or because he wanted something from either or both of them.

I thought about the blackmail letters and the allegations of plagiarism. I thought about the gun Cybil carried in her purse. I thought about the undercurrent of tensions among the Pulpeteers—especially the tension between Ivan Wade and Russ Dancer. I thought about Kerry saying Dancer had been in love with Cybil for more than thirty years. And I thought about Dancer disappearing from the party, about all the whiskey he had poured into himself tonight, about how the moods of a drunk shift and sometimes become irrational, even violent.

Dancer? I thought.

Christ—*Dancer?*

SIX

When I got back to Room 1017, the door was still standing wide open, but there were lamps burning now on a pair of end tables. I did not see Kerry at first and I rapped on the panel and called out her name. She came hurrying out of the bedroom as I entered.

"You didn't catch him," she said in disappointed tones. Her eyes were round and dark, angry, but they softened a little as she looked at me. Which made her disappointed in the fact that the intruder had got away, not in me.

"No. Listen, you shouldn't have left the door open."

"The door? Why not? You don't think he'd come back?"

I bent over and peered at the latch. There were fresh scratch marks on its lip and on the metal plate around the opening, the kind amateurs make when they set out to pick a lock. Professionals—sneak thieves, for example—know how to use tools and seldom leave marks of any kind. I straightened again and shut the door, making sure that the lock still held.

Kerry said, "You didn't answer my question."

"I don't know what to think. Probably not, though."

She came up closer to me and touched my chin gently with the tips of her fingers; her eyes seemed to soften even more, to change shades—dark green to a light emerald green—in the lamplight. "Did this happen when you fell?"

"What is it? A bruise?"

"Just a little one. Did you get a look at him?"

"No. Did you?"

"No, it was too dark, and it all happened so fast. Who do you think he was? A burglar?"

"I don't know. Maybe." I glanced around the room. The coffee table was kicked around at an off-angle near the sofa, but nothing else looked to be disturbed. Nor did anything look out of place in what I could see of the bedroom. There was a connecting door in one wall between this suite and the one on the south side; most of the larger rooms in the Continental had them—an old-fashioned custom for the easy creation of "apartments" for the wealthier clientele. But this one was locked on this side and on the other side too, and it did not look to have been tampered with. "Can you tell if anything's missing?"

Kerry shook her head. "Cybil's suitcase is open, but she might have left it that way herself; it doesn't look rummaged through."

"You'd better call Suite M and tell her and your father what happened. Have them come back here and check things over before they notify the management."

"What are you going to do?"

"There's something I want to check on myself. I'll be back pretty soon." I retreated to the door. "Lock it after me this time, okay?"

"Okay," she said. "But you're making me nervous. Do you know something I don't?"

"No," I said, truthfully enough. "I'd tell you if I did."

I went out, waited until I heard the click of the latch, and then hustled to the elevators and took one up to the sixth floor. Dancer had told me his room was 617; I found the door to it tucked inside one of those little cul-de-sacs you find in older hotels—a blind corridor maybe fifteen feet long, with two doors facing each other across it and a third door, probably to some kind of storage or maid's closet, at the end.

There were no lights showing through the bottom louvers and no sounds from within when I put my ear against the panel. I knocked, waited for fifteen seconds, and knocked again with more emphasis. Nothing. If he was inside he was either passed out or just not opening up for anybody.

For no good reason I went from there back up to the fifteenth floor and poked my head into Suite M. The party was just about over; there were only eight or nine people left, none of them Russ Dancer. I went inside and asked Lloyd Underwood and Bert Praxas if they'd seen him in the past half-hour or knew where he'd gone. They said no.

So what? I asked myself as I hiked back to the elevators. Not being around doesn't make him guilty of anything; he doesn't have to be the one. Hell, it could be anybody. How many people in this city are running around tonight with whiskey fumes on their breath?

But I still wished I knew where Dancer was and where he'd been twenty minutes ago.

I could hear voices inside 1017 when I got back down to there, and it was Ivan Wade who opened up in answer to my knock. If he was upset or worried over what had happened, you could not tell it by looking at him. He wore the same aloof expression he had earlier.

He said, "Come inside. How's your chin?"

"Sore."

"I'm sorry it had to happen."

"Me too. Did you find anything missing?"

"I don't think so. My wife's still checking."

Kerry was standing behind him, near the couch, and when I was all the way inside she said, "Find out much on your errand?"

"No. Nothing."

Wade said, "It was a sneak thief, I suppose."

"Well, that's a possibility."

"Why a possibility? Who else could it have been?"

"Maybe it was your would-be extortionist, Dad," Kerry said. "The one behind those letters and 'Hoodwink' manuscripts."

Wade's eyes narrowed. "That whole business is a hoax," he said.

"Is it?"

"Of course it is. Besides, why would an extortionist break into our room?"

I said, "Did you or your wife bring anything valuable with you from home? I don't just mean money and jewelry; I mean literary material—rare pulps, manuscripts, anything like that."

"No," he said. "Nothing of any special value."

Cybil came out of the bedroom just then with her arms folded, hands against forearms, under her breasts. Her husband may have been taking this thing pretty calmly, but she wasn't; there was anxiety in the way she moved and in the set of her face. Her lipstick was flaked and spotty where she'd worried it off with her teeth.

"Everything still there?" Wade asked her.

"Yes," she said. "I'm sure I closed my suitcase before we left for the party and the lid is raised now; but nothing inside seems to have been touched. I suppose whoever it was didn't have time."

Kerry said, "What could he have been after in your suitcase?"

"God knows." But there was hesitation before she said it.

"Well, no damage done then," Wade said. "Or at least not much damage. The best thing to do is notify the hotel manager and then forget it all happened."

Cybil gave him a sharp bright look. "Why do we have to notify the hotel manager?"

"It's standard procedure, Mrs. Wade," I told her.

She gnawed off a little more paint from her lower lip. She had things preying on her mind, you could see that—and it was not just the breaking-and-entering. Kerry had said she was a tough lady, as tough as Max Ruffe, and I believed it; and tough ladies don't get themselves all worked up over a minor burglary attempt, not unless they suspect it isn't so minor after all.

"Well. I'd rather not make a fuss about it," she said finally.

"There won't be a fuss," Wade said. "We'll ask the manager to be discreet."

"Can't we at least wait until morning?"

Wade glanced at me and I shrugged. He said to Cybil, "All

right, in the morning. It's getting late and we're all tired."

Kerry took that as a cue for us to leave. And a couple of minutes later, after the goodnights, we were alone together in the hallway. She said, "I seem to have lost my appetite. Raincheck on Rosebud's, okay?"

"Sure. But how about a cup of coffee downstairs? It's still early yet."

"Well . . . just one, maybe."

The lobby coffee shop was still open, and we took one of several fancy white wrought-iron tables surrounded by potted plants; the place was called, rather snootily for a hotel coffee shop, the Garden Bistro. Kerry sat studying me as I gave our order to the waitress, and she kept on studying me for some seconds afterward.

"What aren't you telling me?" she said.

"Why do you think I'm not telling you something?"

"Intuition. You don't exactly have a poker face, you know."

"I always thought I did."

"Well, you don't. What did you do on that errand of yours?"

I hesitated. I could be frank with her, but that would mean mentioning the .38 revolver in her mother's purse. If she didn't already know about it, and the odds were she didn't, it might upset her. Still, if Cybil was courting some kind of trouble, she had a right to know about it. And maybe she could help me find out just what it was that was going on here.

"Well?" she said.

"Okay. I went to see if I could find Russ Dancer."

"Why? You don't suspect him, do you?"

"Not actively. But the intruder had alcohol on his breath, and not just the kind from one or two social drinks. That made me think of Dancer."

"You mean because of the way he feels about Cybil? My God, you weren't thinking rape or anything like that?"

"The thought did cross my mind."

"Well, you can forget it, believe me. Dancer would never hurt Cybil; never. He worships her."

"Worship can turn into hatred sometimes."

"Yes, but not in Dancer's case. I can see it in his eyes—how he feels about her."

"Did you know Dancer before you met him here?"

"No. But Cybil told me enough about him to give me a good idea of what to expect. Men like Russ Dancer are easy to read."

Not for me, they weren't. But I said, "Does Cybil do a lot of reminiscing about the old days?"

"Oh, sure. At least she used to when I was living at home. I don't think she's ever been as happy as she was in the forties."

"Why is that?"

The waitress brought our coffee. Kerry stirred cream into hers before she said, "I guess she was happiest back then for several reasons. She was young. She'd just made it through a war and dozens of short separations—my dad was an army liaison officer and did a lot of shuttling back and forth between New York and Washington. And she was writing for the pulps, doing what she'd always wanted to do. She even wrote some pulp stories with Ivan, did you know that?"

"No, I didn't."

"Under a pseudonym. Gruesome stuff about ax murderers and people being buried alive. I loved it when I was a kid."

"They let you read horror fiction as a kid?"

"They didn't know about it. I used to get into their magazine file copies."

"Did Cybil like being one of the Pulpeteers?"

"Sure. Apparently they were a pretty wild group."

"Wild in what way?"

"The forties kind of way," Kerry said. "All-night parties, crazy practical jokes, a fistfight or two once in a while."

"Fistfight? You mean among themselves?"

"Cybil never went into detail. Neither did my dad."

"She never mentioned who was involved?"

"If she did, I don't remember. Maybe Frank Colodny, though."

"Why Colodny?"

"Some of the writers accused him of cheating on what he paid for their stories. He'd promise them one amount, pay them another when they delivered, and claim economic pressures as the reason for the cutback. But the writers suspected he was putting through vouchers for the full amount and then pocketing the difference himself."

I remembered Dancer alluding to the same thing at the party. "Why was Colodny allowed in the Pulpeteers," I asked, "if he was suspected of crooked dealings?"

"Well, the cheating only started at the end of the decade, when Action House was losing money like all the other pulp publishers, because of television and paperbacks. Colodny owned a piece of the company, and Cybil says that he liked money. When he couldn't find anybody else to screw he started doing it to his friends."

"Nice guy."

"But they could never prove it, and it took them a while to even accept that it was going on. One by one they stopped writing for him, and finally they threw him out of the group."

"When was that?"

"In '49, I think. The year before Action House went bankrupt and Colodny disappeared."

"Disappeared?"

"Well, one day he was in New York, and the next day Action House's offices were closed and he was gone. Nobody knew where."

"There wasn't anything shady involved, was there?"

"You mean like embezzlement? No. The company didn't have any money left to embezzle. He just vanished, that's all."

And turned up in Arizona, I thought, with enough money to buy an entire town. A ghost town, sure, but even ghost towns and the land they're on didn't come cheap in 1950.

Where did he get the money, if Action House was bankrupt?

"What did your folks think about Colodny buying a ghost town?" I asked her.

"They didn't know about it until today. But I don't think they were all that surprised."

"Why not? It's not something a person would normally do."

"Not most people, but Colodny was always a flake. Back in New York, Cybil says, his big fantasy was to move out West and prospect for gold. No kidding."

"Some fantasy," I said.

"He'd always been a fan of Western pulp stories; that's probably where he got the idea. He came from a small town in New Mexico and never really liked New York. He went there because an uncle of his got him the job with Action House. But he was always talking about moving back some-day. He had asthma too, that was another reason he wanted to move West—the dry air."

"Then what kept him in New York so long?"

"Money, I guess. He wanted that more than anything else."

"Uh-huh. So where'd he get enough to buy the ghost town?"

"Nobody knows. None of the others had seen him or heard anything about him since his disappearance thirty years ago."

"How did your folks react to the prospect of spending a weekend with him after all that time?"

"They weren't exactly overjoyed. But then, thirty years is a long time to hold a grudge."

"Yeah," I said, "a long time."

There was a silence, during which Kerry gave me another of her long, probing looks. "Are you thinking it might be one of the Pulpeteers who broke into their room tonight?"

"It's possible."

"Frank Colodny?"

"Also possible."

"But why? For what reason?"

I shook my head. "Unless it had something to do with 'Hoodwink' and the extortion letters."

"You mean one of the Pulpeteers behind that too? *Why*?"

"I can't even guess," I said. "But there are all sorts of things going on here, and I don't just mean attempted extortion and breaking-and-entering. Tensions that go back much longer than that."

She frowned down at her cup. "I suppose I got the same feeling tonight. Only I just don't see how my folks could be involved."

I hesitated. Then I said slowly, "Kerry, look, there's something else you'd better know. When Dancer knocked Cybil's purse off the table at the party I got a look at what fell out of it. One of the things was a gun."

"A what?"

"A gun. A .38 caliber snub-nosed revolver."

Strong rushes of emotion seemed to make her eyes change color; they got dark again, almost smoky green, and in them you could see her struggling with what I'd just told her. "A gun," she said. "My God."

"It isn't something she's prone to doing, then."

"Of course not. You think she goes around packing a gun?"

"Some people do."

"She's not one of those paranoids."

"Easy. I wasn't suggesting she was. Do you have any idea why she'd come to the convention armed?"

"No. God, I didn't even know she owned a gun." For half a dozen seconds Kerry stared at a spot just beyond my right shoulder; then she shook herself, and her eyes lightened again, glistening. "I don't like this," she said. "I don't like any of this one damn bit."

"It might be a good idea if you had a talk with her in the morning." I said. "Maybe she'll confide in you."

"You bet I'll have a talk with her in the morning. I'd go back up there right now if it wasn't so late."

And that just about finished the conversation. She was too busy worrying questions around inside her head for any more banter or discussion. I called for the check, and we went out through the lobby and into a warm soft breeze off the Bay.

"Your car close by?" I asked her.

"In the garage just down the street."

"Mine's the other way. But I'll walk over with you."

"No need. Thanks for the coffee."

"Sure. About that raincheck for supper—you could use it tomorrow night if you're not doing anything else."

"Let's see what Cybil has to say." The collar of my standard rumpled private eye trenchcoat seemed to be tucked under, all cockeyed in my standard sloppy fashion, and she reached up and straightened it. She had to stand close to me to do that, and I could smell the faintly spicy scent of her breath. "And what kind of day tomorrow turns out to be."

"Fair enough."

She let me have one of her smiles, patted the trenchcoat collar, and went off toward the lighted front of the parking garage. I watched her for a time, with that spicy scent lingering in my mind, and a kind of afterimage, too, of her coppery hair and the way her mouth looked when she smiled. Then I lifted my head and looked up at the glossy moon hanging overhead—one of those spring moons that bathes everything in silvery light and stirs the blood and makes coyotes stand up all hot and bothered and start baying.

I felt like doing a little baying myself just then. Damned if I didn't.

SEVEN

The convention was already in full swing when I got back to the hotel at ten the next morning. One of the wide central corridors off the reception lobby was crowded with people and lined with tables of various sizes, some of them draped in cloths that read *Registration* and *Banquet Tickets and Seating* and *Tours of Sam Spade's San Francisco*. The people were of various sizes, too, and various ages that seemed to start at about fifteen and extend up to semiold duffers like me. Almost everybody was dressed casually—one young guy in a Shadow cape and slouch hat, no less, and one chubby girl in a short skirt and one of those metal brassieres you used to see on the covers of science fiction pulps. As soon as I quit gawking at the girl, I began to feel overdressed in my suit and tie. But then I spotted Bert Praxas talking to a couple of eager-looking kids, and he was also wearing a suit and tie and looked every bit as stuffy as I probably did.

I didn't see anybody else I knew in the crowd, so I went over to where Praxas was. He saw me, raised a hand in a "just a second" gesture, and finished telling an anecdote about having to make a last-minute change in one of his Spectre novels because of an unintentional double entendre. Then he excused himself from the kids and joined me.

Another teenager trotted by just then, this one wearing a Viking helmet and what looked like a motheaten bearskin, and waving a sword made out of wood and tinfoil. I followed him with my eyes, trying to figure out who or what he was supposed to be.

55

Praxas said, "Conan the Barbarian." He was smiling.

"Pardon?"

"The Robert E. Howard character from *Weird Tales*. That's who the boy is dressed up as." His smile widened. "This *has* to be your first convention. You've got the usual nonplussed look."

"Are there always kids who wear costumes like that?"

"Oh yes. If you think you're seeing strange sights here, though, you should go to a science fiction con. It's an experience."

"I'll bet it is. Why do they do it?"

"Self-expression," he said. "A lot of them are lonely, social misfits in one way or another; they crave companionship and attention, and it's only natural that they gravitate to others with similar interests. But you won't see many of them here. This is more a convention for dealers, collectors, and serious pulp fans."

"Like me, huh?"

"Like you. The huckster room is open, by the way. If you plan to do any buying for your collection, you should go in as soon as possible. The turnover will likely be fast and furious."

"Thanks. I'll do that."

But the first place I went when I left him was to the house phones, to call Dancer's room. There was no answer. I went to the hotel bar next, but it wasn't open for business yet. He still hadn't joined the convention crowd, either, nor had anyone else I knew. Which gave me a good excuse to take Praxas's advice and visit the huckster room.

The woman sitting at the registration table told me it was nearby on the main floor, just turn right at the end of this corridor. So I did that, and it turned out to be a big rectangular room with wide-open entrance doors and a couple of guys checking name tags. A three-foot-square sign to one side said, *Convention Members Only—Shoplifters Will Be Prosecuted.*

It took me thirty seconds to remember what I'd done with

the name tag Underwood had given me last night, and then to consider myself lucky I hadn't changed suits this morning. When I got inside I was confronted with sales tables lining the walls and arranged in a middle square as well, so that pulp magazines—and some hardcover and paperback books —would loom on both sides of you all the way around. The room was almost as crowded as the registration area, but most of the people seemed to be upwards of twenty-five and to have a much more serious mien as they wandered around or bent over the stacks and boxes and trays of plastic-bagged pulps.

The whole place made me feel like a proverbial kid in a candy store. This was something I understood; this was my kind of world. I could feel myself grinning, no doubt in a fatuous way, as I started to do some browsing of my own.

It didn't take long for the browsing to turn into a shopping trip. I found several issues of *Detective Tales, Double Detective, Private Detective,* and *Detective Fiction Weekly* that I didn't have, plus a coverless *Black Mask* from 1931 with stories by Horace McCoy and Frederick Nebel. At the end of half an hour I was fourteen pulps richer and fifty-two dollars poorer.

Then I stopped to admire the display of a Southern California dealer—three 1920s *Black Masks* with Hammett stories, priced at $125 each, the first issue of *Wu Fang* at $650, the first issue of the rare hero pulp *The Octopus* at $800—and to wonder about the incredible inflationary rate of magazines that had sold new forty to fifty years ago for a nickel and a dime. Somebody caught hold of my arm while I was doing that, and when I turned I saw Lloyd Underwood standing there, showing me his stained dentures.

"Finding a lot of your wants, I see," he said. "Good. I picked up a '35 *Shadow* myself a little while ago, got it in trade for an *Operator Five* and a *Spider.* What do you think of it so far?"

I spent a couple of seconds sorting that out. "The huckster room?" I said finally. "I think it's fine—"

"No, I meant the con. Of course we haven't really gotten under way yet. First panel is at one. Have you seen the auction books yet?"

"Auction books?"

"The pulps we're auctioning on Sunday," he said. "To help pay for the con. Some very rare items. Our prize is the first issue of *Weird Tales*—March 23, 1923. You don't own that one, do you? Not many people do. A beautiful copy."

"Sounds expensive."

"Opening bid is twenty-five hundred, but we expect to get three thousand at least."

Three thousand dollars for a pulp, I thought. Suppose I had plenty of money—would I spend that much on just one magazine? Well, maybe. But then, what the hell would I do with it? I'd be afraid to open it, much less read it, and what good was having a pulp or any other reading material if you couldn't enjoy what was in it?

"Come on," Underwood said, "I'll show you the display. Do you know many local collectors and dealers?"

"Not too many, no. I buy mostly through the mail . . ."

I didn't finish what I had intended to say because he had hold of my arm and was maneuvering me through the jumble of people. The auction pulps turned out to be every bit as impressive as I'd expected; in addition to the first issue of *Weird Tales*, there were the first five of *Doc Savage*, the first *G-8 and His Battle Aces*, and several 1930s *Spicy Mystery* and *Spicy Detective* whose stories used to turn on the kids of my generation with descriptions of nubile breasts, alabaster thighs, and lush hips, and with lots of innuendo and three-dot chapter endings. From there Underwood steered me around to meet a bunch of local people, including the head of the San Francisco Academy of Comic Art and the owner of the San Francisco Mystery Bookstore—so many names and faces that they all blended together and flowed right out of my head. One that stayed with me was a big Italian guy who had a name similar to mine. He also had a large collection of pulps, he said, and claimed to be a writer of mystery and detective fiction. Maybe he was, but I had never heard of him.

I'd been in there for an hour by then, and Underwood's antic monologues were beginning to wear on me. Besides which, I was tired of jostling and being jostled and of shaking hands while I tried not to drop or damage the pulps I had bought. It was time I went looking for Dancer and for Kerry. Particularly Kerry.

When I managed to extricate myself from Underwood and the rest of the crowd I went back to the registration area. There were even more people milling around now, among them one kid wearing a futuristic jumpsuit and a holstered plastic raygun, with spaced-out eyes to go with the costume. But I didn't see any familiar faces until I got to the main reception lobby and glanced over at the elevators: both Dancer and the dusty pulp artist, Ozzie Meeker, were standing there, each of them loaded down with armfuls of small, framed oil paintings.

I veered over there and reached them just as one of the elevators opened up and disgorged a bunch of people. Dancer saw me and grinned all over his face—a wet, loose kind of grin. The whites of his eyes had a wounded look, and his breath would have knocked over a horse.

"Hey, shamus," he said, "what's happening?"

"Not much. Where you headed?"

"Art Room up on the mezzanine. Got to help Ozzie here set up his display."

"Mind if I tag along? I want to talk to you for a minute."

"Sure. More the merrier, what the hell."

Meeker was holding the elevator, and he watched me from behind his horn-rims with bright, birdlike eyes as Dancer and I moved inside. Up close, the skin of his face had a brown, sun-cracked look, webbed with tiny crosshatches of wrinkles—the skin of a man who spent a good part of his time outdoors, as Colodny obviously did. There was a whiskey smell on him too, but not half as strong, and his gaze was steady and free of the glassiness that showed behind Dancer's squint.

He said, "I don't think we met at the party last night. I'm Ozzie Meeker. You're the detective, right?"

"Right."

"Best damn detective in the business," Dancer said in his annoying way. "Solved a couple of murders in Cypress Bay a few years back, you know that, Ozzie? Some shamus, bet your ass."

"Interesting," Meeker said, as if he meant it.

The elevator stopped at the mezzanine and we got out and turned into the westside corridor. I said to Meeker, "Couldn't help noticing that you and Frank Colodny had a little altercation last night. Nothing serious, I hope."

He shrugged. "Frank and I don't get along too well anymore."

"How could anybody get along with that bastard?" Dancer said. "Screwed Ozzie out of money back in the pulp days too, just like he screwed his writers. Ozzie was the best damn cover artist the pulps ever had. Drew beautiful stuff. You remember his stuff?"

"Yes," I said.

"Got some of it right here. Originals. Never got the recognition he deserved. Did you, Ozzie?"

Meeker shrugged again. "Do any of us?"

"Not me," Dancer said. "But hell, I never deserved any."

The Art Room hadn't officially opened yet, and the doors to it were closed; another guard-type was posted out front. He let us go inside when Meeker showed his name tag. A dozen or so men and women occupied the room, setting up displays of original oils, reproductions, laminated and framed covers, pen-and-ink interior illustrations, old editorial layout sheets, storyboards, and other pulp artwork and ephemera. According to the convention brochure, the material was all owned by private collectors and was being shown by them; the only ex-pulp artist in attendance was Meeker.

He had been given a place of honor as a result, near the door so his display would be the first you'd see when you came in, and he and Dancer unloaded themselves there. His art, most of which depicted Western gunslingers in various action scenes, was striking; not as good as that done by Eggenhofer, the king of Western pulp artists, but still pretty good. His distinctive signature—his last name inside the loop of a lariat—was prominent on each painting.

Dancer said, "What time's the exhibit open, Ozzie?"

"One o'clock. Same time as Wade's panel."

"Should have time for a couple more belts, hah?"

"I don't see why not," Meeker said.

I did, but I didn't say so. Delivering temperance lectures was out of my line.

"You go ahead and get started, Ozzie," Dancer said. "Soon as I talk to my buddy the shamus, I'll give you a hand."

I told Meeker it was nice meeting him and prodded Dancer over into a corner. "That Ozzie's a hell of a nice guy, you know that?" he said. He gave me one of his sardonic grins, loose and moist at the edges. "Generous with his booze, too. Real generous."

"That where you've been this morning? With him?"

"Yup. Since I ran into him in the hall at eight-thirty. We got adjoining rooms. Damn convenient." He squinted at me. "How long you been here?"

"I came in at ten."

"You ring up my room around that time?"

"Uh-huh."

"Thought it was probably you. I heard the phone but by the time I got through the door it was too late."

"I tried to find you last night, too," I said, "after you disappeared from the party. But you weren't in then, either."

He frowned with a bewildered sort of intensity, the way a drunk does when he's trying to remember something. "What time was that?"

"Around ten-thirty."

"I must've been in," he said. "I went straight there from the party. Maybe I was already asleep."

"Maybe you were. How come you left the party without saying anything?"

"I had to puke. Something I ate; my gut was boiling."

"Sure."

"Okay, so I was a little drunkie too. What the hell."

"You didn't happen to see Cybil Wade on the way back to your room, did you?"

That got me nothing at all. Dancer's reaction was one of dull puzzlement, with flickers of something under it that was probably pain. "No, I didn't see her," he said. "Why?"

"Just wondering." I couldn't see any purpose in mentioning the intruder in the Wades' room; it was liable to stir him up, and he was unpredictable enough as it was. "Are you going to Ivan Wade's panel?"

"Not me. The hell with old Ivan; he's full of bullshit anyway." He squinted at me again. "Speaking of bullshit, you find out anything yet about the big extortion scam?"

"No, not yet. But I'm in there pitching."

"Yeah," he said. "Best damn private eye in the business."

He gave me a broad wink, banged me on the shoulder, and moved back to where Meeker was working with his art display. He was pretty steady on his feet, but the habitual drinker learns how to control his motor responses. I wondered if he'd learned how to control his facial expressions and his tongue too—if he was hiding something, if there were motives or designs perking away inside that shaggy head of his. It didn't seem likely. Still, I had an uneasy feeling about him. He may have been guiltless so far, but if there was any more trouble, I thought, it would be Russ Dancer who was smack in the middle of it.

I had had enough of elevators for a while; I took the stairs back down to the lobby. And the first person I saw when I walked through the door was Kerry.

She was just coming out of the newsstand and tobacco shop across the lobby, alone and wearing a white satiny-looking blouse, a pair of dark blue slacks, and an introspective and faintly agitated look. When she saw me, three or four seconds later, one eyebrow went up and she made a beckoning gesture; then she sidestepped to one of the pillars and stood plucking at her coppery hair—not fluffing it the way women do, just plucking, as if she was restless and her hand did not want to be still.

"I've been looking all over for you," she said when I got to her. "Did you just get here?"

"No, at ten o'clock. But I've been moving around. Did you talk to your mother?"

She nodded. "After breakfast."

"What about the gun?"

"She claims she brought it with her as a joke, to illustrate her panel comments about private eyes. She says it wasn't loaded."

"Do you believe her?"

"I don't know. I got the feeling she might be lying, but I couldn't be sure. Cybil can be inscrutable when she wants to be."

"No reaction when you first mentioned the gun?"

"Hardly any. She's not easily startled, either."

"Did you tell her I'd seen it at the party?"

"Yes. But she was sure you had at the time, she said, and she realized then it was a mistake to bring it with her. She was afraid you might say something to somebody and there'd be a fuss. That's why she left just afterward—to take the gun back to her room and put it away in her suitcase."

"Her suitcase?"

"That's right," Kerry said. "Whoever broke in last night *did* steal something after all, even though Cybil didn't want to admit it. He stole that damned gun."

EIGHT

Ivan Wade's panel started promptly at one o'clock in a small auditorium on the mezzanine. Two other guys flanked Wade at the long dais table—collectors who were authorities on both *Weird Tales* and the Shudder Pulps—and well over 150 people were in the audience. Jim Bohannon, Bert Praxas, and Waldo Ramsey were grouped together with Lloyd Underwood near the back; Frank Colodny sat by himself off to one side, worrying the stem of a corncob pipe and looking just as preoccupied as he had last night; and Cybil Wade was in the front row left, across the center aisle from where Kerry and I had taken seats, wearing an air about as preoccupied as Colodny's.

I had done some more talking with Kerry, over a sandwich in the coffee shop, but to no conclusions. If her mother had another reason for bringing the .38 revolver to the convention, other than using it for demonstration purposes, Kerry had no ideas or guesses as to what that reason might be. And if Cybil was telling the truth about the gun being stolen last night, neither of us had answers to the string of questions that went along with the burglary. Was anything else taken that Cybil refused to mention? Had the intruder been after the gun specifically? If the gun *had* been the objective, how did he know she had it? And what did he want it for?

Then there was the central question: Was he an outsider or someone connected with the convention?

I'd tried to tell Kerry not to worry, but it had come out sounding hollow. I had a nagging feeling that things were bubbling away under the surface, gathering pressure and maybe getting volatile enough to explode. You can't explain intimations like that, but I'd had them often enough over the years to pay attention when one came along.

Once the panel started, however, I quit mulling over the missing gun and tranquilized myself on pulp lore. Wade was a pretty good public speaker and revealed a dry, clever sense of humor that got him rapt attention as well as laughter and applause. He also revealed another talent I hadn't known he possessed: the performance of sleight-of-hand magic. The first illusion he did was to produce a copy of *Terror Tales* out of the air while he was talking, as if to illustrate a point he was trying to make, and it was so casual and so deft that there was a moment of silence and then what amounted to an ovation.

I leaned over to ask Kerry, "How long has your father been an amateur magician?"

"Oh, as long as I can remember. Stage magic is a passion of his; he's written a half-dozen books on the subject. Good, isn't he?"

"Very."

The pulp lore itself—historical facts, anecdotes about writers and editors, bits of inside information—was fascinating. I learned a good deal about *Weird Tales*, and about such sex-and-sadism Shudder Pulps of the thirties as *Dime Mystery*, *Horror Stories*, and *Thrilling Mystery*, whose lurid covers depicted half-naked young women being whipped, clubbed, dipped in vats of acid and molten metal, and otherwise tortured on and with all sorts of devices by a variety of leering fiends.

The panel lasted an hour and a half. Everyone except Frank Colodny seemed to find it as engrossing as I did; he had gotten up about two-thirds of the way through, looking fidgety and with his wattles quivering, and disappeared. Wade ended the session by performing another magic trick— the apparent transformation of another pulp magazine into one of his own books. It was a neat finish and flawlessly done, and it earned him another ovation.

Out in the hall afterward Kerry said, "I've got to call my

office. They gave me the day off but they expect me to check in."

"See you back here for Jim Bohannon's panel?"

"When is it, three-fifteen? I should be back by then." She gave me a critical frown. "Why don't you do something about your tie?"

I looked down. "What's the matter with it?"

"Nothing a dry cleaner can't fix. It looks like something blue died on the front of your shirt."

"Thanks a lot."

"Don't mention it," she said, and grinned at me and went away.

I found a restroom and examined my tie in the mirror. It was a little wrinkled and a little stained, but you couldn't see the stains very clearly against the dark blue background. Or maybe you could, at that. I took the thing off and opened my shirt collar and stuffed the tie out of sight in my coat pocket.

Damn, but she had a knack for making me feel self-conscious.

I took the stairs down to the lobby, went from there out into the balmy afternoon to where I had parked my car. The pulps I had bought in the huckster room went into the trunk; so did the tie. On my way back, with the sun beating down on me, I decided I was thirsty and that a cold beer would taste good. There were still twenty minutes left before Bohannon's panel.

You got into the Continental Bar by way of a longish corridor, both sides of which were lined with glass-enclosed relics of the Victorian period; it opened off one corner of the lobby. I was just entering the corridor when the commotion started: the banging sound of a chair being overturned, several voices raised and chattering at once. The loudest of the voices, thick with a boozy rage, belonged to Russ Dancer.

Christ, now what? I thought, and half ran the rest of the way into the bar. It was dark in there—dark wood paneling and furnishings, high shadowy ceiling, lighting so sedate it was almost nonexistent—and it took a second for my eyes to adjust. Then I saw Dancer. He had Frank Colodny back up against one of the walls, fist bunched hard in Colodny's shirt-front, standing nose to nose with him and yelling something incoherent. Waldo Ramsey was there, too, dragging at Dancer's arm without accomplishing much and telling him to lay off. The rest of the half-dozen people in the room, including the bartender, weren't doing anything except gawking.

I hustled over and caught hold of Dancer's other arm, and together Ramsey and I managed to make him turn loose. Colodny put a hand up and rubbed his throat and made a gurgling sound; his whole body seemed to be quivering, but with a rage equal to Dancer's, not with fear.

"Let me go, goddammit!" Dancer yelled. "I'll fix this son of a bitch, I'll fix him!"

I said, "You're not going to fix anybody," and he swiveled his head and seemed to see me for the first time. Some of the combativeness faded out of his expression; he ran his tongue loosely over his lips, muttered something under his breath, and glowered at Colodny.

"What's this all about?" I asked Ramsey.

"Hell, I don't know. He came charging in here a minute ago, hoisted Frank up out of his chair, and started accusing him of being a crook and a swindler."

"That's what he is," Dancer said, "damn right."

Colodny was making a visible effort to keep himself under control. He glared back at Dancer and said, "You're a crazy drunk, you know that? You ought to be in an institution."

"So should you, bastard. San fucking Quentin."

"Cut it out, Russ," I told him. "If you want to stay out of trouble, watch your temper and your mouth. This is a public place."

"He's the one who's gonna have trouble, not me."

"Why? What are you so stirred up about?"

"He's behind the extortion scam, that's what."

Ramsey blinked at him. Colodny said, "You're a liar."

"The hell I am. You slipped the note in my pocket, all right. Upstairs, when you ran into me in the hall a few minutes ago."

I said, "What note?"

"Let go my arm and I'll show you."

I eased my grip a little first, to see if he had any more rough ideas, then released him when I decided he didn't. He dug out a folded square of paper from his jacket pocket, handed it over without taking his eyes off Colodny. There were three sentences typed on the paper, in a different typeface from either the previous letter or the "Hoodwink" manuscript; no salutation or signature.

"What does it say?" Ramsey asked me.

"'There's no mistake now, I know you're the one. My price has gone up—ten thousand dollars, to be paid by midnight Sunday. Otherwise your plagiarism will be made public on Monday morning.'"

"I didn't write that," Colodny said. "It's nonsense."

I looked at Dancer. "Are you sure he put this in your pocket?"

"Sure I'm sure. It wasn't there a little while ago, and I haven't been close to anybody except him. Damn straight he's the one."

"*Delirium tremens,*" Colodny said. "The man's hallucinating."

"Do you know anything about this extortion ploy, Mr. Colodny?" I asked him.

"No." The anger seemed to have drained out of him; he looked fidgety again. "I don't have to answer questions or take any more abuse, not from any of you." And he pushed away from the wall, did a wary sidestep around Dancer, and headed over to the bar. He had it all to himself when he got there; the other patrons had disappeared.

Dancer said to me, "You just going to let him go?"

"What else can I do? There's no evidence against him. It's your word against his."

His mood shifted and turned sullen; you could see it happen in his face, even in the semidarkness of the bar. "He won't get away with it, I'll tell you that. Not this time."

I started to tell him to take it easy, not to go off half-cocked, but he was already moving away. It looked for a second as if he would try bracing Colodny again. Then he veered off, walking in hard, bullish strides, and vanished down the corridor.

Ramsey said, "Christ, but he's a lush," and shook his head.

"You don't think he's right about Colodny?"

"I doubt it. I don't see Frank pulling a stunt like 'Hoodwink.' It's got warped overtones—the work of somebody who's at least half a whack. Colodny may be a lot of things, but a whack isn't one of them."

"It's been a long time since you knew him, hasn't it?"

"Yes. But he hasn't changed much; I'd bet on that. This sort of gambit just isn't his style."

"Then where do you suppose Dancer got the note?"

"Beats me," Ramsey said. "Lushes aren't particularly attentive, and you can't trust their memories or their time perception. Seems to me anybody could have slipped him the note at any time."

"You're probably right."

There was an antique chiming clock above the lounge's Queen Anne fireplace, and it started to bong just then. Three times: three o'clock. I decided I didn't want a beer after all and left Ramsey and started out. Colodny watched me in the backbar mirror, holding a glass in one hand and stroking the six strands of hair on his scalp with the other. Maybe it was a trick of the faint lighting, but he looked frightened sitting there, almost cowering, like somebody trying to hide in a roomful of shadows.

When I got out into the lobby I spotted Dancer again, standing together with Cybil Wade near the reception desk. He had his head bent forward, saying something to her in an intense sort of way; I could not see his face from where I was, but hers was visible in three-quarters profile. And it was blank, void of expression—one of those plastic, dimpled doll's faces.

I started toward them. The shape Dancer was in, he was capable of saying or doing anything, and I was afraid of another scene. But I had only taken a couple of steps when he raised his head and clumped past her to the elevators. I caught a glimpse of his face then: he was laughing. There was not much mirth in it, though. Part of it was sexual leering and part of it seemed to be a kind of painful release. The way a man laughs when something is tearing him up inside.

Cybil stayed where she was, looking after him. She didn't notice me until I came up beside her and said, "Anything wrong, Mrs. Wade?" Then the tawny eyes blinked and looked at me, and animation came back into her face.

"Oh," she said. "Hello."

"Everything all right?"

"Yes, fine. Will you excuse me?"

"Sure, of course."

She hurried across the lobby, vanished into one of the elevator cars. And it was my turn to stand looking at nothing, thinking about her and Dancer and Colodny and the second extortion note—and all the things that had happened in the past twenty-four hours.

And this is only Friday afternoon, I thought gloomily. The convention still has two full days to run.

Where does it all go from here?

Kerry and I went out for dinner at seven o'clock.

Nothing much happened in the four hours before then. When I met her at the auditorium for Jim Bohannon's panel I didn't show her the new note or tell her what had happened in the Continental Bar. She was worried enough as it was, without me adding fuel. Besides, she had a nice smile for me and I did not want to make it go away.

Frank Colodny was a no-show; so were Dancer and Ozzie Meeker. But Cybil was there, sitting with her husband and looking less remote and more composed than she had downstairs. Most of the 150 or so people in the audience seemed to have a grand old time once the panel got rolling. I should have and didn't, really, but that was no fault of Bohannon or the two collectors of adventure and Western pulps who shared the dais with him. Bohannon was a quiet, amusing speaker, without Ivan Wade's theatrical flair, but with just as much expertise. And the pulp lore, as always for me, was stimulating: historical perspectives on *Adventure, Argosy, Blue Book, Wild West Weekly, Western Story;* ancedotes about Leo Margulies, Rogers Terrill, and other pulp editors. But I just could not seem to keep myself mentally involved. My mind kept wandering, shuffling through the events of last night and today as if they were a deck of cards—strange mismatched cards that didn't seem to add up to much yet.

After the panel was over, Kerry and I spent a little time browsing through the huckster room again. I bought two more issues of *Dime Detective* and an autographed copy of one of her father's books on stage magic. Then Lloyd Underwood appeared and reminded us that there was another cocktail party in Suite M, beginning at six.

The party started out all right. I got myself a beer, and Kerry had a vodka gimlet, and we mingled. After a while Dancer showed up with Ozzie Meeker, looking twice as squiffed as he had in the bar earlier, and I quit mingling to keep an eye on him. But he was in pretty good spirits and seemed to have forgotten the incident with Colodny, who was the only one of the Pulpeteers not present. He was as obstreperous as ever, but he left Cybil alone, and he didn't make trouble for anybody else.

More and more people began to file in, until finally the room was jammed to overflowing. That was when I decided I didn't need to be a watchdog any more today and reminded Kerry of her dinner raincheck. She said, "Okay, good idea; I'm starved," and we found her folks so she could tell them we were leaving. Ivan Wade gave me a speculative look, as if he were wondering what sort of intentions I had toward his daughter. But he had nothing to say to me.

We opted for an English-style pub called The Coachman because it wasn't far away—over on the far side of Nob Hill— and because Kerry said it was one of her favorite restaurants. A two-block walk past Union Square and then the Powell-Mason cable car got us there in twenty minutes. And another twenty minutes after that we had a table, pints of Bass ale, and orders in for steak-and-kidney pie.

We talked over the drinks, over dinner, over the coffee afterward—nice, easy, relaxed talking, as if we were two people who had known each other for two years instead of two days. Yet at this point or that one, there were small silences, and each time she seemed to study me with those frank green eyes, and each time it made me aware of the way I looked, my posture, the difference in our ages. There had only been a few women in my life I had felt quite as comfortable with—and none who made me feel so damned awkward and self-conscious. And she knew it, too. It seemed to amuse her, but not in a perverse or unkind way; as if it was part of whatever appeal I held for her.

She was thirty-eight, she told me, and she had been divorced for four years and married for eleven before that to a schmuck named Ray Dunston, who was a Los Angeles criminal lawyer. Those were her words: "a schmuck named Ray Dunston." She was candid about the marriage; it had started out good, begun to slide gradually year by year, and finally become a thing of cold convenience. She suspected that he had been seeing other women almost from the first, which made him a schmuck in my book, all right. As soon as she found out for sure, she left him, filed for divorce, applied to Bates and Carpenter for a job—she had worked for a Los Angeles ad agency for five years—and here she was. No children, although she would have had kids if the schmuck had been willing; no involvements and no obligations. Enjoying San Francisco, enjoying her freedom, enjoying life again. And what about me? What was *my* life story?

So I told her about growing up with the pulps, wanting to emulate the detectives I spent so many vicarious hours with. About my tour of duty as a military policeman in the South Pacific and how I had taken my civil service exam and gone through the Police Academy after the war. About all the years on the San Francisco cops and the brutal ax murder in the Sunset District that had given me the excuse I needed to quit the force and open up my own agency. I told her about Erika Coates, and about another woman named Cheryl Rosmond that I had loved—or thought I'd loved—for a while. I told her about the lesion on my lung, the struggle I had gone through to come to terms with the spectre of cancer.

Things seemed to be getting a little grim at that point, and I switched the subject to the convention. But that wasn't much better. So then, by tacit agreement, we did the rest of our talking about neutral topics—books, movies, sports—until the time came to pay the check.

Outside I said, "It's a nice night. Why don't we walk back?"

"Fine."

"We can stop somewhere for a nightcap if you like."

"How about your place?"

I did a small double take. "Are you serious?"

"Sure. I'm curious about your pulps."

"Not my etchings, huh?"

She laughed. "I'll bet you don't have sixty-five hundred of those."

"Nope. Uh, what I do have, though, is a pretty messy flat. I'd better tell you that now, in case you're easily shocked."

"I'm not. Besides, I expected you to have a messy flat."

"How come?"

"The way you dress," she said, and gave me one of her smiles. "Okay, come on—take me to your pulps."

We walked back to the hotel, picked up my car, and I took her to my pulps. Her eyes widened a little when I opened the door and put on the lights and the dustballs winked at her from under the furniture; but she took it pretty well. She said, "You could apply for disaster relief, you know?" and made straight for the bookshelves flanking the bay window, where I keep the pulps in chronological order by title.

While she was making impressed noises, I opened the curtains over the window. Pacific Heights is an expensive neighborhood primarily because of the view, and on a night like this, you had it all: the Golden Gate Bridge, the lights of Marin, the revolving beacon on Alcatraz, the luminous pinpoints strung across the East Bay. Romantic stuff—but maybe I shouldn't be thinking about romance. Except that I was. Ivan Wade could have popped me on the nose for what

I was thinking right then, and I wouldn't have blamed him much.

I found some brandy in the kitchen, poured a snifter for her and a companionable dollop for me, and we sat on the couch and talked about pulps and looked at the view. Then we stopped talking and finished the brandy. Then we just sat there and looked at each other.

"Well?" she said.

"Well what?"

"Aren't you going to tear my clothes off?"

"Do what?"

"Tear my clothes off. Isn't that what private eyes do when they get a woman alone in their flat?"

"Not this private eye."

"No? What do you do, then?"

"Conventional things, that's all."

"Not *too* conventional, I hope."

"Well . . ."

"Well," she said. "Do something conventional."

So I kissed her. "Mmm, you taste good," she said, and I said, "You too" and kissed her again—a good long hot kiss this time. It was starting to get even hotter when she ended it and leaned back to look at me.

"Well?" she said.

"Well what?"

"Oh for God's sake. Ask me if I want to go to bed."

"Do you want to go to bed?"

"I thought you'd never ask," she said, and took the hand of the tough private dick, the last lone wolf, the suave seducer of beautiful women, and led him like a kid into his own bedroom.

NINE

I woke up a little past seven in the morning, and there she was beside me, lying on her back with her hip thrust over against mine—all smooth and soft-looking with that coppery hair sleep-touseled around her face. I lay looking at her for a time. There was a good warm feeling inside me, and a kind of tenderness, and a kind of wonder, too, that my bed should be full of so much woman.

Pretty soon I rolled toward her and kissed her and did a couple of other things. She opened one eye and said sleepily, "Mm."

"Morning," I said.

"Morning yourself."

"You feel good, you know that?"

"Mm."

"I'm not used to waking up with a lady in my bed."

She yawned and opened the other eye. "So I gathered."

"I guess I was pretty eager, huh?"

"Pretty eager."

"Well, it's been a while, I admit it."

"For me, too," she said.

"Really?"

"Really."

"How long?"

"A while. Months."

"So why me, then?"

"Why not you?"

"Any old port in a storm, right?"

"No, not right," she said seriously.

"Then why me?"

"What's wrong with *you*?"

"Plenty. I've got a beer belly—"

"I don't mind that."

"—and the general appearance of a bear—"

"I like bears."

"—and I'm an old man. Getting there, anyway."

"Sure you are. Hah."

"So what do you see in me?"

"God, you're persistent. All right—a nice man, that's what I see in you. A nice, gentle, pussycat private eye. Okay?"

"Pussycat," I said and laughed.

"Pussycat. You attract me; I can't tell you exactly why, but you do. Every time I looked at you the past two days, I found myself wondering what it would be like to go to bed with you. Haven't you ever looked at somebody and just wanted to go straight to bed?"

"Lots of times. You, for instance."

"Mm-hmm. And you know something?"

"What?"

"I wouldn't mind doing it again right now."

"Mutual," I said. "But I guess we can't."

"Why not?"

"I don't think I'm up to it."

"You will be," she said. "Oh, you will be."

She was right: I was.

What with one thing and another, it was almost noon before we got down to the Hotel Continental.

One of the things was stopping off at her apartment in Diamond Heights Village, at the crest of Twin Peaks, so she could change into fresh clothing. It was a nice apartment, with one of those 180-degree views from a rear balcony or through a combination picture window and sliding glass door; she had it decorated with modernistic furniture, accent on chrome and sharp angles. and huge paintings done in blacks. whites. and oranges. A warm. comfortable place. the kind you want to come back to. And I wanted to come back there. all right. just as I wanted her to come back to my flat—time and again. I wanted it more than I was willing to admit to myself just yet.

As we entered through the main lobby doors of the hotel I said. "How about something to eat?" All we'd had for breakfast was coffee and some toast made out of two-day-old bread. and my stomach was making ominous rumbling noises.

"Lord, yes. I'm famished." Kerry said. "But I should say hello to my folks first."

The bank of house phones was nearby. so we went over there and she rang up 1017. Somebody came on the line: she talked for maybe fifteen seconds before she replaced the receiver. When she turned to me her forehead was ridged and those chameleon eyes of hers were starting to change color again.

"I think I'd better go up and talk to Cybil," she said.

"Something wrong?"

"I don't know. She sounded . . . odd."

"In what way?"

"Just odd. Subdued, worried. Maybe I can find out what it is if I see her in person. Meet you in the coffee shop?"

"Okay. I want to check on Dancer anyway."

She went away to the elevators. And I went across and into the corridor toward the convention tables. wondering if something else had happened last night after we'd left—something to do with the missing .38 revolver, for example, or with Russ Dancer. Or both.

But if that were the case, it couldn't have amounted to much, judging from the crowd and the general atmosphere of cheerful camaraderie. There were even more people than yesterday, and a proportionately greater number of kids dressed in unconventional costume. The chubby girl in the brass brassiere had brought a boyfriend dressed up as a bug-

78

eyed monster: green scaly papier-mâché head and eyeballs dangling and bobbing at the end of six-inch springs. But I was used to it by now. It was only three or four seconds before I quit staring this time.

The first Pulpeteer I saw was Jim Bohannon, making his way in my direction through the crowd. When we neared each other I motioned him off to one side, out of the traffic stream.

"Mob scene this morning," he said. "I didn't know this many people even remembered the pulps."

"There are plenty of us. Maybe they'll make a comeback someday."

"No chance of that, I'm afraid. Damn country's too sophisticated these days." He made a wry mouth. "We were sort of virginal back in the thirties and forties, if you know what I mean. But we've been screwed a whole hell of a lot since."

"That's the truth," I said. "Anything exciting happen last night? I left the party a little before seven."

"Not much. Bunch of us got together for a poker game in Bert Praxas's room after dinner. I dropped thirty bucks, and Ivan Wade won fifty. He always was lucky at cards."

"Did Dancer play too?"

Bohannon's mouth got even more wry. "He wasn't in any shape to do more than puke on himself. He and Ozzie Meeker were both loaded." He shook his head. "Picked up again this morning right where he left off, too, the damn fool."

"How early this morning?"

"Pretty early."

"Did you talk to him?"

"For a minute or so. He said he'd just telephoned his ladyfriend, the one he lives with down the coast, and a letter came for him yesterday from his agent. He had a deal pending to do some Adult porno Westerns, but it fell through. So he was celebrating another defeat, as he put it." Bohannon shook his head. "Adult porno Westerns, of all the abominations."

"You have any idea where he is right now?"

"Not right this minute, no. He came stumbling in through the lobby about twenty minutes ago, with one of the convention people. Pretty obvious he'd latched on to the fellow, and they'd been out drinking their breakfast. But I didn't notice where he went. Off to freeload some more drinks, maybe."

I nodded. "I think I'd better have a little talk with him."

"Trying to talk common sense to a drunk," Bohannon said, "is like trying to talk Shakespeare to the back end of a horse."

"Yeah," I said. "But I guess I'll try it anyway."

I went back into the lobby to the house phones. There was no answer in Dancer's room. With Meeker, maybe? I thought. But when I got Meeker's room number from the switchboard and dialed it, that line buzzed in the same empty way.

Just as I was replacing the receiver, somebody said "Good morning" a little stiffly to one side of me. I turned, and it was Ivan Wade—dressed in a pair of doeskin slacks and a dark blue blazer, mustache twitching and eyes full of ice. He was not smiling.

"Morning, Mr. Wade."

"Did you and Kerry have a nice time last night?"

Uh-oh, I thought. "Yes, very nice."

"The two of you seem to be quite friendly."

"Well . . ." I stopped and cleared my throat. "We get along pretty well, yes."

"Evidently," Wade said, and the ice was in his voice now. Along with something that might have been distaste.

I stood there trying to think of something intelligent to say while he watched me in his cold way. He was not keen on the idea of Kerry and me having a relationship, that was plain enough; but for what reason? The fact that I was fifteen years older than she? The fact that I was a private detective? My passion for pulp magazines? The way I parted my hair or the way my belly drooped over my belt? Maybe he just didn't like anybody messing around with his daughter after the way her schmuck of a former husband had treated her.

I said, "Look, Mr. Wade," and then stopped again, blank-headed, and I probably would have found something stupid to say if one of the elevator cars hadn't reached the lobby just then and discharged Kerry. She saw Wade and me and came straight over. Whatever her mother had had to say to her, it couldn't have been very pleasant; her eyes had a dark, angry look and the set of her face was a little grim.

She said to Wade, "What happened to Cybil last night?"

He glanced at me, then back at her with sharp meaning.

Kerry ignored it. "My mother," she said to me in a deliberate way, "has a big fat bruise on one cheekbone. She says she fell down, but I don't believe her. I think someone hit her." And she looked hard at Wade.

His mouth was tight and you could tell he was building up a pretty good anger of his own. "I've never laid a hand on Cybil in forty years."

"Then who did it?"

"I don't know. She wouldn't tell me."

"Well, when did it happen?"

"Sometime last night. She was all right when I went to play poker with Bert Praxas and some of the others; she had those marks when I came back a few hours later." He glanced at me again, with something close to open hostility. "Do we have to discuss private matters in front of a stranger?"

Kerry linked her arm through mine. "He's not exactly a stranger, Dad."

"So I gathered," Wade said. "I'd like to see you later, if you don't mind. Alone."

Kerry and I watched him stalk away. She said, "I love him, but God, he can be stuffy sometimes."

"He doesn't seem to like me very much," I said.

"Well, he's always been overprotective. But I can handle him, that's no problem. It's my mother I'm worried about."

"What did she say to you just now?"

"Not much. She's hiding something and she wants to confide in somebody. But she can't seem to let it come out."

"You think your father was the one who hit her?"

"No. But I almost wanted it to be him. I could cope with that; it's not so . . . I don't know, ominous."

"Did she tell you anything at all about last night?"

"Nothing that wasn't a lie. It must have something to do with that gun—with why she brought it with her. Don't you think?"

"Maybe," I said, but that was what I thought, all right. Something to do with the gun, and possibly with its theft from her room. Something to do with Russ Dancer, too? I wondered. Suppose he got Cybil alone somewhere last night, made a pass at her, and swatted her one when she rejected him?

Kerry seemed to be reading my mind. She said, "It could be Russ Dancer who beat up on her. He was drunk again at the party."

"Yeah."

"If it was him, I want to know it."

"So do I. I've been looking for him since you left."

"I'll help you find him."

"No. Better let me handle him alone."

"Tough-guy stuff?"

"I hope not. Why don't you go ahead and have lunch? I'll join you as soon as I can—or meet you in the auditorium for Colodny's panel at one if I run late."

She said all right, not without reluctance, and I went off to check the Continental Bar. No sign of Dancer there. And no sign of him in the registration area or the huckster room. I went up to the mezzanine and looked into the auditorium and the Pulp Art room. He was not in either of those places. Which meant he'd left the hotel again, maybe to do some more drinking, or he was up in his room after all, passed out or partying.

I got back into the elevator and rode up to the sixth floor. When I turned along the east corridor, a middle-aged maid with loose piles of butterscotch hair was just coming past the little cul-de-sac that contained the entrance to Dancer's room, pushing one of those big all-purpose hotel carts loaded with fresh linen, detergents, trash receptacles, and the like. She looked harried, the way most hotel maids always seem to, and as I moved toward her she lifted one hand and rubbed the back of it across her forehead.

That was when the gun went off.

The flat, banging sound seemed to erupt ahead of me and to my right, behind where the maid was—Dancer's room. The maid had stopped dead and so had I, and for an instant we were staring at each other across twenty yards of empty carpeting. Then there was a low cry and a series of other sounds muffled by the walls that I couldn't identify.

The hackles went up on my neck, and there was a prickling sensation along my scalp like something scurrying through dry grass. I uprooted myself, went charging ahead along the hall. The gunshot had come from Dancer's room, all right; I was sure of it. Ahead of me the maid had backed off and was peering into the cul-de-sac with a seriocomic expression of confusion and fright. I pounded past another of the cul-de-sacs, past her cart. More noises came from behind the thick corridor wall, still deadened and unidentifiable. When I neared the maid she scrambled aside, but she was slow doing it and I almost collided with her. We veered off from each other, her squeaking a little, stumbling, and I caught hold of the wall at the corner and pulled myself around it into the cul-de-sac.

Nobody was in the passageway. All three doors—the entrances to 617 and 619 and the one to the storage closet at the end—were shut. I ran to Dancer's door and grabbed the knob and twisted hard; it bound up halfway through the rotation. I hung onto it, rattled the door in its frame. Then I quit rattling and held a breath to listen.

Silence inside there now.

"Dancer?" I shouted. "Open the door!"

Nothing.

I looked back toward the corridor. The maid was still poised there, watching me huge-eyed, like one of the children in a painting by Keane. "I'm a detective!" I yelled at her. "I need your passkey!"

I had to yell it a second time, moving back toward her, before it got through and she responded. She held the key out at arm's length, timidly, as if she were afraid I might want to take her arm along with it. I jerked it out of her hand, ran back to 617, and slotted it into the lock. The latch clicked; the knob rotated all the way in my hand this time and the door popped inward. I shoved it all the way, tensing, and took two quick steps into the room.

Dancer was ten feet away, in the middle of the carpet near the couch, swaying a little. His face was gray, blotchy, and his eyes were only half focused and so red-rimmed and red-lined they looked bloody. The smell of raw whiskey coming off him and from the open quart bottle of rye overturned on the couch, mingled with the stench of cordite, was nauseating.

And lying back-sprawled at his feet, one leg drawn up and both arms wrapped across his chest, was Frank Colodny. You only had to look at him once—the position he was in, the facial rictus and the blank staring eyes, the blood showing beneath the crossed arms—to know that he was dead.

Dancer turned his head toward me, blinked, blinked again, and seemed to recognize me. "I didn't do it," he said in a sick, slurred voice. "Christ Almighty, I didn't kill him."

But the gun he held pointed downward in his right hand said otherwise.

Cybil Wade's gun, I thought—the missing .38 revolver.

TEN

I said slow and careful, "Put it down, Russ."

"What?"

"The gun. Put it down."

He squinted along the length of his arm, and his face registered confusion, as if he hadn't known he had anything at all in his hand. A belch came out of him, an ugly sound in the stillness. Then he grimaced and threw the .38 at the couch, the way you throw something too hot to hold, or too foreign. It hit one of the back cushions and plopped down next to the overturned rye bottle.

"It was lying on the floor next to him," he said. "I must have picked it up. But I didn't kill him."

I eased over past him, still tensed, not taking my eyes off his face, and caught up the gun by the tip of its barrel. Still warm. Dancer had not moved and he still didn't move as I backed off again to the door, dropped the .38 into my jacket pocket.

"What's he doing here?" he said, meaning Colodny. He sounded amazed. "How did he get in here?"

"Stay where you are," I told him. "Don't move."

I backed out into the passageway. The maid had not gone anywhere, nor was she alone; three other people I didn't know, all of them gawking, were grouped at the far corridor wall. I called out to the maid, keeping Dancer in my line of sight, "What's your name, Miss?"

"Greta."

"All right, Greta. Go downstairs and tell the manager

there's been an accident in Room 617 and a man's been killed."

Her eyes got even wider. I could hear her suck in her breath.

"Tell him I'm going to call the police." I said. I gave her my name. "But don't say anything to anyone else; just the manager. And don't leave the hotel. The police may want to talk to you."

I waited for her to hurry away. Then I went back inside and shut the door. The lock on it was a deadbolt, not one of those spring jobs with a button you can push on your way out so the door will lock automatically; you had to use a key from the outside to lock this one, or turn the handle on the deadbolt latch from inside. I turned the handle now, and then went over near Dancer again. But not too near because I had no way of knowing how he would react when he came out of his daze.

He was no longer looking at the body; his eyes had shifted toward the bottle on the couch. "I need a drink." he said. "Christ. I need one bad."

"No more drinks." I said.

"I'm getting the shakes . . ."

"No more liquor. Sit down in that chair over there."

The chair was a Victorian replica; he sat on the edge of its plush seat and got a tight grip on both knees. His chest kept jumping, and his mouth worked as if he were trying not to vomit.

In the wall beyond him, the bedroom door stood wide open. I went over to it and looked inside. The windows in the outer wall were undraped, giving me a view of Telegraph Hill and Coit Tower; they were also closed and locked. The bed was rumpled, blankets kicked into a tangle at the foot end, but there was nothing else to see. And nothing to see in the bathroom, either, most of which was visible through another open door across the bedroom.

One of the suite's two telephones sat on an end table next to the couch. I sidestepped around to it and lifted the receiver and dialed nine to get an outside line. While I did that I remembered to check my watch. The time was 12:37, which put the time of the shooting at approximately 12:30.

When I got the Hall of Justice on the line I asked for the Homicide Squad and Lieutenant Eberhardt. I had not talked to Eb in over a week—he was my closest friend on and off the force and had been for more than three decades—so I did not know if he was on duty this weekend or not. But it would make things a little easier for me if he was.

And that was the way it worked out. Eberhardt came on after thirty seconds, and I told him where I was calling from and gave him a quick rundown of what had happened as far as I knew it. When I was done he said angrily, as if something was biting on him, "A homicide at a pulp convention. Another one of your dillies. What the hell's the matter with you?"

"It's not my fault, Eb."

"Did I say it was? Fifteen minutes, maybe twenty."

The line buzzed in my ear. I put the receiver down and looked at Dancer. He was still gripping his knees, rocking back and forth a little now with his eyes squeezed shut and his face scrunched up tight. You could almost see the pain he was suffering, mental and physical both.

I moved to where Colodny lay on the rose-patterned carpet, steeled myself the way I always had to do in the presence of violent death, and went to one knee beside the body. As far as I could tell without touching him, he had been shot in the heart region at close range; scorched-powder marks were mixed with the blood on his white shirt-front. There weren't any other marks on him that I could see.

When I straightened again I made an automatic inventory of the room. No indication of a struggle; nothing out of place and no damage except for the whiskey spilled over the couch. There was another door in the inner wall opposite the entrance, which figured to be a connecting door with the adjacent suite. Ozzie Meeker's? I moved over there to have a look at it, and it was locked. I could tell that without touching the knob, by peering into the crack between its edge and the jamb: parts of the bolts were visible in there—two of them, one thrown on this side and one thrown on the other side, both deadbolt locks similar to the one on the entrance door, except that you couldn't open it from the other suite with a key.

Dancer made a funny, low, keening sound, and I looked over at him. He had quit rocking and was sitting motionless, staring at nothing; a line of spittle dribbled from one corner of his mouth. He made the sound again, kept on making it, and I realized that it wasn't keening at all—it was a familiar, tuneless singing.

> *"No tengo tabaco,*
> *"No tengo papel,*
> *"No tengo dinero—*
> *"Goddammit to hell . . ."*

I went over to him and punched his arm. The chanting cut off in midverse; his eyelids fluttered, and his eyes focused again, slowly, as if he were coming back from a long way away. His gaze settled on my face and clung there, moist and pain-edged.

"Talk to me, Russ," I said.

"Talk?"

"What happened in here?"

"I don't know," he said thickly. "Don't know."

"Tell me what you do know."

"Nothing to tell. Loud noise woke me up. Then more noises. I came out here, there he was. Lying there with the gun next to him. I thought it was booze at first. DT's. Things crawling out of walls. Jesus."

"Are you saying you didn't let him in here?"

"No. Wasn't me."

"Then how did he get in?"

"Must've got a key somewhere."

"How long ago did you come up here?"

"Don't remember. Right after Benny and I got back from the bar. Goddamn Bloody Marys hit me hard."

"Who's Benny?"

"Convention guy."

"You came up here alone?"

"Yeah. Alone. Must've passed out."

"And stayed passed out until you heard the noises?"

"Yeah."

"Listen to me, Russ," I said. "I heard the shots too; I was right out in the hall. Nobody left this suite afterward, and there wasn't anybody in here but you when I came in. The hall door was locked, probably from the inside; the connecting door is locked on this side and on the other side too; and even if it were possible for somebody to get in or out through the bedroom windows, which it isn't, they're all locked. You tell me how somebody else could have killed Colodny."

"Don't *know*." He grimaced and jammed the heels of both hands against his temples. "Jesus, my head's coming apart."

"This is only a sample of what you'll get from the police."

"I didn't do it; how many times I have to tell you? Maybe he did it himself. Shot himself."

"Sure. In your room instead of his own. And in the chest, not the head like most gun suicides. And with a gun stolen from Cybil Wade because it was easier than taking a bottle of sleeping pills, say, or throwing himself out a window."

"Cybil?" Dancer said. "Sweeteyes with a gun?"

"You don't know anything about that either, huh?"

He made an anguished sound that turned into a half-cough, half-retch. "Leave me alone. Leave me the hell alone, will you?"

Somebody started banging loudly on the hall door. Not enough time had passed for it to be Eberhardt, so that meant the hotel manager. I crossed to the door and asked who was there, and a voice said, "Security officer. The manager's with me."

I unlocked the door and let them in. The security officer looked about as much like an old-fashioned hotel dick as I did like Bogart in *The Maltese Falcon*; he was a neat, dapper little guy with graying hair and delicate-looking hands, dressed in an expensive Wilkes-Bashford suit. The manager, on the other hand, looked just as you'd expect the manager of a Victorian throwback like the Continental to look: tall, prim, reserved, and right now wearing an expression of fluttery horror. His name was Mr. Rigby, and his prominent Adam's apply never did stop bobbing up and down his neck like a yo-yo on a string. The security officer's name was Harris.

Rigby did not stay long. He took one blanching look at what was left of Colodny, listened to Dancer start in again with his *"No tengo"* chant, made shocked noises about the Continental's reputation, and went away to do something administrative. When he was gone, Harris asked me for an account of what had happened. I gave him one, omitting the more involved details. He looked, sounded, and acted neutral and businesslike, which made him easy to deal with. He knew as well as I did that guys like us, hotel cops and private cops, were better off not trying to get too involved in a homicide case.

But he did prowl around a little, the way I had, looking at the doors and windows without touching anything. While he was doing that, I stood off against one wall and kept an eye on Dancer. And waited. And wished to Christ I was somewhere else.

Harris was just coming out of the bedroom when the banging started again on the hall door. He opened up, and I heard Eberhardt identify himself. Then he came trooping inside with an inspector I knew named Klein and two other plainclothesmen outfitted with a lab kit and photographic equipment.

Eberhardt looked tired. There were puffy bags under both eyes, and the sharp angles and contrasting blunt planes of his face seemed less defined than usual, as if the features were all beginning to melt together. It made me wonder if there was anything wrong with him, or if it was just that he was being overworked again.

He spent the first couple of minutes examining the body.

Then, while the lab boys went to work and Klein started asking Dancer a few preliminary questions, he came over and glowered at me around the battered old briar clamped in one corner of his mouth.

"You okay, Eb?" I asked him.

That got me a sharp look. "Rum dandy. Why?"

"You look kind of beat."

"Yeah, well, never mind how I look. This is business. So let's have the details—everything you didn't go into on the phone."

"Sure. But it's a little complicated."

"It always is when you're mixed up in it."

I went over it all step by step, beginning with Dancer's visit to my office on Thursday afternoon and finishing with what I had done since entering this suite. Eberhardt listened without interrupting and without changing expression. "That's all of it?" he said when I was done.

"All of it as far as I know."

"Uh-huh. Well, it looks pretty cut-and-dried to me. Your boy Dancer, there, broke into the Wade woman's room Thursday night and swiped her gun. Today he gets drunk and uses the gun on Colodny, because of this 'Hoodwink' crap and because they were old enemies." Eberhardt shrugged. "An easy one for a change."

Sure, I thought, an easy one. Cut-and-dried. Dancer's been in trouble and asking for more for three days; and nobody else could have shot Colodny. He's guilty no matter how much he protests otherwise. So what if a lot of other people might have hated Colodny enough to want him dead? So what if it doesn't feel right? Dancer killed him and that's that. An easy one for a change. . . .

ELEVEN

Eberhardt shooed me out of there before long, with instructions not to leave the hotel for the next couple of hours in case he wanted to talk to me again. There was a uniformed cop stationed at the entrance to the cul-de-sac, and two more in the east corridor, to keep gawkers from cluttering up the area. A fourth cop somewhere near the elevators was having trouble with one citizen; I could hear their raised voices as I started up the hall.

The citizen turned out to be Lloyd Underwood. I recognized his voice before I saw him, querulous and more manic than ever, saying, "Why can't I see Russ Dancer? Everyone is waiting for him in the auditorium; he's forty minutes late for his panel already. Has something happened to him? Why won't you tell me what's going on?"

"It's not my job to tell you anything, buddy," the cop said. "If you want to wait around and talk to one of the inspectors, that's fine so long as you keep quiet. Otherwise, back on the elevator."

I made the turn out of the corridor, toward where they were. Underwood spotted me immediately, waved a fistful of mimeographed papers in my direction, and ran over to paw at my arm.

"You came from Dancer's room, didn't you?" he said. "What's going on? This officer won't tell me anything—"

"Take it easy," I said, "calm down."

"But something's happened, I *know* it has."

"Something's happened, all right. We'll talk about it on the way down to the auditorium."

I prodded him to the elevator panel, pushed the down button. The cop watched me without saying anything; he looked more bored than anything else. A car came pretty soon, and when Underwood and I were inside, I punched the button for the mezzanine and waited until the doors slid shut and the car began to descend before I said, "Frank Colodny is dead."

"What?" he said. "What?"

"You heard me right. He was killed in Dancer's room."

Underwood gaped at me. "Dead? Killed? Oh, my God! How did it happen? You don't mean that Dancer—"

"It looks that way. Maybe not, though. It's too soon to tell just what took place."

The car stopped and the doors whispered open. Underwood stayed where he was, looking horrified, so I had to take his arm and steer him out. He said then, "What am I going to tell everybody? They're all waiting; I have to tell them something . . ."

"That's up to you. But don't use the word *murder,* and don't imply anything against Dancer. Keep it as low-key as you can."

"Low-key," he said. He still looked horrified, but he sounded flustered and aggrieved. "The convention is ruined. You know that, don't you?" As if it were my fault. "All the work we put into it, all the time and money . . . *God.*"

"Yeah," I said.

"And not just for this year—ruined for good. How can we put on a con again after a thing like this? Who would want to come?"

I said sourly, "Not Frank Colodny, that's for sure."

There were maybe a dozen people standing around in the hallway outside the auditorium, smoking, talking in low voices. Through the open doors I could see the rest inside, most of them on their feet too; Kerry was one of the few sitting down. The general atmosphere seemed to be one of agitation and annoyance: the most popular object in the room was the clock on one wall.

As soon as we stepped inside, Underwood broke away and

made straight for the dais. I moved over to hold up the side wall. Kerry had got up as soon as I appeared and she came over to join me. So did Bert Praxas and Waldo Ramsey, both of whom had been standing nearby.

Kerry put her hand on my arm. "What's going on?" she said. "Is Dancer drunk again?"

"He's drunk, all right. But it's worse than that."

Underwood was up on the dais now, calling for attention through one of the table microphones. The rumble of conversation in the room died away into an expectant hush; you could almost see necks craning forward. I picked out the ones belonging to Cybil Wade and Ozzie Meeker and kept my eye on them. Ivan Wade was nowhere to be seen. Neither was Jim Bohannon.

"I'm sorry to say I have some tragic news," Underwood said into the microphone. "Frank Colodny has been . . . killed in an accident here in the hotel."

It rocked them pretty good, as that kind of news always does. Voices rose, people looked at each other in disbelief, a couple of those sitting down popped up like jack-in-the-boxes. I was still watching Cybil Wade and Ozzie Meeker. Beyond a slight head jerk Meeker didn't show any reaction at all, but Cybil seemed to go through a whole series of them. First she stiffened and her eyes got wide and her mouth came open; then her mouth closed, and she raised one hand to touch the makeup-faded bruise on her cheek; then the hand dropped and the rigidity left her; then the near corner of her mouth lifted slightly in what might have been a grim smile; then her whole body appeared to sag and she slumped lower on the chair, the way a person does at a release of tension. All of this in no more than six or seven seconds.

Kerry's hand was tight on my arm. When I heard her say, "My God!" in a low voice I transferred my gaze from her mother to her. She wore a shocked and frightened expression, and her eyes were full of questions. Ramsey and Praxas looked shocked too; neither of them could seem to decide whether to give his attention to Underwood or to me.

People were clamoring at Underwood for more information. He kept saying. "I don't know any of the details. It has something to do with Russ Dancer, and the police have been called in. They're upstairs now. That's all I know."

"But that's not all *you* know, is it?" Kerry said to me. "What happened to Colodny?"

"He was shot. In Dancer's room."

"Shot? You mean murdered?"

"The police think so." I was not going to tell her he'd been shot with Cybil's stolen gun, not here in front of Praxas and Ramsey and the others milling around.

Ramsey said, "Did Dancer do it?"

"Maybe. He says no, but I found him alone with the body a few seconds after it happened. I heard the shot as I was coming down the hallway."

"But why?" Praxas asked. "Why would Russ do such a thing?"

"He didn't like Colodny much. And he thought Colodny was behind the 'Hoodwink' extortion."

"That's not much of a motive for murder."

"It might be if a man was drunk enough and had violent tendencies to begin with."

"I guess so. But my God, a cold-blooded murder . . ."

Underwood made another announcement, this one to the effect that the rest of today's program would have to be cancelled; he looked pained as he did it. Then the buzzing crowd began to file out of the auditorium. But Ozzie Meeker kept on sitting in his chair, the only person in the room who was. Behind his horn-rimmed glasses his bird-like eyes seemed fixed on a spot somewhere to the left of the dais. He looked about as unconcerned as a man can look in the middle of general upheaval. I wondered if maybe he was drunk again, or if maybe he was savoring Colodny's demise for reasons of his own. I had not forgotten the angry words the two of them had had on Thursday night.

I said to Ramsey and Praxas, "You'd better keep yourselves available. The police will want to talk to you and the others."

"I wasn't planning to go anywhere," Praxas said.

"Neither was I," Ramsey said. "Except maybe to the bar."

Kerry had gone over to talk to Cybil. I gestured to her to wait for me, and when she nodded I made my way through the rows of empty chairs to where Meeker was sitting. He looked up when I stopped in front of him and blinked at me a couple of times. Up close his eyes had a faint hangover glaze, but he smelled of breath mints, not whiskey.

"Well," he said, "the detective."

"Hell of a thing about Colodny, isn't it?"

"Is it?"

"You don't think so?"

"I'd be a liar if I said I did. I hated his guts."

"Why?"

"He was a man people hated," Meeker said, and shrugged. "All the Pulpeteers hated him, you know. Did Dancer kill him?"

"What makes you think he was murdered?"

"Wasn't he?"

"Maybe. What did you and Colodny argue about on Thursday night?"

The question got me what passed for a sly look. "Thursday night?"

"At the cocktail party. You had words."

"Did we? I don't remember."

"Sure you do. He warned you to stay away from him."

"Did he?"

"Was that because you'd threatened him?"

"Not me. Why would I threaten him?"

Yeah, I thought. Why?

I said, "The police'll be around to talk to you pretty soon, Meeker. Maybe you'll be a little more cooperative with them."

"Maybe I will." He grinned at me. "And maybe I won't."

I went back and collected Kerry—Cybil had disappeared— and we went out into the hallway. She said, "Why did you want to talk to Meeker?"

"Because I think he's got secrets."

"What kind of secrets?"

"I don't know yet. What did Cybil have to say about Colodny's death?"

"Not very much. She seemed kind of wilted."

Relieved was the proper word, but I didn't correct her.

The area in front of the elevators was crowded with people waiting for cars to take them up or down; we opted for the stairs. In the lobby I went over to the front desk and found the prim manager, whose name I'd forgotten, deep in conversation with the security officer, Harris. I told them I would be in the Garden Bistro if Lieutenant Eberhardt wanted to see me, and Harris said, "Fine," and the prim guy favored me with a prim nod. But he looked at me as if I was one of those he held responsible for scandalizing his hotel.

The lobby did not look scandalized so far. The police had evidently been ushered in through the service entrance and taken upstairs in one of the service elevators, and word of the homicide had not yet spread among the guests and general staff. A few of the convention people were hanging around in knots, looking nervous and furtive, but nobody seemed to be paying much attention to them. Kerry and I made our way across to the coffee shop and found a table in the rear. Neither of us said anything until we'd ordered coffee.

"Are you going to tell me the details?" she asked then. "Or do I have to read them in the papers?"

"I'll tell you what I know," I said, and did that. I still did not mention the fact that the murder weapon was her mother's missing .38, but I might as well have; she seemed to intuit it and asked me flat out if it was. So I admitted it.

She said, "Then it was Dancer who stole the gun."

"If he killed Colodny, it must have been."

"Why do you say 'if'? Didn't you just tell me that all the doors and windows in his room were locked from the inside and you got there only a few seconds after the shot was fired? He *must* be the killer."

"So it would seem. But I keep having doubts."

"Why?"

"The way he looked, the things he said. He was drunk and it's hard for a drunk to lie convincingly."

"That's pretty flimsy against all the evidence. How could Colodny have been killed in his room if Dancer's not guilty?"

I shook my head.

"Who else could possibly have done it?"

"Just about anybody, I suppose."

"You mean one of the other Pulpeteers."

"Well, that's how it would add up."

Ridges formed on her forehead. "You're not thinking of Cybil?"

"No," I said, but it could have been Cybil, all right. She might have lied about the .38 being stolen. The sneak thief could have been after something else and she could have hidden the gun somewhere, with the intention of using it on Colodny. The question then was, why? What would her motive be? But this was a game you could play with Ivan Wade and the other Pulpeteers as well. Any of them *could* be guilty, and if you dug deep enough, you'd probably find more than one suitable motive. To make that reasonable, though, you had to eliminate Dancer as the primary suspect, which meant providing an answer to the one big question Kerry had just posed.

How could Colodny have been shot in that locked room if Dancer wasn't the killer?

Our coffee came and Kerry toyed with hers for a time, mostly in a kind of brooding silence. Pretty soon she said, "I think I'll go find Cybil and have another talk with her. My father, too."

I nodded. "Are we having dinner tonight?"

"If I say no, you won't take it as a rejection, will you?"

"Not unless you mean it that way."

"I'm just not in the mood, after all this. Tomorrow or Monday, okay?"

"Okay."

"But call me tonight if you want. I'll be home."

I said I would. And after she was gone, I sat there and drank coffee and did some meditating, none of which got me anywhere. At the end of fifteen minutes, I decided I had had enough of sitting around; I paid the check and went out and prowled around for a time, down by the huckster room—it was closed now—and back again.

When I returned to the reception area, Eberhardt was over at the desk, scowling at the prim-faced manager. As soon as I came up, the scowl switched in my direction and hung on me like a dark cloud. It made me think, irrelevantly, of one of the worst lines I had ever read in a pulp: "Mister, I'm gonna cloud up and rain all over you."

"Where the hell have *you* been?" he growled.

"Wandering around the lobby. Why?"

"You left word you'd be in the goddamn coffee shop. You think I got nothing better to do than play hide and seek?"

"Lighten up, Eb, will you?"

"Yeah, lighten up. The hell with that. Listen, I'm finished here, and as far as I'm concerned, so are you. Come down to the Hall tomorrow or the next day and sign a statement."

"Sure. What about Dancer?"

"What about him?"

"Is he going to be charged?"

"What the hell do you think? Of course he's going to be charged. He's guilty as sin, and you know it."

"Has he confessed?"

"Do most of them confess? He did it and that's that; don't go making a big mystery out of this. Just go home and try to keep your fat ass out of trouble."

"I don't go looking for it, Eb."

He made a snorting sound and took his scowl away to the elevators.

There was no reason for me to hang around the hotel. Besides, its somber Victorian good taste was beginning to depress me. I got out of there, claimed my car from the garage down the block, and pointed it across town to Pacific Heights. Eberhardt's odd behavior nagged at my thoughts part of the way. He was always irascible, but today there had been none of the affection that underlay his gruffness. Something was weighing heavy on him, and I was not going to be satisfied until I found out what it was.

The day was getting on toward dinnertime, so I stopped at a place on Union that makes pretty good pizza and ordered a pepperoni-and-extra-cheese to go. In my flat I opened a bottle of Schlitz and sat eating in front of the bay window, where I could look out over the Bay and watch the sunset bathe the hills of Marin in a soft reddish glow. It made me feel kind of pensive. And aware of how quiet and empty the flat was.

I went into the bedroom. Kerry had insisted on making the bed this morning, and it had never looked so neat. The whole damned room looked neat for a change; it wasn't half bad that way, either. A different perspective. I sat down on the bed, hauled up the phone receiver, and dialed Kerry's number. The thing buzzed ten times, emptily, before I put the handset down again.

To pass the time, I decided on some reading. But instead of taking a pulp off one of the shelves, I dragged out the "Hoodwink" manuscript, which I had carted home from the office, and had another go at that. I went all the way through it without feeling any more enlightened than the first time I'd read it—but when I put it down there was a funny scratching sensation at the back of my mind. Over the years I had had enough similar itches to recognize them as insights trying to be born: there was something about the novelette—plot, style, something—that I was overlooking.

I read it a third time. But the insight, whatever it might be, stayed in labor. There was no use in trying to force it through; it would get itself born eventually.

Damn, but it was quiet in there. I turned on the little portable television, something I seldom do, just to have some noise. A little while later, I went into the bedroom and dialed Kerry's number again. Still no answer. The nightstand clock said that it was after ten. She told me she'd be home tonight, I thought. So where is she?

So she's out somewhere. She's a big girl; she doesn't have to answer to you if she decides to stay out on a Saturday night. What's the matter with you? Mooning around here like a lovesick jerk. You're fifty-three years old, for Christ's sake. Go to bed, why don't you? You old fart, you.

I went to bed.

But I didn't sleep right away. The damn bed felt empty, too, and I could still smell the sweet musk of her perfume on the other pillow.

I dreamed I was in a room where half a dozen guys were playing poker. They were all private eyes from the pulps: Carmady, Max Latin, Race Williams, Jim Bennett—some of the best of the bunch. Latin wanted to know what kind of detective I thought I was; his voice sounded like Kerry's. I said I was a pulp detective. Carmady said, "No you're not, you can't play with us because you're not one of us," and I said, "But I am, I'm the same kind of private eye you are," and Bennett said, "Private eyes can't fall in love with younger women because they can't be dirty old men," and I said, "But I'm not in love with her," and Williams said, "You old fart, you," and the phone went off six inches from my ear and put an end to all this nonsense.

I sat up in bed, rubbed at my eyes until I could focus on the dial of the clock. It was 8:40. Welcome to a new day, I thought, and fumbled the handset up to my ear.

A male voice I didn't recognize made a question out of my name. I confirmed it, and the voice said, "My name is Arthur Pitchfield. I'm the public defender assigned to represent Russell Dancer."

"What can I do for you, Mr. Pitchfield?"

"You can't do anything for me, I'm afraid. I'm calling for Mr. Dancer. He'd like to see you as soon as possible."

"He would, huh?"

"Yes," Pitchfield said. "I told him there's very little a private investigator can do for him—no offense—but he insists you're a friend of his."

Sure I am, I thought. "He's still at the Hall of Justice?"

"Of course. Even if bail had been set, he couldn't meet it." A pause. "I'm advising him to plead guilty, you know."

"What does Dancer say?"

"He says no," Pitchfield said. "He claims he's innocent."

"Tell him I'll be down around ten," I said, and hung up on him.

I sat there for a little while, waking up. Well, I told myself, you might have known it was coming. Maybe you did know, huh? You agreed fast enough. But it could be the poor bastard *is* innocent, despite all the circumstantial evidence. What can it hurt to talk to him? Nothing much you can do for him, Pitchfield may have been right about that, but at least you can listen to what he has to say.

Then I thought, wryly: An old fart, a lovesick jerk, a brother-figure to an alcoholic ex-pulp writer. *Some* private eye. Is it any wonder Carmady and Latin and the rest of the boys want to kick you out of the fraternity?

TWELVE

The Hall of Justice was a massive gray stone building on Bryant Street, south of Market, not all that far from Skid Row and the Tenderloin. It looked just like what it was: you could take away all the signs and bring somebody in from Iowa or rural New Hampshire and ask him what the building was, and he'd tell you in two seconds flat. On gray days it looked even more austere, and this was a gray day. The fog had come in sometime during the night, along with a chill wind, and built a high overcast that wiped out the nice summery weather we'd been having.

It being Sunday, there was available street parking on Bryant. I put my car into a slot a half-block away, went down and inside, and rode one of the elevators up to where they had the holding cells on the top floor. I filled out a form, and one of the cops on duty took it and went away somewhere. It took him ten minutes to find his way back. Five minutes after that, I was ushered through a metal detector and then into the visitors' room, where I sat myself down in one of the screened-off cubicles. And another three minutes after that, Dancer was brought in.

He was wearing one of the orange jumpsuits the city and county provide for their prisoners; it looked as incongruous on him as a dress. He walked like a man in pain, and one look at his eyes told you he was suffering plenty. The whites were gray and bloody, the pupils a runny brown color. The effect was of something—eggs, maybe—that was spoiled and decomposing. He winced as he sat down, dug the heels of his hands into his temples, and grimaced. Then he put those eyes on me. And through the wire mesh and the hangover dullness, I was looking at a frightened man.

"Thanks for coming," he said. His voice sounded hoarse, brittle. "I wasn't sure if you would."

"I figured I owed you this much."

"What did that prick Pitchfield say to you on the phone?"

"Not much. Just that he wanted you to plead guilty and you weren't having any."

"Fuck him. I didn't kill Colodny; why should I plead guilty? 'Cop a plea,' he says. 'They'll let you off with second-degree, and you won't do more than six or seven years in jail.' Jesus!"

"It doesn't look good for you, Russ, you know that."

"I don't care how it looks. I'm no murderer."

"You were pretty drunk yesterday . . ."

"So I was drunk. I've been drunk a thousand times in my life, and I never killed anybody. Why would I want to kill Colodny? I didn't have any motive."

"The police must think you did."

"Sure—that 'Hoodwink' crap. They say I got him to come to my room on some pretext and then shot him. They found a portable typewriter in Colodny's room that matches the typeface on that note he slipped me, so they know he was behind the extortion scam. And one of the others told them about the scuffle we had in the hotel bar and that there was bad blood between us back in the pulp days. That was all the cops needed."

"You *did* attack him in the bar," I said.

"Yeah, all right. But there's a big difference between cuffing somebody around and shooting him."

"What about the gun? You'd never seen it before?"

"No. The cops think I stole it from Cybil, but that's crazy too. I never knew she had a gun. Why would she pack one around with her?"

"She claims she brought it with her for demonstration purposes on her private eye panel. But she might have had another reason."

"What reason?"

"I thought maybe you could tell me that."

He wagged his head.

"Did you talk to her Friday night? Have an argument with her?"

"No. What kind of argument would I have with her?"

"The kind where you lose your head, maybe, and swat her one."

"Are you nuts? I'd never lay a hand on Cybil."

"Somebody did Friday night. She's got a bruise on her cheek to prove it."

"Colodny," Dancer said.

"Why Colodny?"

"He was the kind to hit women. He did it once, with this love-pulp writer he was bedding back in the forties, right in front of everybody at a Pulpeteers meeting. Just because she was kidding around. Ivan Wade took a poke at him for it. Ivan's a bastard but he respects women."

"But why would Colodny have hit Cybil?"

"Maybe she said something to him and he didn't like it. He screwed her out of money, too, just like he did the rest of us."

"I know all about that. But it's not enough; there has to be a specific motive for his murder. Did Cybil or any of the others have one that you know about?"

"No."

"Something from back in the forties, maybe?"

"How would I know what went on between Colodny and anybody else, back then or since? I hadn't seen him in thirty years, for Christ's sake. Or any of the others in almost that long."

His voice had risen until it was a scratchy whine. The guard, standing against the wall behind Dancer, frowned over at us. I said, "Take it easy, Russ. I'm listening to you and I'm willing to give you the benefit of the doubt. I'm on your side."

He ran his tongue over lips that looked blistered. The fear in him settled below the surface again, but it was plain that he was having to struggle to maintain his control. The hangover was not helping matters; his hands kept plucking at each other, and you could almost see his nerves jangling.

I said, "Do the others have alibis for the time of the shooting?"

He nodded jerkily. "The cops say so."

"Unshakeable alibis?"

"They didn't tell me that. They can't be, can they?"

"Let's hope not. Suppose we go over again what happened yesterday. Can you remember it any better today?"

"Part of it, yeah. I've been over it a dozen times in my head."

"All right. You were out drinking Bloody Marys with one of the convention people—"

"Benny. His name was Benny something."

"Benny, right. What time did you get back?"

"I'm not sure. Around eleven, I think."

"Then what?"

"We split up and I went upstairs to my room."

"Did you talk to anybody on the way?"

"No. I think I stopped to bang on Ozzie Meeker's door, see if he wanted to buy me a drink. But he wasn't in."

"Did you lock your door after you went inside?"

"I can't remember."

"Can you remember if the room was empty?"

"It must have been. Why? You think somebody could've been hiding in there when I came in?"

"It's possible. But if there was anybody there or anything out of the ordinary, you were too drunk to notice."

"Yeah. Too frigging drunk to notice."

"After you came in, did you go straight into the bedroom?"

"I can't remember."

"Or maybe you sat down to have a drink first."

"Uh-uh. No."

"Why are you so sure?"

"Because I didn't have any booze in the room."

I frowned at him through the mesh. "What about the bottle that was on the couch? You remember that, don't you?"

"Yeah," he said, and frowned back at me. "A quart of rye."

"How did it get there if it wasn't yours?"

"I don't know."

"You're sure you didn't carry it up with you?"

"Pretty sure. I don't drink rye; it's an Eastern hooch."

"Who does drink it among the Pulpeteers?"

His mouth pulled down at the corners. "The only one I know of was Colodny. That's all he drank in the old days."

"Well, he could have brought the bottle in with him. But why? Why come to your room in the first place? And how did he get in, if you didn't let him in?"

"I *didn't*. Maybe he got a key somewhere."

"Maybe. But that still doesn't explain why he was there."

Dancer shook his head: a study in raw misery.

"Did you see Colodny yesterday morning, before you went out drinking with Benny?"

"No."

"Was he around when you got back to the hotel?"

"No."

"Then the last time you saw him was when?"

"At the party on Friday night."

"Did you say anything to him there?"

He pressed knuckles across the bridge of his nose, trying to remember. "I was a couple of sheets to the wind then, too; a deal my agent had been trying to put together fell through. And I was still pissed about that note he'd slipped me. I think I said something to him about watching his step or I'd fix his wagon . . ." He broke off as he realized the significance of that. Then he said, "Ah, Christ," and pawed his mouth out of shape.

"Lots of people overheard this, I suppose?"

"Enough. Bohannon and Ramsey and Ozzie Meeker were all there. One of them probably told the cops about it. But I didn't mean it like it sounds. I wasn't threatening his life."

I said, "What did Colodny say in response?"

"He didn't say anything. He just walked away."

"Did you have any other contact with him that night?"

"No. He didn't stay long at the party."

"Let's get back to yesterday. You said the gunshot woke you up."

"Yeah. It was loud as hell."

"Did you know what it was right away?"

"No. I was still drunk."

"But you got up right away."

"A few seconds, maybe. I'm not sure."

"Did you hear anything else?"

"Some noises, I think."

"Before you got into the other room."

"Yeah."

"What sort of noises?"

"Just noises. A cry or yell or something, then some other sounds. None of it is clear in my head."

"Okay, you went into the other room after a few seconds. What did you see?"

"Colodny lying there dead."

"Anything else? Movement, anything out of place?"

"No."

"What did you do then?"

"I guess I picked up the gun. Stupid goddamn thing to do but I did it. Then you started beating on the door and came inside. That's all."

"I hope so, Russ," I said. "I hope you've told me everything and all of it is the truth. If I find out different, it's quits."

He brightened a little. "You'll help me? You'll find out what really happened?"

"I'll do what I can, as long as the police have no objections. But don't expect miracles. I'm not all that good."

"Sure you are. I saw the way you handled things in Cypress Bay; I read about those other cases of yours in the papers. If anybody can get me out of here it's you."

"I'll do what I can," I said again. "No promises."

"I don't have any money," he said, "you know that. But you clear me of this, I'll find a way to pay you. I mean that—I will."

"That's something we can talk about later." I got up on my feet. "I'll let Pitchfield know I'm working for you so he won't keep after you to enter a guilty plea."

I left him there like a supplicant behind the wire mesh and took the elevator down to General Works. One of the homicide inspectors on duty was Klein; I asked him if Eberhardt had come in today, and he told me yes and that he was in his office. "But he's in a foul mood," Klein said. "He's liable to bite your ass if you go in there."

"I'll take my chances. What's eating him, anyway?"

"I don't know. He's been like that all week."

Klein buzzed him for me, got growls I could hear across the desk, and passed word that I'd have to wait. I waited twenty minutes, watching nothing much going on in the squadroom. Then Eberhardt buzzed out and let me go have an audience.

The air in his office was layered blue with pipe smoke and hot enough to grow orchids. A portable heater glowed on one side of his desk—that in addition to the building's heating system. Eberhardt was in his shirt sleeves, pawing through a mess of papers, puffing away on a scarred apple briar. Grayish beard stubble coated his cheeks; his shirt was wrinkled and had a stain of some kind on the front, and his tie was askew. His features still had that blurred look I had noticed yesterday. The bags under his eyes were heavier, too, as if he had slept little or not at all last night.

As soon as I shut the door he said, "You got ten minutes, no more. I'm up to my ass in paperwork today."

"Sure. How come you've got it so hot in here?"

"It's not hot in here."

"It must be eighty, Eb, with that heater on."

"It's my office, I'll keep it as hot as I like."

"Are you feeling okay?"

He took the pipe out of his mouth and pointed the stem at me, glaring. "You come here for a reason? If you just want to ask dumb questions, get the hell out."

He was beginning to worry me. But prodding him about it would only make him more close-mouthed. Eberhardt was not a man you could prod about anything.

I went over and sat down in one of the chairs before his desk. "I'm here about Russ Dancer."

"Klein's got your statement outside for you to sign."

"I already signed it. I don't mean that."

"What then?"

"I've been upstairs talking to Dancer," I said. "He swears he didn't kill Frank Colodny."

"So?"

"I believe him, Eb."

"I might have known it." He put the pipe back in his mouth and made angry gnawing sounds on the bit. Then he said, "I suppose you want permission to conduct your own investigation."

"That's what I had in mind."

"You're a pain in the ass sometimes, you know that?" It was something he'd said to me before, many times, but this time there was real rancor in the words. "Always getting mixed up in murder cases, always playing the champion role like one of your lousy magazine private eyes. And I'm supposed to hop to it every time you come sucking around for a favor. You think I like any of that? I got enough grief in this job without stumbling over you every time I turn around."

I didn't say anything. Just sat there looking at him.

"Ah, the hell with it. What's the use in talking to you? You don't listen."

"I'm listening now," I said.

"Sure you are. Well, listen to this. Dancer is guilty; he's as guilty as they come. And its *your* testimony that makes it conclusive."

"The locked-room angle," I said.

"That's right, the locked-room angle. Dancer's room was

on the sixth floor, for starters. The windows were all locked from the inside, and there's nothing outside any of them except a sheer wall and thin air. The access hall is a cul-de-sac, and that door was locked when you got to it. The connecting door with Oswald Meeker's room was locked on both sides. You and the maid were out in the main hallway, with a clear view both ways along it, and you both swear the shot came from inside Dancer's room. Less than a minute later you let yourself in and found Dancer with a gun in his hand and the body on the floor behind him. Okay, bright boy. Go ahead and tell me how he can be innocent and somebody else knocked off Colodny."

"I can't tell you how. Unless one of the doors was gimmicked . . ."

"Well, you can get that idea out of your head. The lab boys went over them; they fit snug in the jamb, both of them, and both bolts turn hard, and there's no indication of tampering. They're willing to swear that nobody could have pulled any of that fancy fictional crap, like strings on the deadbolt, even if there had been time for it. Which there wasn't. You think this is a fancy killing? Like hell it is. It's a crime of passion, just like ninety percent of all homicides. Premeditated, maybe; that's up to the courts to decide. But you can't make one of those goddamn impossible crime things out of it."

"I'm not trying to," I said. "I'm just trying to figure angles. Suppose the killer—somebody other than Dancer, for the sake of argument—came out through the hall door and slipped into the room opposite, six-nineteen? There was enough time for somebody to do that; it was at least ten seconds from the time I heard the shot until I got to where I could see into the cul-de-sac."

"Oh sure, right. And Dancer waved bye-bye to him and locked up again after he left."

"What if the killer had a key? That hall door can be locked from the outside with a key."

"Yeah. He came out, locked the door, and disappeared—all in ten seconds. Where did he go, wise guy? Room six-nineteen was vacant, and there aren't any missing keys to it, and that door wasn't tampered with either. The maid and a bunch of other citizens were out in the hallway, so he couldn't have gone by them. You think maybe he hid in the storage closet for a couple of hours and then slipped away when nobody was looking?"

I held up my hands, palms toward him. "Okay, I'm convinced. But *was* there an extra key to Dancer's room—on Colodny's body, maybe?"

"No. The only key he had was the one to his own room. He got inside Dancer's because Dancer let him in."

"Well, not necessarily. He could have bribed somebody to let him in with a passkey. The maid, for instance."

"Nuts. We checked her out; she's been at the hotel twenty-five years. Nobody lasts that long in a ritzy joint like the Continental without being honest."

"Somebody else, then. The point is, Colodny *could* have already been inside the room when Dancer showed up."

"The hell he could."

"Why couldn't he? Eb—"

"Two reasons, that's why." He pointed the pipe stem at me again. "In the first place, the maid knocked on Dancer's door about fifteen minutes before the shooting because it was her time to go in and clean the room. When she didn't get any answer she assumed nobody was home and used her passkey to let herself in. She found Dancer passed out in the bedroom and beat it out of there. But she was around long enough to swear that the front room was empty and the bathroom, which she could see into because the door was open, was also empty. And if you say anything about a guy hiding under the bed, I'll laugh in your face."

"She could have been lying," I said doggedly.

"Why would she lie?"

"It was just a thought. How long was she in the hallway before I showed up?"

"Half a minute or so. She'd just come out of the next room past the cul-de-sac, six-twenty-one."

"Did she see or hear anything?"

"Not until you appeared and the gun went off. Listen, get the hell off the maid; her story's straight, and she's not involved." Another jab with the pipe. "And here's your second reason why nobody could have been hiding in Dancer's room: how would he have got out after Colodny was dead? What do you think this mythical killer did—wave a magic wand and dematerialize?"

The smoke in there was beginning to irritate my lungs; I could feel my chest tightening up. Now that I had been off tobacco for a couple of years, I no longer had any tolerance for it. I felt like getting up and opening the window to let in some air. But if I did it would only make Eberhardt more antagonistic than he already was.

I said, "Dancer told me all the other Pulpeteers have alibis for the time of Colodny's death."

"That's right," he said, and then pulled a face. "Pulpeteers. Of all the silly damn names for a bunch of grandfather types. Where's the dignity in something like that?"

"They were young when they thought it up."

"Pulp writers," he said. "And private eyes. Bah."

"Eb, will you tell me how the alibis break down?"

"No. Listen, I've had enough of your questions."

"If none of them is airtight, somebody could have slipped away for a few minutes. Or somebody could be lying to protect somebody else—"

"Don't you hear good?"

"Look, Eb, I'm only—"

"I said that's enough!" He slapped the pipe down on his desk; ashes and half-burned tobacco sprayed out over the litter of papers. "Your time's up. Get the hell out of here. And don't come sucking around again for free information. I'm sick of looking at your goddamn wop face."

There were still some things I wanted to know about besides the alibi breakdown: the typewriter that had been found in Colodny's hotel room; the bottle of rye whiskey in Dancer's room. But he was pretty upset, face all blood-dark, and provoking him would only get me upset too. His cutting remarks had already begun to fray the edges of my temper—the one about my "goddamn wop face" in particular. We had traded ethnic insults for thirty years, but this was the first time either of us had ever put malice into one.

"Okay," I said, "I'm going. Maybe you'll decide to be a human being again one of these days. Not to mention a friend. Let me know if that happens."

I shoved up out of the chair, pivoted around it, and went over to the door. I had my hand on the knob when he said, "Wait a minute," in a much quieter voice.

I came around. "What?"

The anger had drained out of his face; he was sitting slump-shouldered now, and all of a sudden he seemed old and tired and wasted-looking. He had let down his defenses finally—and what I was looking at was naked anguish.

"Dana left me," he said.

It was a flat statement, without inflection, but there was so much emotion wrapped up in it that I could feel the skin ripple along my back. "Ah Jesus, Eb . . ."

"Last Sunday. Week ago today. I went out to Candlestick to watch the Giants play, I came home, she had all her bags packed."

"*Why?*"

"Twenty-eight years we've been married. Not all of them good, but most of them. I thought it was a good marriage. I thought I was a decent husband." He let out a heavy breath, picked up the apple briar and stared at it blindly. "I think she's been having an affair," he said.

I tried not to wince. "Is that what she told you?"

"Not in so many words. But there've been signs, little things, little signals for three or four months. And she wouldn't tell me where she was going. All she'd say was that the marriage wasn't working, she was going to file for divorce—'I'm sorry, Eb,' she said, and out the door. Twenty-eight years, and 'I'm sorry, Eb,' and out the door."

"Do you . . . have any idea who it is?"

"No. Does it matter? I figured, okay, she's having a fling. I didn't like it but I could accept it. I had a couple of things in my time, I never told you about them but I did. So did Dana, once, a long time ago. She told me about that one, everything, and I forgave her, and I told her about it both times I strayed, too. It was a good marriage, goddamn it. It *was*."

"Maybe she'll change her mind, come back . . ."

"Not this time. She's gone. It's over, finished, she's gone. But I still love her, you know? I still love the bitch."

I did not say anything. What can you say?

He looked up at me—big, stolid, tough Eberhardt, the original Rock of Gibraltar. And in his eyes there was some of the same mute appeal that I had seen in Dancer's eyes only a little while ago.

"What am I going to do?" he said. "What the hell am I going to *do*?"

THIRTEEN

It was one o'clock when I got out of that hot smoky office and out of the Hall of Justice into the cold afternoon wind. I picked up my car and took it over to Sixth and turned uptown toward the Hotel Continental. The heat and the pipe smoke had combined to give me a headache, and what Eberhardt had told me only made me feel worse. A kind of grayness moved through me, thick and heavy like the fog roiling overhead. It had been some while since I had felt this low down.

Eb and Dana. Christ, I had been best man at their wedding. I had spent hundreds of hours with them over the years. I had suffered through Dana's good-natured attempts to fix me up with various women and get me married off. I had watched them banter with each other and share the cooking duties at Sunday afternoon barbecues and walk hand in hand at Ocean Beach, Kezar Stadium, Golden Gate Park. Twenty-eight years. Half a lifetime, almost. They had been my friends all that time, and I had thought I knew them; I had thought that if ever there was a perfect marriage, two people made for each other, this was it. Yet all the while they'd been having problems, they'd strayed from each other in more ways than one.

Standing up there in Eberhardt's office, listening to him talk about it, I had felt shocked and sad and painfully awkward. And aware of a bitter irony: I had heard it all before, from dozens of clients and prospective clients, men and women both. The same old story—the age-old story. They

approach a private detective the way they approach a priest;
they make you into a kind of father-confessor, and they tell
you everything. And then they ask you to help them do this
or do that to repair their shattered lives. Or they say, as
Eberhardt had said, "What am I going to do? What the hell
am I going to do?"

I never knew what to say to all those others, and I had not
known what to say to Eberhardt. I had no answers for him; I
couldn't do anything for him except to be around if he
needed somebody to talk to or somebody to get drunk with.
You had to get through it by yourself. It was a little like
dying: ultimately you had to face it alone.

But the trouble with me was, I empathized too much with
Eberhardt and all the rest of them; I knew too much about
that quality of aloneness. They hurt, so I hurt. The feeling
private eye, the tough guy riddled with *Weltschmerz*—the fictional stereotype. And the hell with those who thought in
terms of stereotype rather than in terms of humanity. I cared,
that was all. I was *me*, not any other detective, pulp or otherwise. I was me, and Eb and Dana had split up, and I hurt for
both of them.

I had worked myself into a funk by the time I parked my
car and walked down to the Continental. One of those
moods where cynicism keeps vying with melancholy and you
feel like going off somewhere by yourself to brood. But I had
made a commitment to Dancer. I would have to deal with
people today whether I felt like it or not.

There was no one in the lobby I knew. I went over and
took a look along the corridor where the convention tables
had been set up; they were gone. So much for the first annual Western Pulp Con. I tried the Garden Bistro, didn't find
any familiar faces among the late-lunch trade, and tried the
Continental Bar next. That was where I found Jim Bohannon and Ivan and Cybil Wade.

They were sitting at a table near the Queen Anne fireplace,
working on what appeared to be Ramos fizzes. Bohannon
gave me a solemn smile as I came up, and Cybil let me have

one that was not solemn at all. What I got from Ivan Wade was a blank stare. It was dark in there and I couldn't see his eyes clearly, but I thought that they showed hostility. Because of my relationship with Kerry? I wondered. Or for some other reason?

Bohannon said, "Didn't expect to see you today. Rest of the convention's been cancelled, you know."

"So I gathered."

"Haven't you had enough of pulp writers?" Wade said. His tone was the same one he had used on Dancer at the party Thursday night: quiet, even, but with an overcoating of venom. "Not to mention their offspring."

Cybil said, "Ivan, please."

The mood I was in made me bristle a little. But I was not going to get anywhere, or do myself any good, by indulging Wade and making a scene. I said to Cybil, "All right if I join you for a bit?"

It wasn't all right with Wade; his expression made that plain even in the murky light. But Cybil said, "Of course," and he offered no objection. So I took the only empty chair, between Bohannon and Cybil, and sat myself down in it. That put me opposite Wade, who glared at me over the rim of his glass.

Nobody had anything to say for a few seconds. Wade kept glaring at me, but I told myself again that I was not going to be provoked and ignored him. Bohannon looked vaguely uncomfortable. Cybil, on the other hand, looked to be in good spirits, as if a burden had been lifted from her and nothing much could bother her as a result. Colodny's death? It would seem that way, judging from her relief at the news yesterday.

Bohannon cleared his throat. "Have you heard anything more about Dancer?" he asked me. "Has he confessed?"

"No, he hasn't confessed."

"I suppose the police have charged him by now."

"They have, but they could be making a mistake."

"Mistake?"

"I don't think he's guilty," I said.

That sat them all up on their chairs. Wade said, "What kind of nonsense is that? Of course he's guilty."

"Not until it's proven in court."

"But you were there just after it happened," Cybil said. "You found him with the body . . ."

"I also talked to him then, and again this morning. He says he's innocent and I'm inclined to believe him."

"How could he be? All the doors were locked, and Russ and Frank were the only people in the room. How could someone else have done it?"

"I don't know yet. But I'm going to try to find out."

"You mean you're working for Dancer?" Bohannon asked.

"On his behalf, yes."

Cybil said, "Do you think one of the other Pulpeteers killed Frank?"

"That's the logical assumption, I'm afraid."

"It's also a ridiculous assumption," Wade said in his supercilious way. "Dancer killed him and that's that. All your stirring around won't prove any different."

Ignore him, I thought. He's Kerry's father, remember?

Bohannon had begun to look thoughtful. "I don't know, Ivan," he said to Wade. "None of us liked Colodny worth a damn."

"True enough. But I wouldn't have killed him. Would you?"

"Only people I'm likely to kill," Bohannon said, "are rustlers and outlaws. Which Colodny was, come to think of it—but I mean the fictional kind."

"But Dancer would have," Wade insisted. "It's obvious he hated Colodny, and he's always been prone to violence when he was drinking."

"Now that's not true," Cybil said. "Rowdiness yes, but violence?"

He gave her the same kind of look he'd been giving me. She gave it right back to him. You could tell just from that what kind of marriage they had; neither of them backed down an inch.

I said, just to see what would happen, "I understand you and Mrs. Wade were together at the time of the shooting—is that right?"

Wade put his glare on me again. "What kind of question is that?"

"A reasonable one."

"I suppose you think we weren't together."

"I didn't say that, Mr. Wade."

"I suppose you think one of us was off committing some sort of locked-room murder right under your nose. Of all the damned—"

"Oh Ivan, for God's sake be civil. The man has a right to ask simple questions. Particularly so if Russ Dancer *is* innocent. Do you want to see an innocent man go to prison?"

"For all I care," Wade said, "Russ Dancer can go to hell."

Cybil made an exasperated gesture. "Well, I care," she said. And to me, "We were together, yes, but I left the room a few minutes past twelve. Ivan didn't want to attend Frank's panel, and I did."

"You don't remember exactly what time you left?"

"No, I'm afraid I don't."

"It was twelve-thirty," Wade said. "The same time Colodny was shot, according to the newspapers."

"You happened to check the time, did you?"

"Are you calling me a liar?"

Kerry's *father,* damn it. "All right," I said evenly. "Do you mind telling me what you did after your wife left?"

"I do mind but I'll tell you anyway. Nothing. I was reading a book and I went on reading it."

Bohannon said, "If you want my whereabouts at twelve-thirty, I was up in the room with my wife. She wasn't feeling well—still isn't; arthritis acting up—and I didn't want to leave her alone."

I nodded and looked at Cybil again. "Did you see any of

the others when you went downstairs? Praxas, Ramsey, Ozzie Meeker?"

"No."

"Afraid you're out of luck on those three," Bohannon said. "As far as talking to them goes, anyhow."

"How so?"

"They've checked out already. Police gave us all permission to leave after they talked to us."

"I see."

"Meeker left last night for the Delta. Waldo headed back to L.A. this morning—he's driving, so he wanted an early start—and Bert's spending a few days with one of the convention people."

"Do you know which one?"

"Nope, but Lloyd Underwood could tell you. Some fellow in the Bay Area who runs a small-press publishing house. He's going to reprint a couple of Bert's Spectre novels."

"Did any of them happen to mention what they were doing when Colodny was killed?"

"Well . . . I think Waldo said he was with Underwood around that time, in the auditorium. Meeker was with Underwood, too, just before that—something about Ozzie's art display."

"How about Praxas?"

"I don't recall. Bert say anything to you, Ivan?"

Wade picked up his drink and said flatly, "No."

"It seems to me," Cybil said, "that he did say something about being downstairs talking to some fans. But I'm not sure."

I asked Bohannon, "Are you also planning to leave today?"

"Not much reason to stay now," he said. "We're booked on a five-o'clock flight to Denver."

"What about you, Mrs. Wade?"

"We're staying on until Tuesday or Wednesday," she said. "We don't get a chance to see Kerry that often, you know."

"Where is Kerry today?"

"Home working on one of her accounts. She'll be down this evening; we're having a late dinner." She smiled at me. "Would you like to join us? We—"

"The hell he's going to join us." Wade said in a voice full of fire and ice, and thumped his glass down on the table. "I've had enough of his questions, and I've had enough of him. I have no intention of taking a meal with him."

I said, "I'm sorry you feel that way."

"Well I do, and I don't like it. I don't like you, either."

It's mutual, brother, I thought.

"Ivan," Cybil said. Warningly.

But he was not having any of that. His eyes bit into me across the table. "A man your age, a fat, scruffy private detective, sucking around a woman young enough to be your daughter. I won't have it. You understand me? I won't have it."

Fat, scruffy private detective. "That's her decision, Mr. Wade," I said thinly. "Not yours."

"We'll see about that."

I still had the lid on my control, but it was rattling like one on a pot of boiling water. Either I got away from him right now or I would start to backtalk him, and that would only make things worse between us. And worse for Kerry, too. If the animosity got strong enough, and push came to shove, how could I expect her to make a choice between her father and me?

I slid back my chair and stood. "I think I'll be going," I said. "Thanks for your time. You have a good trip home, Mr. Bohannon."

He nodded, looking embarrassed. Cybil showed embarrassment too, but it was sharing space with anger; her eyes were like whips against the side of her husband's face. I put my back to all three of them and made myself walk slowly out of there.

Fat, scruffy private detective.

I went straight to the public telephone booths and shut myself inside of one. It took a minute or so for me to get calmed down; then I found a dime and dropped it into the slot and dialed Kerry's number. She answered on the fourth ring.

"Hi," I said. "It's me."

"Well, hello. I've been wondering if you'd call."

"I've had kind of a busy morning."

"You must have. I rang up your apartment at nine-thirty and you were already gone. I thought maybe you were miffed at me."

"Why should I be miffed at you?"

"Because I wasn't home last night. Or didn't you try to call?"

"I tried to call."

"My folks insisted I go out to dinner with them," she said, "and it got to be pretty late. I didn't get home until after eleven."

"You don't have to answer to me for your time."

"Hey, you sound grumpy. What's the matter?"

"Not too much," I said. "I just had a nice little session with your father, that's all. He called me a fat, scruffy private detective and said I didn't have any right to be sucking around a woman young enough to be my daughter."

"Oh, God."

"Yeah."

"He's impossible sometimes. He thinks I'm still a child who has to be protected from myself."

"I suppose he gave you the same routine last night."

"Not in the same words, but yes."

"What did you say?"

"I told him I was a big girl now and he'd realize what a nice guy you were when he got to know you."

"What'd he say to that?"

"I don't think you want to hear it."

"Terrific," I said. "This has been some damn day. First I let myself get talked into going to work for Dancer—"

"Dancer?"

"Yeah. I went down to see him at the Hall of Justice this

morning, and I'm still inclined to believe his story; so I'll try
to do what I can for him. Then I find out my best friend's
wife just left him after twenty-eight years. Then I come down
here to the hotel and get into a verbal battle with your old
man."

"Have you seen the newspapers yet?"

"No, I don't bother to read them most of the time. Why?"

"You won't like what they have to say about you either."

"What do they have to say?"

" 'Murder-prone private detective gets involved in another
slaying. Pulp collector attends pulp convention where ex-
pulp editor fatally shot by ex-pulp writer.' That's about the
gist of it."

"Bastards. They're having a field day at my expense."

"I told you you wouldn't like it."

"Miserable damn day."

"What are you going to do now?" she asked.

"I don't know. I'm fresh out of ideas."

"Why don't you come over here?"

"I'm not sure I'd be very good company."

"I'll take the chance. Maybe we can think of something
cheerful to do together."

So I went over there and we thought of something cheerful
to do together.

Twice.

I was feeling better when I got home around eight o'clock.
Kerry had had to keep her dinner date with her folks, but
that was okay; there was the promise of other nights to be
shared. Whether her father liked it or not, we seemed to have
a thing going. And nuts to him. She liked it and I liked it and
we were the only two who mattered.

But after I had been home an hour or so, while I was
swilling down a can of Schlitz and some leftover pizza, I

started to brood again. Why should I be so down on Ivan Wade? From what Kerry had told me, he was a decent enough guy who cared about her welfare and her happiness. So maybe he had a legitimate gripe. Maybe I *was* a fat, scruffy private detective and maybe I *was* too old for her. And maybe I had gone to her apartment and her bed this afternoon as much to spite him as to be with her—prove I could lay his daughter if I damned well pleased and the hell with him. I did not want to think about what sort of person that would make me, down in the depths of the subconscious.

Then I started to think about Eberhardt and Dana, and what a lousy thing the breakup of their marriage was, and pretty soon I had managed to brood myself right back into a funk. I had another beer and went to bed, which is one good place to take a funk. But then I made the mistake of reading the news story on Colodny's murder—I had bought a Sunday paper on the way home, against my better judgment—and it enraged and depressed me all over again. They'd had a field day, all right. The facts were at a minimum: Colodny had died from a gunshot wound, Dancer had been arrested and charged with homicide. The rest of the story focused on the convention, on the Pulpeteers, and on me, and was written more or less tongue-in-cheek. Somebody dies by violence and the journalists treat it as a kind of black-humored joke.

So I brooded about that for a while. And some more about Kerry, Ivan Wade, Eberhardt and Dana, Dancer caged up down at the Hall of Justice, sweating out a murder rap. Then I got up and had one more beer. But all it did was give me a headache and put a bad taste in my mouth. I took three aspirin and brushed my teeth, and when I crawled back into bed it was almost midnight.

Tomorrow couldn't get here soon enough to suit me . . .

FOURTEEN

The empty packing boxes were waiting for me when I got down to my office a little past nine on Monday morning.

I looked at them without much relish. Last day in the old digs, like it or not. The end of an era; a kind of milestone in the long and illustrious career of Lone Wolf, the last of the red-hot private snoops. From now on it would be business in sedate surroundings. No more dingy office in a dingy building in a dingy neighborhood. No more forties-style atmosphere; no more Spade and no more Marlowe. Retire the trenchcoat, throw out the slouch hat, get rid of the shiny-bottom suits with the frayed cuffs. The times, son, they are a-changing. Image is everything these days. Nobody pays much attention to anachronisms in the 1980s, especially red-hot private snoop-type anachronisms, except for a bunch of smartass newspaper reporters who ought to know better. And that's another thing: cut it out with calling yourself private snoop and keyhole peeper and lone-wolf private eye. What you are, you know, is the head of an investigative services firm.

Nuts, I thought.

So the old lone wolf took off his trenchcoat, hung it up along with his slouch hat. Then he shot the frayed cuffs on his shiny-bottom suit and ankled across to his desk, where he winked a cynical private eye at the *Black Mask* poster on one dingy wall. After which he settled down to the business of a new day.

There weren't any messages on my answering machine. I disconnected the thing and took it over and plunked it down

125

inside one of the packing cases; that was a start, anyway. While I brewed coffee I wondered if Ben Chadwick had dug up anything yet on Rose Tyler Crawford and the *Evil by Gaslight* film. But if he had, I decided, he'd have called by now. There was just nothing to do on that angle except to wait it out.

I shuffled some papers around while the coffee water heated. Opened up my portfolio case and shuffled through the "Hoodwink" manuscript again while I drank my first cup. I had brought the manuscript with me from home because that elusive oddity about it kept scratching at my mind, and I thought if I went over it enough times, I could eventually get a handle on it. Not this time, though. All I got was a coffee stain on one of the pages.

It was nine-fifty before I finally convinced myself to quit procrastinating and get the damn packing over and done with. I had to be out of here by five o'clock, which meant I had to have everything boxed up and a moving company called in by midafternoon. And the longer I hung around here being nostalgic or maudlin or anachronistic, the less time I would have today to do something constructive in Dancer's behalf.

I started with the file cabinet and got both drawers empty of files—what was left of them after the office rape—and packed away in short order. After which I took down the poster and the framed photostat of my license and wrapped them in a blanket so the glass would at least stand a chance of survival. Then I went into the alcove, dragging one of the cases after me, and began unloading the miscellaneous crap from the shelves in there.

That was what I was doing when somebody knocked on the office door. I heard it open a moment later, silence for a couple of seconds, and then Kerry's voice say, "Hey, anybody here?"

I poked my head around the corner, over the top of the packing case. "In here."

She came through the rail divider, peering around the way

a woman does the first time she enters a place, and stopped in the middle of the office. "Busy busy, aren't we?" she said.

"Never a spare moment."

I stood up, wiped my hands on a rag. She was wearing a gray business-type suit with a frilly green blouse under it, and she had her hair fluffed out in a way that was a little different. She looked pretty fine standing there, so I went over and kissed her. That was pretty fine too—at least for me.

"Ugh," she said. "What did you have for breakfast?"

"Why? Bad breath?"

"Well, a little garlicky."

"I guess it's the pastrami."

"Pastrami? For *breakfast*?"

"I don't like eggs much," I said.

"My God. It's a wonder you don't have bleeding ulcers."

"Not me. I've got a bachelor's stomach—made out of cast iron." I resisted an impulse to kiss her again and maybe nibble a little on her ear. How would it look if somebody else came in and found a fifty-three-year-old lone wolf nibbling on a pretty woman's ear? "So how come you came all the way over here from Bates and Carpenter?"

"It's all of a dozen blocks," she said.

"Long blocks," I said.

"I came over because I've got an early appointment for lunch and some free time, and I wanted to see this office of yours before you move out of it. I've never been inside a private eye's office before."

"What do you think, now that you're here?"

"I think you made a very wise decision to move somewhere else. Have you really spent twenty years in this place?"

"Yep. It's not all that bad, you know. I mean, it looks more respectable when it's cleaned up."

"I doubt that."

"You'll like the new offices a lot better," I said with some irony. "Very modern and businesslike."

"Oh, I'll bet. Plush carpets, soft lighting, and tasteful paintings on the walls. The artistic touch, no doubt."

I didn't open my mouth for three or four seconds. Then I said, "What did you say?"

"Weren't you listening? I said plush carpets, soft lighting—"

"No. The artistic touch. That's what you said."

She gave me a funny look but I barely noticed it. Somewhere inside my head a door had opened up, and the thing that had been scratching at it the past two days, the odd thing about the "Hoodwink" manuscript, came popping through. I took a good long look at it. Then I hustled over to the desk, dragged the manuscript out of the portfolio again, and took a good long look at that.

Kerry came over next to me as I was riffling through the pages. "What's the matter with you?" she said. "Do you have seizures like this very often?"

"Not often enough," I said. "I think I know who wrote the 'Hoodwink' novelette. And it wasn't Frank Colodny."

That got her attention. "Then who was it?"

"Ozzie Meeker."

"But he's not a writer—"

"Maybe he wanted to be one. It adds up."

"What adds up?"

"Here, look." I spread the manuscript out on the desk and pointed to the first paragraph on page one. "This sentence: 'In that moment of silent motionlessness, man and hansom had the aspect of two-dimensional shadows newly sketched on night's dark canvas, with ink still wet and glistening.'" I flipped over to the last page, indicated the second sentence in the final paragraph. "'The stationary objects in the room seemed to swirl past her, shading into distorted and colorless images much like those in a surrealist composition.'"

Kerry looked at me sideways. "Artistic references?"

"Right. The manuscript is full of them. Most writers, professional or amateur, wouldn't use phrases like 'two-dimensional shadows,' 'night's dark canvas,' 'stationary objects,' 'shading into distorted and colorless images,' 'surrealist composition.'" I riffled the pages again, pointing out a few more at random. "Or 'the elements of perspective.' Or 'the good strong odor of linseed oil.' Or 'the overall effect was of something painted with a dry brush.' "

"I see what you mean," Kerry said thoughtfully. "Whoever wrote this almost has to be an artist. And an amateur writer too. But it *doesn't* have to be Ozzie Meeker."

"No. Except that Meeker is a member of the Pulpeteers. And knows everybody involved. And was here at the convention. And had at least one altercation with Frank Colodny."

"Do you think he was involved in Colodny's death?"

"If he wrote 'Hoodwink' and those extortion letters, it's a good bet he was."

"But how?"

"I don't know yet."

"What motive would he have for wanting Colodny dead?"

"Some sort of revenge angle, maybe."

"After thirty years?"

"Colodny disappeared for thirty years, remember?"

"Mmm. Which could mean that Meeker wrote 'Hoodwink' back in the forties and it really was plagiarized for *Evil by Gaslight*—by Colodny?"

"Possible. It would explain his sudden disappearance. But Colodny was just an editor, wasn't he? He didn't do any writing himself?"

"Not as far as I know. My folks could tell you."

"They're still at the hotel?"

"Yes. Dad has a date with some sort of amateur magician's group today, but Cybil might still be in."

I went around behind the desk and rang up the Continental. The line to the Wades' room buzzed half a dozen times and I was just getting ready to break the connection when Cybil's voice answered a little breathlessly; I must have caught her on the way out. I told her who was calling and then asked about Frank Colodny.

"No," she said, "he never wrote anything himself. Or if he did, it was a well-kept secret. Some editors are frustrated writers, but not Frank; he was satisfied doing what he did."

"What about Ozzie Meeker? Do you know if he ever tried his hand at fiction?"

There was a small silence, as if she were searching her memory. "Well, it seems to me he did say once that he had ambitions along those lines. But not pulp; I think he wanted to do something more serious. I can't remember if he ever said what it was."

"Did he follow through? Write something for publication?"

"He never spoke of it if he did. Why do you ask?"

"Just an idea I've got. Thanks, Mrs. Wade."

Kerry was watching me as I put down the receiver; she had perched herself on the front edge of the desk. "No on Colodny?" she said.

I nodded. "But yes on Meeker."

"But then who wrote *Evil by Gaslight*? Not one of the other Pulpeteers?"

"Could be. If 'Hoodwink' was plagiarized in the first place."

"Then why was it Colodny who was killed?"

"I wish I knew."

"And why were extortion letters and manuscripts sent to *all* the Pulpeteers?"

"I wish I knew that too."

I picked up the phone again and put in another long-distance call to Ben Chadwick's office in Hollywood. More than ever now I wanted to know the background details on *Evil by Gaslight*; there was little doubt in my mind that the film, the "Hoodwink" manuscript and extortion letters, and Colodny's murder were all connected somehow. But all I got was Chadwick's answering machine and his recorded voice saying he was out of the office. I thought about leaving a message asking him to get in touch as soon as possible because the matter had become urgent, but decided against it and said only that I would call again later today or tomorrow. Chances were I would not be spending much of the day here—and I had already disconnected my own answering machine.

When I hung up this time Kerry said, "What are you going to do now? About Ozzie Meeker, I mean."

That was a good question. I could take all these suppositions and half-truths to Eberhardt, but what good would it do? They were inconclusive, and they had no direct bearing on Colodny's murder or his case against Dancer. Besides which, his marital problems were keeping him from being as open-minded as he usually was.

"I think what I'd better do," I said, "is have a talk with Meeker. If I handle him right, I might get him to admit something definite."

"Talk to him in person, you mean?"

"Well, if I tried it on the phone he'd probably hang up on me. And I couldn't gauge his reaction either." I stood up and came around the desk. "It's only a two-hour drive up to the Delta. I can be there by midafternoon if I find out his address and get the rest of my stuff packed in a hurry."

"Damn," she said. "I'd like to go with you."

"You would, huh?"

"Yes. It's fascinating watching you work."

"Sure it is. Just like watching plumbers plumb."

"No, I'm serious. It really is."

"Is *that* my attraction for you? The fabled mystique of the private eye?"

"Frankly, yes—part of it. Private eyes have fascinated me ever since I first read one of Cybil's pulp stories. You're not offended, are you?"

"No," I said, and I wasn't. It did not make any difference why she had picked me as a lover; she had picked me, and that was enough. "Fact is, you're pretty nice to have around. If you hadn't come around this morning and made that comment about artistic touches, it might have been days before I made the connection. When I get rich I'm going to hire you away from Bates and Carpenter as my secretary."

"Oh you are?"

"Sure. I wouldn't mind having you around all the time."

That last sentence seemed to hang in the air between us for three or four seconds, heavy with implication that I hadn't really meant. Or had I? Our eyes locked for those few seconds; then we both moved at the same time, Kerry straightening up from the desk, me hiding my big, awkward hands inside my trouser pockets. Oddly, for the first time in months, I had a craving for a cigarette—and whatever that meant psychologically, I didn't want to pursue.

"Well," she said, "I'd better go have my business lunch. Will you be back in time to have dinner with me tonight?"

"I should be. If there's a delay, I'll call you."

When she was gone I telephoned East Bay information, asked for a Hayward listing on Lloyd Underwood, and then dialed the number I was given. Underwood was home and surprised to hear from me. He was also as antic as ever, nattering away at top speed.

"Ozzie Meeker?" he said. "Yes, he lives on Yoloy Island up in the Delta. Is there any special reason you want to talk to him? Does it have anything to do with poor Frank Colodny being shot through the heart at the convention?"

"It's a private matter, Mr. Underwood. Where would Yoloy Island be, do you know?"

"Near Grand Island, I think, east of Rio Vista. I've never been there myself. It's an Indian word meaning a place thick with rushes. *Yoloy,* I mean. Did you know that?"

"No," I said, "I didn't know that."

"Yes. I still can't believe Russ Dancer is a murderer. Do you really think he did it?"

"I have my doubts."

"You do? Who do you think it was, then?"

"I don't know. But I'm trying to find out."

"Well, if it wasn't Russ Dancer I hope you do." He made a clucking sound. "What a tragic end to the first Western Pulp Con. Don't you think so? Of course, the publicity might work in favor of a second Western Pulp Con and bring the dealers and fans out in droves next year. You just never know about people—"

"Thanks for your help, Mr. Underwood," I said. And hung up on him.

It took me another ten minutes with the telephone to locate a small trucking outfit that charged reasonable prices and was willing to pick up this afternoon and deliver right away to the new address on Drumm Street. Then I finished cleaning out the alcove, emptied my desk, and pushed all the packing cases together in the middle of the floor. Then I went down the hall to the office of a CPA named Hadley, told him I'd given the moving company his name, asked him if he'd let them into my office when they came, and turned my key over to him. Then, not without reluctance, I got out of there for the last time.

I had my car on the Bay Bridge, headed east, before the noon hour was half gone.

FIFTEEN

The weather was better on the east side of the Bay: mostly clear with scattered banks of wind-driven clouds. Traffic bunched a little heavy on Highway 24 coming out of Oakland, but when I picked up 680 outside Walnut Creek, it thinned down quite a bit. I turned the radio on, just to have some noise, and let my thoughts wander the way you do on an easy freeway drive.

Where they wandered to first off, and lingered on, was Kerry. Our relationship. We were pretty fine together in the sack, but there was more to it than that. How much more I wasn't sure yet. Ego was part of it; ego always is when an old fart gets himself an attractive woman a dozen or more years younger than he is. The depth of her personality was part of it too; and her sense of humor; and that knack she had of making me feel like a dumb little boy one minute and a hell of a man the next. All those things, yes—but still something more?

I remembered what she'd said to me on Saturday morning, after the night we'd spent together: "You're a nice man, a nice gentle pussycat private eye." More than that for her too, though—and more than the sex and my great wit and charm. Hell, she'd confessed it herself this morning—she had been fascinated by the mystique of the fictional private investigator ever since she was a kid. Rock stars and athletes have groupies; why shouldn't a private eye have one?

Hey, come on, I told myself, that's not fair. So she's attracted to private detectives, so what? Are you any better?

Maybe the bottom-line attraction for *you* is that she's the daughter of a pair of pulp writers, one of whom wrote your favorite detective series. Maybe you're a pulp groupie. Think about that one, wise guy.

I thought about it, and it began to make me feel uneasy. There seemed to be a certain element of truth in it—maybe more truth than I cared to accept—and it opened up disturbing possibilities. The pulps had been a central part of my life for three and a half decades; I had already admitted to myself that from my own youth I had tried to emulate the pulp detectives I admired. Suppose those pulps had become so central that I had subconsciously allowed them to govern my emotional and sexual responses? Suppose the only woman I was capable of loving now was one with a connection to those yellowing old magazines and the people who had written for them?

Suppose it was the pulps, not Kerry, that I had gotten off on Friday night and Saturday morning and yesterday afternoon?

No, I thought, no. No. I'm a lot of things but that kind of abnormal isn't one of them. Is Kerry abnormal because she likes private cops? Was it Sam Spade or Phil Marlowe she had her orgasms with instead of me? Bullshit. We had pulps and private detectives in common—they were what had drawn us together in the first place—but that was all there was to it. It was me, the man, she cared for; it was her, the woman, I cared for, and wanted, and was touched by inside.

With an effort I herded all the psychological nonsense into the back of my mind and walled it off there, the hell with it. Think about something else—Eberhardt's marital crisis, what I would say to Ozzie Meeker when I got to Yoloy Island, theories on the murder of Frank Colodny and the solution to the "Hoodwink" enigma. Too much self-analysis only led you into ugly little byways you had no business exploring. And ended up driving you half crazy.

I picked up Highway 4 above Concord, and when I got past Antioch I stopped at a service station and bought a tankful of gas and a map of the Delta area. A couple of minutes with the map was all I needed; Yoloy Island didn't look to be too hard to get to. And it was small enough so that I probably would not have to chase around checking streets and asking a lot of directions to Meeker's place.

It was getting on toward two o'clock when I crossed the San Joaquin River at the westernmost edge of the Delta, near where it merges with the Sacramento River on a course to San Francisco Bay. Highway 160 began there and wound up through the network of islands, villages, marinas, picnic spots, levee roads, seventy bridges and drawbridges, and more than a thousand miles of waterways that make up the Delta. It was pretty nice country, full of willow trees and mistletoe-draped cottonwoods, cultivated farmland and jungley backwater sloughs where you could pick wild blackberries and catch catfish and Delta crayfish, shanty-towns occupied by elderly Chinese who looked as though they'd stepped out of the nineteenth century, places with colorful names like Dead Man's Slough, Poker Bend, Jackass Flat, some of the best restaurants in California, and any number of houseboats, speedboats, sailboats, rowboats, skiffs, rafts, and old freighters. About the only inland water craft you wouldn't find, in fact—and ironically enough—were the steamboats that had opened up the Delta in the days following the Gold Rush, carrying passengers and freight to and from Sacramento, Stockton, San Francisco, and new settlements in between.

The area was steeped in history and legend. Ghosts were said to walk on foggy nights in Dead Man's Slough; there was supposed to be a treasure of gold specie buried on Coarsegold Island; oldtimers would tell you straightfaced that there had been so many corpses consigned to watery graves in the Delta—miners murdered for their pokes, cheating gamblers, claim-jumpers, outlaws and outlaw victims, Chinese slaughtered by whites and by their own in tong battles, passengers and crewmen killed when steamboat boilers exploded—that if you drained all the rivers and sloughs, you could walk from Sacramento to San Francisco on the layers of muddy bones.

During the summer the Delta was one of the most popular recreation and resort areas in Northern California. In the spring, though, cold winds still blow steadily across the flat alluvial plain and keep most people away. And this year, because of serious flooding and land erosion during heavy winter rains, even foul-weather fishermen were said to be looking elsewhere.

With the light traffic conditions, I made the twenty-odd miles to Grand Island in just under forty-five minutes. The turnoff I wanted, according to the map, was Poverty Road. I found it easily enough, went along there for another three miles, made another turn on Yoloy Road, and followed that to where an old-fashioned latticed-metal bridge spanned the gunmetal-gray waters of a channel. When I came off the bridge I was on Yoloy Island.

If *yoloy* meant "a place thick with rushes," as Lloyd Underwood had told me, the island was well named: Tules grew all along the shoreline, below the levee road that looped along its perimeter. The other side of the road was lined with willow and pepper trees. Toward the center of the island, well apart from each other on higher ground partially hidden by brush and trees, I could see a couple of frame houses, one of them in tumbledown condition; unpaved access roads led up to each property, and at the foot of each drive was a mailbox with a name lettered on it. I slowed at both of them and pulled over close enough so that I could read the names. Neither one was Meeker.

The whole island could not have been more than three-quarters of a mile in circumference. Halfway around it the levee road veered inland past a rocky point on one side and a stretch of windswept grassland on the other. Beyond the point was a stand of cottonwoods, and beyond the cottonwoods was another house, this one built between the road and the slough and shaded by more cottonwoods and a couple of droopy willows. I came up near the drive and squinted through the windshield at the mailbox standing there. The lettering on this one was artistically done in three colors: Oswald J. Meeker.

I turned up the drive. The house was an old two-story frame with galleried porches and looked even more tumbledown than the one back near the bridge: white paint chipped and faded, upper gallery sagging in the middle, railings and Victorian latticework broken in places. The remains of a covered pioneer wagon, maybe authentic and maybe not, sat off to one side; the high grass growing up around it made it look as if it were sinking into the earth. Parked between the wagon and the house was a Plymouth station wagon, Korean War vintage, that had part of its right rear panel caved in and rust spots all over its chrome.

Meeker may have been a pretty successful artist for the pulps, I thought, but he didn't seem to be doing too well these days. Unless the ramshackle appearance of everything was an eccentricity or some sort of calculation. For all I knew, the inside of the house was as opulent as any in the wealthy neighborhoods of San Francisco.

I parked my car behind the Plymouth and got out. The wind here was raw and blustery, swaying the grass and the willow trees, building little choppy waves in the slough behind and below the house. It had scraped the sky clean of clouds, leaving it a slatey blue with the sun off-center in it like a frozen yellow eye. I pulled up the collar on my coat, stuffed my hands inside the pockets. Then I went up onto the porch, stepping gingerly because the old boards creaked and gave under my feet, and pushed the doorbell button.

Nothing happened. The door stayed closed and there weren't any sounds except for the echoes of the bell and the low whistling cry of the wind.

Maybe he's not home, I thought. Maybe I should have called first instead of driving all the way up here on faith. But unless he owned two cars, how about the Plymouth wagon sitting there?

I came down off the porch and made my way around to

the rear; it could be he had a studio back there and hadn't heard the bell. Past the house, I saw more grassy earth that sloped down to a tiny natural cove flanked on both sides by thick tule patches. Two beaten-down paths led through the grass. One went to a rickety pier that bisected the cove, extending twenty feet or so into the channel; the other went to some kind of shed with a window on the near side, built triangularly between the house and the pier.

A screened-in porch with a glass roof had been tacked onto the back of the house. I thought that the glass roof probably made it a studio, all right, and climbed three steps to the screen door. It was unlatched and standing open a couple of inches. I caught hold of it and poked my head through and called Meeker's name.

No answer.

It seemed a little funny that Meeker would leave the door open like this if he wasn't around. Maybe he was eccentric enough not to care about things like locking doors—but it still made me wonder. You'd think he would want to protect his personal belongings, particularly the original oils and charcoal and ink sketches that were hung all over the inner wall of the studio. They had to be worth quite a bit of money to collectors.

I debated going inside. But I did not want to do that; trespassing was one trait of the fictional private eye I had always considered dumb as well as illegal, and I cared for it less than ever since I'd broken into a fish processing company in Bodega Bay on that Carding/Nichols case a few months back, against my better judgment, and nearly got myself killed for it. Instead I settled for a look around the studio from where I stood outside. Which told me nothing. The place was even sloppier than my flat, cluttered with easels, jars of paint, brushes, blank canvases, and other artist's supplies, and a farrago of papers, maps, books, tattered Western pulps, fishing equipment. It was also empty of human habitation.

I pushed the door shut and stood for a couple of seconds

looking out at the empty slough. Then I went down along the path to the pier. Tied up on the lee side was a fourteen-foot skiff with an outboard engine tilted up at the rear and a tarpaulin roped over most of its length. I took a couple of steps out on the pier, to where I could look both upstream and downstream along the slough. There wasn't anything to see in either direction, or across the channel at the opposite bank.

The wind gusted and made the skiff bob in the choppy water, bang against the side of the pier. I could feel my cheeks and ears getting numb. It could be Meeker had a second skiff and had gone fishing in one of the other sloughs; he *was* a fisherman, judging from the gear I'd seen inside the studio. But it was a damned cold day—too cold and too rough for the fishing to be good at any hour, much less the middle of the afternoon. And why would he leave the studio door unlocked?

When I stepped off the pier the shed caught my eye. It was about twelve feet square, made out of weathered gray boards, with an asymmetrical roof covered in tarpaper There was a window on this side too, facing the channel. On impulse I headed over that way through the marshy grass. At the door I stopped and reached out to try the knob. Locked.

I started to turn away—and stopped again, for no reason except that a length of fishing twine lay curled in the grass like a scrawny snake. A hollow jumpy feeling started up in my stomach; then the back of my scalp began to crawl, and not from the wind or the cold. Ah no, I thought, not again, not another one. But that kind of feeling had come over me too many times before. It had got so I could almost feel the psychic after-tremors of violence, the presence of death, when I got near enough to them.

I put my teeth together and moved around to the window on the side nearest the house. The glass was streaked with dirt; I had to lower my face close to it to get a clear look inside. The interior was shadowed and cobwebby, but enough daylight penetrated through the windows to make the shapes within discernible.

Ozzie Meeker was lying crumpled on the wooden floor near the door, next to an overturned stepladder and a double-bitted ax. There was blood and gray matter on him and on the blades of the ax: the back of his head had been split open.

Bile kicked up into my throat; I turned away and took three or four deep breaths. When my stomach settled down again I had another look through the glass—not at the body this time but at the door. There was a key in the old-fashioned latch, one of those big, round-headed ones; I could see it plainly. I caught hold of the window sash and tried to force it upward. It wouldn't budge. I hurried around to the other side, made the same effort with that window, and got the same nonresults. Both windows were either stuck fast or locked from inside like the door. And as far as I could tell, there was no other way in or out of the shed.

Another damned sealed-room killing.

SIXTEEN

I called the county sheriff's office from Meeker's studio, using my handkerchief to hold the phone receiver and not touching anything else. A guy with a voice like a file on metal took my name and Meeker's address, told me to stay where I was, somebody would be out within twenty minutes, and clicked off before I could offer an acknowledgment. He sounded pretty excited; they probably didn't get many homicide cases up here, and this one would be the highlight of his week. Some highlight.

I debated ringing up Eberhardt and filling him in on this latest turn of events, but that would have been premature. Maybe Meeker's death would get Dancer off the hook and maybe it wouldn't; it was too soon to tell. If Meeker had committed suicide, and if there was a note somewhere saying he'd done it because he had been responsible for Frank Colodny's death, then that would tie everything off in a nice little bundle. The problem with that was, Meeker *hadn't* committed suicide. Suicides don't lock themselves inside sheds and split their heads open with double-bitted axes. No, it was either an accident—which was more convenient coincidence than I cared to swallow—or it was murder. And if it was murder, it would either uncomplicate things or complicate them even more; it all depended on the mitigating circumstances and on what sort of evidence the local authorities came up with.

Or that I could come up with myself, I thought.

Here I was, alone in the studio with nothing to occupy my

time until the county sheriff's men arrived. I could go outside and wait for them, but it was pretty cold outside. I was
not supposed to touch anything in here, but I didn't have to
touch anything—not with my hands, anyway. There was
nothing to stop me from sniffing around like an old blood-
hound, was there? Nothing to stop me from *looking*?

I went over to the screen door and looked out to make sure
the rear yard was still empty. Then I turned to look at the
disarray of things in the studio. And it struck me that the
mess in there might not have been made by Meeker—that
maybe the place had been searched. It had that kind of look,
the more you studied it. Nothing overt, like slashed uphol-
stery or upended furniture, but a messiness that went beyond
sloppy. About the only things that weren't slung around hel-
ter-skelter were the pulp magazines stacked along one wall.

But if it had been searched, why? What did Meeker have
that somebody wanted?

The pulps didn't tell me anything; they were all late forties
issues, except for a couple of coverless *Wests* from the thirties, and all Westerns. The artist's supplies and fishing equipment didn't tell me anything either. I gave my attention to
the scattered papers. Most of them were leaves from various-
sized sketch pads, containing partially finished drawings of
one kind or another, and letter carbons dating back several
years. All of the face-up correspondence related to Meeker's
commercial artwork. None of it was addressed to anyone I
knew or mentioned the names of any of the Pulpeteers.

Spread out over one of the tables were two maps, one half
open and the other open all the way. The half-open one was
city map of San Francisco and on it was a circled X, made
with a black felt-tip pen, at the approximate location of the
Hotel Continental downtown. The open map was a comprehensive of the state of Arizona. That one had a circled X on
it too, some distance southeast of Tucson, in Cochise County.
I bent over for a closer look. The area beneath the X showed
blank—no town, no road or railway or body of water—which
meant that it was open land of some kind: desert, maybe, or

foothills. The nearest town was a place called Wickstaff, and that was at least ten miles from the X.

Why would Meeker have marked a piece of barren land on a map of Arizona? Well, there was one answer: Frank Colodny, according to testimony, owned a ghost town in Arizona called Colodnyville. So maybe the land wasn't barren after all; ghost towns were seldom included on even the most comprehensive of state maps.

I started to straighten up from the table, and as I did that I noticed another mark on the map, down in the lower right-hand margin, half-hidden by a crease in the paper. What it was, I saw when I got one eye down close to it, was a pair of names written in a small crabbed hand, one above the other and both circled, like the names of lovers inside a heart. The bottom name was also underlined several times and had a string of question marks after it.

The upper name was Frank Colodny.

And the lower one, with all the question marks, was Cybil Wade.

The county sheriff's men showed up in just about twenty minutes, as advertised. I was outside by then, sitting in my car with the engine running and the heater up full blast to take the chill out of my bones. The first car contained a pair of patrol deputies, and the second, on the tail of the first, contained a deputy sheriff named Jeronczyk, who was the acting officer in charge until the arrival of the sheriff's investigators from Rio Vista.

I took them around to the shed and showed them the body through the window. Jeronczyk asked me questions and I answered them; I also gave him some references, including Eberhardt. He was not particularly impressed. But neither was he hostile or suspicious. Just a wary cop investigating an evident case of homicide.

So I got sent back to my car, which was fine with me, while he and the others set about jimmying one of the shed's windows. A lot of empty time passed. I keep an overnight bag in the trunk, in the event I get caught out of town unexpectedly, and inside the bag I keep a couple of pulp magazines. I got one of them out and tried to read a story by John K. Butler, but my mind was elsewhere. I kept having mental flashes of Meeker's body inside that shed, twisted into a stiffened posture with his head opened up and bloody. And I kept thinking about the two names, Colodny's and Cybil Wade's, presumably written by Meeker on the map of Arizona.

A second sheriff's car showed up after a while, this one containing a couple of plainclothesmen and a guy carrying a doctor's satchel. The younger of the cops was outfitted with a field lab kit and a camera. All three of them went to where one of the deputies had been stationed by the house, and were shown around to the rear. Ten minutes later the older plainclothesman came back alone and made straight for my car and me inside it.

He was about my age and had a notch out of his right ear, as if somebody had taken a bite from it; his name was Loomis. And he was so polite it made me wonder if he was putting on an act: he called me sir every second sentence, and apologized twice for the inconvenience of having to detain me. But he also copied down all the information from my investigator's license as well as the names and addresses and telephone numbers of my references, and made me tell twice how and why I happened to come here today and find Meeker's body.

We were just finishing up round two when a country ambulance pulled into the drive. Loomis thanked me again for my cooperation, touched his hat like John Wayne in a Three Mesquiteers movie from the thirties—you had to see it to believe it—and went over to conduct the two attendants around to the shed. That left me alone again. I got out of the car and walked around it a couple of times, dog-fashion, and then got back in and looked at the truss and the you-too-can-be-a-detective ads in the back of the pulp.

Another twenty minutes crept off into history. At the end

of which Loomis and Jeronczyk reappeared and headed my way again. Behind them the ambulance attendants, with the doctor or coroner's assistant alongside, came slogging into view carrying Meeker's sheet-covered body on a stretcher. I got out of the car one more time and stood with Loomis and Jeronczyk, watching the attendants load the body inside the ambulance.

Jeronczyk said, "Well, that's that."

Loomis nodded and looked at me. "You're free to leave now, sir. We'd appreciate it, though, if you'd stop by the office in Rio Vista and sign a statement. It's necessary in cases of accidental death."

"Accidental death?"

"Yes, sir."

"Are you *sure* it was an accident?"

"Reasonably sure," Jeronczyk said. "He was up on that stepladder, fussing with one of the wall hooks, and he either slipped or the ladder gave way under him. He had the ax in his hand, or maybe it was lying on the floor; either way, he fell on it, and it split his head wide open. Happens once in a while, that kind of thing. Just a freak accident."

"Then how come he had the door locked?"

Loomis said, "Sir?"

"Why would a man go into a small shed like that, on his own property, and lock the door before he climbs up on a stepladder? It doesn't make sense."

Jeronczyk shrugged. "People do strange things sometimes. Have strange quirks. Maybe he was paranoid about security."

"The door to his studio was unlocked," I said. "That's how I was able to get in to use the telephone."

"You seem to think he met with foul play," Loomis said mildly. "Why is that?"

"I told you before, he was mixed up in a killing in San Francisco over the weekend. It's a funny coincidence he should get himself killed in a freak accident two days later."

"You say he was 'mixed up' in this San Francisco murder. If that's so, why didn't the police detain him?"

"I explained that, too: they've arrested somebody else."

"But you don't believe this other person is guilty."

"No, I don't."

"And yet you have no evidence of any wrongdoing against Mr. Meeker. Speculations only. Isn't that true, sir?"

"It is unless you found something among Meeker's papers to connect him to the extortion matter."

"We didn't," Loomis said. "We found nothing at all incriminating among his papers."

"Besides," Jeronczyk said, "there's no way he could have been murdered inside that shed. The door was locked from the inside and both windows were stuck fast. It took us five minutes to jimmy one of them open so we could get in ourselves."

"There are all sorts of locked-room gimmicks," I said.

He gave me a skeptical look. "Such as?"

"I don't know offhand. I'm not John Dickson Carr."

"Who's John Dickson Carr?"

"All right, look, here's one way. That shed is pretty small; suppose the walls aren't fully anchored to the ground or the floor; suppose there's a way you can tilt the whole thing off its foundation—against a couple of heavy braces, say, to keep it from toppling over. One man could kill another inside, walk out through the door, tilt the shed, crawl back inside under the tilted end, lock the door, crawl out again, and then push the shed back into an upright position around the body."

Neither Loomis nor Jeronczyk said anything. They were looking at me now as if they suspected I might not be playing with a full deck.

"Sure it's farfetched," I said, "and I don't believe it happened that way. But it's the kind of thing I mean by a locked-room gimmick—something that *could* be done to make murder seem impossible."

"Nothing like that happened here," Loomis said. His voice was patient and his eyes said that he really didn't mind standing around and humoring a half-wit private detective from San Francisco. "That shed is solid all the way around and top to bottom. Nobody could tilt one end of it except maybe with a crane."

"I never doubted that. Look, it was only an example—"

"There wasn't *any* gimmicking done," Jeronczyk said. "The door was locked from the inside and the key was in the lock. You saw that yourself through the window, right? And there were two clear latent prints on the key, both of which belonged to the deceased. Now what does that tell you?"

"That he handled the key at one time or another," I said, "but not necessarily that he was the one who locked the shed door. The killer could have worn gloves, couldn't he?"

Loomis sighed. Patiently. "How would this killer of yours have gotten out of the shed?"

"Maybe he wasn't *in* the shed when he locked the door."

"You mean he was already outside?"

"Yes."

"And how did he lock the door on the inside?"

"Maybe he used a couple of pieces of twine. It's an old trick: You tie the cord around the key, using slip knots, and run the two lengths under the bottom of the door; then you close the door and manipulate the twine to turn the key in the lock. When you're through all you have to do is jerk hard to loosen the slip knots and then pull the cord out under the door."

"Interesting idea," Jeronczyk said, as if he thought it wasn't.

"There's a broken piece of fishing twine near the shed door, in the grass. I noticed it; you must have too."

"We noticed it, yes, sir," Loomis said.

"The killer could have used it the way I described and dropped it there afterward."

"No, I'm afraid not. It would have been impossible for anyone to lock the shed door using pieces of twine."

"Why would it?"

"Because the key turns hard in the lock," Loomis said. "I know that because I turned it myself, several times. No one could possibly turn it with twine. Or even with clothesline or rope. using slip knots and manipulating from under the door. No, sir—the only way that key could have been turned was by hand."

So much for that theory; he'd shot it down pretty good. But I said, "I don't suppose there was anything inside the shed that might point to foul play?"

He shook his head. "No signs of a struggle, no foreign objects to indicate another's presence—nothing whatsoever."

"How long has Meeker been dead?"

"Several hours. Rigor mortis had already set in."

"Sometime this morning?"

"Early this morning, yes."

"What about other marks on the body?"

"A bruise on the jaw and lacerations of the right forefinger and the left elbow, all of which the coroner's assistant says were the result of the fall."

"Couldn't that jaw bruise have been caused by a blow of some kind? With a fist or some type of weapon?"

"It could have but it wasn't," Jeronczyk said. He did not have as much patience as Loomis; he was beginning to sound annoyed. "Now why don't you just drop the matter, all right? Mr. Meeker died in a freak accident and that's all there is to it."

"He's right, you know," Loomis said. "You can't make malice where none exists. Suppose you just follow me to Rio Vista, sign your statement, and go on home and forget the whole thing."

What could I do? I followed him to Rio Vista, signed my statement, and went on home. But I was damned if I would forget the whole thing. No matter what Loomis and Jeronczyk said, no matter what the evidence seemed to indicate, I was convinced that somehow Ozzie Meeker had been murdered.

When I entered my flat, it was a few minutes past seven o'clock and San Francisco was full of pea-soup fog. I opened a bottle of beer, took it into the bedroom, and dialed Eberhardt's home number. No answer. So I called the Hall of Justice, but he wasn't there either; one of the Homicide inspectors told me Eb had taken the day off. I left a message for him to call me when he came in in the morning—and wondered if he was out somewhere tying one on. Well, what if he was? He was entitled, wasn't he?

I sat there working on my beer and staring at the phone. I had already called Kerry from a pay phone in Rio Vista to tell her the news about Meeker and to cancel our dinner date for tonight. She'd taken it well enough, but underneath the calmness in her voice I could tell she was frightened. Two deaths already—would there be more? Were her folks in any danger? Maybe she was even worried about me; I wanted to think so, anyway. And I wanted to see her tonight, except it was more important that I see her mother instead. I had not told her that; I had said only that I didn't expect to make it back to the city until late. I also hadn't said anything about the map of Arizona in Meeker's studio, or what was written on it in felt-tip pen.

After a time I caught up the handset again and called the Hotel Continental and asked for the Wades' room. I had called there, too, from Rio Vista, but Cybil and Ivan had both been out. I'd left a message for her, saying that it was urgent I talk to her and that I would call again around seven-thirty.

The line buzzed five times before she picked up. "Yes?"

I told her who was calling. "Are you alone, Mrs. Wade? Can you speak freely?"

"Why, yes. Ivan's been out all day, at a meeting with some local amateur magician's group. What is it you want to talk about?"

"I don't think we should discuss it over the phone," I said. "Can I see you tonight?"

"Is it about Frank Colodny's murder?"

"Yes. And there's been a second homicide; Ozzie Meeker was killed today."

An intake of breath. Then silence for six or seven beats.

Then "Oh my God" in a voice not much louder than a whisper.

"I can meet you in the hotel bar in thirty minutes," I said.

"No, not here. You don't live far away, do you? Kerry said something about Pacific Heights . . ."

"Would you rather come here?"

"If you don't mind."

"Not at all." I gave her the address. "When can I expect you?"

"Right away. As soon as I can get a taxi."

We rang off, and I got up and took my beer into the living room. I felt more apprehensive than anything else. Cybil Wade seemed to be a key factor in this tangled business, and there was no sense in denying it any longer. Or in not sitting her down and asking her some fairly blunt questions. I had backed off from her before because she was Kerry's mother; but now Meeker was dead, and there was that notation he'd made on the Arizona map, and Dancer was still locked up with a murder charge hanging over him. It was time to bite the bullet.

I rummaged around in my file of *Midnight Detectives* until I found one with a Samuel Leatherman story. Then I sat down on the couch, communed a little with Max Ruffe, and waited for his maker to come by and tell me a tale that was fact, not fiction.

SEVENTEEN

She got there at 8:05. She was wearing a gray coat and a gray pantsuit made out of some kind of shiny material, and her coppery hair was pulled back into a chignon. On most women that kind of hairdo is severe; on Cybil Wade it highlighted the shape of her face and the still-smooth texture of her skin. The face, with the bruise almost gone under light makeup, and the sweet tawny eyes were composed, but below the surface, like a rippling undercurrent, you could see anxiety. She was a woman with secrets, and she was afraid that I had gone poking around and found out what some of them were. She was wrong about that, but if I had my way, she wouldn't be wrong much longer.

I showed her inside and took her coat and hung it up in the closet. Like Kerry, she did not feel ill at ease in strange surroundings. She had herself a look around, her eyes lingering longest on the shelves of pulp magazines; if she felt any distaste at the room's untidiness, she didn't show it. Then she went over and took a closer look at the plastic-bagged rows of pulps.

"You really do have an impressive collection, don't you?" she said when I came over to the couch behind her.

"Substantial, anyway."

She turned. "Kerry said it was impressive and it is." Pause. "She also seems impressed with you."

"Does she? Well, it's mutual."

"I thought it was. That's part of the reason I wanted to come here tonight, you know, instead of meeting at the hotel.

152

To see where you live, find out a little more about you. Motherly interest, I guess you could call it."

Uh-huh, I thought. Maybe she was sincere, but maybe she was trying to con me a little, too, so I would go easier on her. But it was not going to work. If she was mixed up in murder, I wasn't about to let her off the hook just because she was Kerry's mother. I could be as hard-boiled as Max Ruffe if it came down to that.

I said, "Why don't you take a seat, Mrs. Wade. I'll get us something to drink. Brandy, beer, coffee?"

"A beer would be fine."

I went into the kitchen, opened up two bottles of Schlitz, got a glass for her out of the cupboard, and carried them back to the living room. She had gone to sit in one of the chairs and picked up the issue of *Midnight Detective* with her Samuel Leatherman story; she was looking at the interior illustration. There seemed to be a kind of sadness in her expression, but it went away as I crossed over and set one bottle and the glass on the table in front of her.

She put the magazine down again. " 'My Body Lies Over the Ocean,' " she said. "Frank had a positive genius for concocting the worst titles. But he was a good editor. He knew when a story didn't work and why it didn't work, and he never fiddled with copy. Some editors fancied themselves writers and were forever changing sentence structure and tampering with style, but not Frank."

"But he was also dishonest, wasn't he?"

"Oh, he was a bastard there's no question of that." Nothing changed in her face, but the words were bitter. "Not at first, when the pulps were flourishing and he didn't have to worry about money. But later—yes."

I sat down on the couch. "How well did you know him in those days?"

"As well as any of the other Pulpeteers, I imagine."

"But not intimately?"

Her gaze flicked away from me, down to the beer on the table. Then she leaned forward and began to pour from the bottle into the glass. I couldn't see her eyes when she said, "What do you mean by intimately?"

"Just that, Mrs. Wade."

She poured the glass half full, lifted it, and drank until there was nothing but foam left. Foam made a thin white mustache on her upper lip as well; she licked it off. "I never used to like beer," she said. "I still don't very much. But once in a great while it tastes good. Do you know what I mean?"

"Yes."

"There are other things like that," she said. "Things that aren't good for you, things that you don't like or care to do except once in a great while. Then something inside you, some sort of craving, makes you want it. Just once, or maybe twice, and then you don't want it any more. But that once or twice, you have to have it, no matter what."

This time I did not say anything.

She crossed her legs, put one hand on her knee. The other hand began toying with the blouse button between her breasts. She said, "You know about Frank and me, don't you?"

"Yes," I lied.

"The whole story?"

"Not all of it, but enough."

"How did you find out?"

"There were some things at Ozzie Meeker's place," I said. "Notations he'd made linking you and Colodny."

"Yes, Ozzie would know if anybody did. I tried to keep it a secret, God knows, and Frank was bound to do the same. But Ozzie was the closest thing to a friend he had during the war; he was always hanging around Frank's apartment, and he must have seen us together."

"And now he's dead."

"Dead," she repeated. "How did it happen? Where?"

"At his place up in the Delta. I found him this afternoon, inside a tool shed. His head was split open with an ax."

She seemed to shiver. And poured more beer and drank it off the way she had before, in one long swallow.

"The police think it was an accident," I said, "because the shed door was locked from the inside. But I think it was murder."

"But why? Why would anybody want to kill Ozzie?"

"Maybe because he wrote 'Hoodwink' and sent those extortion letters."

"Ozzie did? But I thought Frank—"

"No, it wasn't Colodny."

Pause. "You don't think *I* had anything to do with Ozzie's death?"

"Did you?"

"Of course not. I was out shopping part of the day and at the hotel the rest of it; I certainly didn't go up to the Delta."

Which was probably true enough. Meeker had died early this morning, according to the coroner's estimate, and I had talked to Cybil myself around ten-thirty. I said, "Does your husband know about your affair with Colodny?"

"Ivan? God, no!"

"Are you positive of that?"

"Yes. He'd have confronted me if he knew. He'd have . . . I don't know what he'd have done. But he'd never keep it to himself." Her fingers had opened the blouse button and were trying to get it closed again. You could see her Adam's apple working in the slender column of her throat. "I was terrified back then that he'd find out. That's why I paid Frank his filthy blackmail money. He'd have told Ivan if I hadn't, just as he threatened to do."

"Blackmail?"

It got quiet for a few seconds. Then her mouth opened and made a little *O*. "You didn't know about that? I thought you'd found that out, too."

"No. You'd better tell me about it."

"Why? My God, Frank is dead—it's all ancient history."

"Is it? Meeker's dead, too, and Russ Dancer is in jail charged with a crime he didn't commit, and the real murderer is running around loose. Suppose he decides to go after somebody else?"

"I don't see how my relationship with Frank could have anything to do with murder . . ."

I could, if her husband was the person who had killed Colodny. But I didn't say that to her; I said only, "Maybe it doesn't. You tell me the truth, all of it, and I'll take it from there."

The blouse button opened again, closed again. "You won't let it go any further than this room, will you? You won't tell anyone—especially not Kerry?"

"Not if you haven't done anything criminal."

"No, nothing criminal." Her mouth turned wry. "Just foolish, that's all. Very, very foolish."

"Everybody's foolish once in a while," I said.

"Yes. It's not a very pretty story, you know."

"I'm not in a very pretty line of work."

"I suppose not. But I feel . . . cheap. You seem to care for Kerry, and I know she cares for you. And here I am, waving a lot of dirty family linen in front of you."

"That isn't going to change how I feel about Kerry," I said. "Or about you, for that matter. I'm not here to sit in moral judgment, Mrs. Wade. All I'm interested in is finding who killed Colodny and Meeker, and getting Russ Dancer out of jail."

"All right," she said, and took a breath and let it out with her lips pursed, as if she were blowing out a match. "It happened during the war—World War II, I mean. Ivan was in the Army and stationed in Washington, but there was a housing shortage there, and we decided it would be best if I stayed in New York. My pulp writing career was going well, and all our friends were in Manhattan, and it was just easier all the way around. Ivan used to come home once or twice a month, which was fine; but sometimes his military duties kept him away for months at a time. I was young in those days and . . . well, warm-blooded. I could stand the short separations but the longer ones were . . . difficult."

She was looking past me now, at a spot somewhere beyond my right shoulder. Or maybe she was not looking at anything in this room. Her eyes had taken on a remoteness, as if she might be peering down a long, dark tunnel into the past. I wanted some of my beer, but I was afraid that if I moved I would disturb the confessionary mood she was in. I just sat still and listened.

"I had plenty of opportunities, God knows," she said. "But I wasn't promiscuous; I loved Ivan—I've never stopped loving him. I turned down all sorts of offers, from all sorts of men. Including Russ Dancer. I had my writing and I had Kerry to take care of, she was just a baby then. I might have stayed faithful except that Ivan was sent out to California for six months, some sort of secret work that didn't allow me to join him or even to talk to him on the telephone. It got terribly lonely after a while. And I had this craving inside me. I needed someone. I just . . . needed someone.

"And Frank was there, always there. I found him attractive and he knew that; he'd made passes at me before, and I'd turned him down before, but it was always in a bantering way. Then one night after an editorial meeting, he offered to take me to dinner and I accepted. We had several drinks, we went to his apartment for another one, and it suddenly occurred to me that I didn't have to go home that night because my mother was looking after Kerry, out in Brooklyn—she did that sometimes to give me a little freedom . . . I didn't have to go home. So when Frank made his pass, as I knew he would, I didn't turn him down; it wasn't bantering any more. And I slept with him.

"It happened one more time after that, about a month later. Just those two times, never again. If Frank had had his way, it would have become an all-out clandestine affair—he was after me about it all the time. But there was never anything serious between us. He wanted my body and those two times I wanted his. That was all.

"Then Ivan came back to Washington and began to make regular trips home to New York, and Frank stopped pestering me. He had other women, droves of them, so he didn't need me to bolster his ego. The war ended not long after that and we were all excited and busy with the adjustment to peacetime living. I saw Frank fairly often at Pulpeteer meetings, we stayed friends; there were no recriminations. It had been just one of those brief war romances that didn't mean anything, that after a while you could pretend never happened at all.

"But then the pulp markets began to collapse in the late forties. Action House started to lose money on *Midnight Detective* and their other titles and had to fold all but *Midnight* by the end of 1949. That was when Frank got desperate and turned into a thief—and worse. When *Midnight* folded in 1950, that was the end of Action House; Frank was broke and out of a job. So he came to me and asked me for five hundred dollars.

"I had the money. My own writing had slacked off, but Ivan was doing well with his pulp work and with books and radio scripting. But the money was in savings for Kerry's education, and I turned Frank down. We'd become much less friendly anyway by then, because of the way he'd been cheating writers. Only he wouldn't take no for an answer. He said he had proof we'd been intimate during the war—that damned photograph. He said that unless I gave him the five hundred dollars he'd tell Ivan about us, show him the photo, make it all seem more intense and sordid than it had really been. I had no choice. Ivan is insanely jealous and there's no telling what he might have done. I gave Frank the money.

"That wasn't the end of it, of course. He came back three months later and demanded another five hundred. There was that much and more still in the savings, but if I took it out I knew Ivan would become suspicious; he'd asked me about the first five hundred and I'd had to invent a story about one of my relatives being ill and needing a loan. So I went out alone to my mother's for a three-day weekend, on a pretext, and wrote fifty thousand words of detective pulp and managed to sell all of it to the surviving magazines under pseudonyms. I kept on writing on the sly like that because I knew Frank would be back for more. I did it for four months, half frantic all the time—well over three hundred thousand words—and I think that, more than anything else, was what burned me out as a writer.

"Frank did come around again, twice more. And then, all of a sudden, he disappeared: one day he was there, hanging around publishing, looking for work that nobody would give him, and the next he was gone. I couldn't believe it at first. I kept waiting for him to get in touch with me, to make more blackmail demands. But he didn't, not for almost thirty years."

She stopped talking and sat statuelike for a time, still peering down that long, dark tunnel. Then she came out of it, blinked several times, and finally focused on me. She ran her tongue over dry-looking lips, fumbled at the blouse button again.

"You see?" she said wryly. "Not a pretty story."

I hauled up my beer and had a long pull from it. When I put the bottle down I said, "Do you have any idea why Colodny disappeared as he did?"

"No. And I didn't care enough to try finding out. All that mattered was that he was out of my life."

"Did any of the other Pulpeteers know?"

"None of them indicated it if they did."

"What about this ghost town Colodny is supposed to have bought in Arizona? Was any mention made of that in New York?"

"Well, he was always talking about moving back to the West—he came from New Mexico—and prospecting for gold. But none of us took him seriously; we all treated it as a joke."

"Did he say anything along those lines before he disappeared?"

"Not that I remember. Russ told me the other day Frank bought the town right after he left New York—that was what Frank had told him—but if he did, I can't imagine where he got the money."

I could, but I did not want to go into it with her. I didn't much want to ask the next question, either, but I had to know the answer. "You said something about a photograph, Mrs. Wade. What sort of photograph?"

Her eyes flicked away from me again. Two small spots of color, like the marks a pair of pressed-in dimes would leave, appeared on her cheeks. "Frank took it that first night we were together, after we . . . afterward. I refused to let him at first, but I'd had a lot to drink, and he promised he'd never show it to anybody, and the idea of it was . . . exciting, wicked." Her gaze came back to my face. "Do I have to tell you what pose I was in when he snapped it?"

"No," I said. "I wish you wouldn't."

"Thank you. I think you can understand why I couldn't let Ivan see it. I'd have done anything to prevent that."

"Including murder?"

"Yes," she said without hesitation. "If it had come to that; if I'd had no other alternative. But I didn't kill him. I'm glad he's dead—I felt a tremendous relief when I heard about it. But I did not kill him."

It seemed stuffy in there; I got up and went over to the thermostat and turned it down. Cybil was looking at her beer glass with distaste when I sat down again, as if remembering the analogy she had drawn earlier and equating beer with her ill-advised affair.

I said, "The first time you saw Colodny since 1950 was at the convention?"

"No. Not quite."

"Oh?"

"He called me in Los Angeles one night about three weeks ago, out of nowhere. God, I nearly had a heart attack. He said he'd been approached about attending the convention, and when he learned that Ivan and I were on the program he'd accepted. He said Lloyd Underwood had given him our address and telephone number, and he was in Los Angeles and thought it would be nice if he and I got together for a little preconvention reunion. I tried to put him off but he insisted; there was nothing I could do except agree to meet him. I thought he might try to blackmail me again, and I was right. But it wasn't money he wanted this time. It was me."

"He made a pass at you?"

"Yes. A vulgar pass. If I didn't go to bed with him, he said, he'd have a talk with Ivan and he'd show him the photograph; he'd kept it all these years, and he was sure Ivan would still be interested. I almost gave in to him—I don't have much shame left—but you saw the way he looked: the years hadn't been good to him. He was repulsive. I just couldn't bring myself to do it. I put him off with promises, all sorts of promises and told him I'd make arrangements to be with him at the convention."

"Did you mean that, or were you just buying time?"

"Just buying time. But I also had an idea I could drive him away, force him to leave me alone."

"How?"

"By threatening him," she said. "With a gun."

"The .38 you brought with you, the one that eventually killed him."

"Yes. I bought it from a friend who has a gun collection."

"Did you go ahead with the threat?"

"Yes. I went ahead with it."

"And?"

"He laughed at me. He said I didn't have the courage to shoot anybody. I told him I did and I meant it; I think I *could* have killed that man. But I swear to you again that I didn't."

"Did your husband know you'd brought the gun with you?"

"No. Not until after it was stolen. Then I had to make up that story about bringing it with me for demonstration purposes."

"Did anyone else know you had it?"

"Not unless someone saw it when Russ knocked over my purse at the party on Thursday night. *You* saw it then, didn't you?"

"Yes."

"But if nobody else did, then it had to be Frank who broke into our room later and took it."

"Assuming the thief wasn't after something else," I said, "and stealing the gun was incidental."

"Nothing else was missing."

Not unless Ivan had played the same game as she and brought along something he hadn't told her about. "Did Colodny say anything to indicate that he might want your gun?"

"No. But he did seem nervous about something, almost frightened."

"Could it have been the 'Hoodwink' extortion business?"

"Well, it could have been. He didn't seem to want to talk about it."

"Did he approach you again after the theft?"

"About sleeping with him? Yes."

"What did you say?"

"I said no. He called me names and I slapped him."

"And that was when he hit you and gave you that bruise?"

"How did you know it was Frank who hit me?"

"I didn't, but it's not much of a deduction after what you've told me."

"Well he did it, yes. With his fist. He said I'd better not lay a hand on him again, or try to threaten him again, or he'd fix me. He said I'd better come across for him, too. Not that weekend—he had too many things on his mind—but as soon as I got back to Los Angeles. Then he shoved me out of the room and slammed the door."

"Were there any more run-ins with him?"

"No. I saw him Saturday morning, but we never said another word to each other."

"All right. Is there anything else you can tell me that might be pertinent?"

"I don't think so, no. I've told you everything—much more than I could ever tell anyone else." A faint smile. "But I feel better for it. It's been festering inside me much too long."

"Sure," I said, "I understand."

"I *can* trust you not to say anything, can't I? If any of this gets back to Ivan or Kerry . . ."

"It won't. I just hope you've been honest with me."

"I have. Painfully honest." Cybil uncrossed her legs and got to her feet. "I'd better go. I left a note for Ivan that I was having dinner with a friend, but he starts to worry if I'm out late."

"He's been gone all day, has he?"

"Yes. Since seven this morning. Magic is his great passion these days. May I use your phone to call a taxi?"

"That's not necessary," I said. "I'll drive you back to the hotel."

I got her coat for her and helped her into it. She let me have another smile, a little brighter than before, and said, "I'm glad I came here tonight. I wasn't sure about you before I did, but now I am. You're a decent man and I think you're good for Kerry."

"I hope so, Mrs. Wade."

"Please call me Cybil. And I wouldn't worry about Ivan's disapproval. He's terribly stuffy sometimes, and overprotective, but he'll come around."

I said I hoped that too, but I was not worried about Ivan's disapproval. What I *was* worried about was that he was the one who had killed Frank Colodny and maybe Ozzie Meeker too, which was a hell of a lot more dismaying prospect. Because the way things looked to me now, no one fitted the murderer's role half so well as stuffy Ivan Wade.

EIGHTEEN

Somebody kept ringing the damned door buzzer.

At first the sound got mixed up with a jumbled dream I was having; then it broke all the way through and woke me up, brought me jerkily upright. Disoriented and grumbling, I pawed at my eyes until I got them unstuck. There was morning light coming through the window, but it was pale and gray and gave the room a dingy look, like something out of an old B movie. I squinted at the nightstand clock. And the time, for Christ's sake, was 6:46.

Who the hell would come calling at 6:46 in the morning?

The buzzer kept blaring away, long and short, long and short, until the noise began to rattle around inside my head like a marble in a box. I said a few things under my breath, most of them obscene, and fumbled my way out of bed and into an old robe from the closet. Then I lumbered into the front room and jammed down the talk lever on the intercom unit.

"Who is it?"

"It's me—Eberhardt."

Eberhardt? "You know what time it is?"

"Yeah, I know. Buzz me in, will you?"

So I buzzed him in, scowling about it. Then I unlocked the door, opened it, and went back into the bedroom to put my pants on I heard him come in—he made some noise with the door—and pretty soon he yelled my name.

I yelled back at him to keep his pants on, finished putting

164

mine on, and went out there. I don't know what I expected to see—Eberhardt as he usually was, I suppose, wearing a business suit, with his hair combed and a pipe poking out of his face—but what I did see brought me up short and made me gawp a little. He was standing over by the couch, none too steady on his feet, and you could smell the liquor on him from across the room. He wore sports clothes instead of a suit, but the shirt was rumpled and one of the buttons was missing, and the fly on his trousers was at half-mast. His cheeks were stubbled, his hair stuck up at sharp angles like the stubby spokes on a mace; his face was red and glazed-looking, and his eyes were a couple of wounds with streaks of blood in them. I had known him more than thirty years, and I'd never seen him like this. Never.

"What the hell, Eb?"

"What the hell, yourself. You got any coffee?"

"I'll put some on. What're you doing here?"

"I was in the neighborhood," he said. "Just thought I'd drop in."

"Yeah."

I went into the kitchen and ran some tap water into a kettle. He followed me, propped himself up against the wall next to the door, fumbled around in his jacket until he found one of his old briars. He put the thing in one corner of his mouth and left it hanging there.

"You went out and tied one on, huh?" I said as I plopped the kettle down on the stove and turned on the gas flame.

"Better believe it," he said.

"You feel any better?"

"No. I feel lousy."

"You look lousy. Why aren't you home?"

"Told you, I was in the neighborhood."

"What does that mean?"

"I spent the night down on Greenwich."

"Who do you know on Greenwich?"

"Lady, that's who. Lady I met last night."

"Uh-huh. Like that."

"Like that. You think I'm too old to pick up broads in bars? Not me, hot shot. You, maybe, with that flabby gut of yours. Not me."

I spooned instant coffee into two cups. "Congratulations. So you got laid. How're you going to make it to work today, the shape you're in?"

"No," he said.

"No? No what?"

"No, I didn't get laid."

"That's too bad. Wasn't she willing?"

"Oh, she was willing. So was I."

"Well, then?"

He pushed away from the wall, moved to one of the chairs at the dining table. When he sat down he did it heavily, and the pipe fell out of his mouth and clattered on the table, spilling a trail of ash and dottle. He sat there looking at it, frowning.

"Shit," he said.

"If you didn't come here to brag about your conquest," I said, "why did you come?"

"Coffee. And I was in the neighborhood."

"Come on, Eb. I know you better than that. You've got a reason or you wouldn't be here looking like you do."

"You think you know me? Nobody knows me. Dana least of all. You want to hear something funny? She called last night. I'm home two minutes and she calls, first I've heard from her since she moved out. Reason is, she thought I might be worrying about her and she wanted to let me know she's all right. Didn't ask me how I was, how anything was, just wanted to let me know she's all right and staying with a friend. That's what she said, 'I'm staying with a friend.' Asshole lover of hers, that's who she's staying with."

"So you went right out and got drunk and got laid."

"No. Don't you listen? I *didn't* get laid."

"Okay, you didn't. Go back and see the lady tonight. Maybe you'll get lucky."

"Get lucky. Yeah. She threw me out."

"What?"

"She threw me out."

"Why?"

"Because she didn't get laid."

"Eb . . ."

"Called me a sorry excuse for a man and threw me out."

The kettle commenced a whistling shriek. I reached over and shut off the gas.

"Figured it was the booze last night," Eberhardt said. "Nothing to worry about. But this morning . . ." His face screwed up and for an awkward moment I thought he might start to bawl. But then he passed a hand over his eyes and his expression cleared; he looked up at me with the same sort of appeal as on Sunday. "You understand me? You're the same age I am, you been around . . . you understand?"

I understood, all right. Why he had come, what it was he really wanted to talk about. And the whole thing—the way he looked, what he was saying, what he was about to say— would have been comical if it had not been so tragic.

"I couldn't get it up," he said. "I couldn't get the son of a bitch to stand up and salute."

I spent an hour filling him full of coffee and talking to him like a Dutch uncle, reassuring him, telling him it was a temporary thing—stress, the psychological blow of Dana leaving him, maybe the woman and circumstances of last night as well. He knew all that, of course, but he was beaten down and lonely—about as beaten down and lonely as a man like Eberhardt could get—and he needed to have it all said to him by a sympathetic friend. He seemed to feel a little better afterward, which made one of us; it was the wrong kind of start for my day, and coming on the heels of last night's dirty-laundry session with Cybil Wade, it left me feeling as morose as I had on Sunday.

Eberhardt was in no shape to go traipsing down to the

Hall of Justice or even to drive to his house in Noe Valley. I convinced him of that, and got him to take a cold shower and crawl into my bed to sleep it off. Then I rang up the Homicide Squad for him and told one of the inspectors that Eb wouldn't be in until later today, maybe not at all. When I got out of there at 8:40 he was snoring away in bed, with one of the pillows clasped against him as if it were Dana in the days before the walls came tumbling down.

I took my depression downtown through wispy fog that had put a sheen of wetness on the streets. I was on Taylor Street, just crossing Eddy and about to swing into the lot on the corner, when I remembered that I no longer had an office here. My new offices, as of today, were located on Drumm Street. For Christ's sake, I thought, and wondered if I was becoming senile. The memory lapse, and the fact that I wouldn't be working in this lousy neighborhood anymore after two decades of calling it a second home, made me even more morose. It was one of those days when you should never get out of bed. When you should crawl under the sheets and huddle there like a rabbit under a newspaper until it goes away.

I drove all the way up the hill to California, turned right, and drove all the way down the hill to Drumm. Amazingly, there was a parking space near Sacramento; I put my car into it and walked back to the nice, shiny, renovated building where I had my new offices.

The offices were nice and shiny too: two rooms, one waiting area and one private office; pastel walls and a beige carpet on the floor; some chrome chairs with corduroy cushions; and Venetian blinds over the windows in case you didn't want to look out at the Embarcadero Freeway monstrosity looming nearby. The only things out of place were crap that belonged to me—the piles of boxes in the middle of the anteroom, the desk in the private office, that the moving company had delivered yesterday.

It was a fine new set of offices, all right. And it tied a nice black ribbon on my depression: I was going to *hate* working here, image or no image, changing times or no changing times.

The telephone company had come in and installed a phone—as promised, for a change—and it was sitting in the middle of my desk. It was a yellow phone, with a push-button dial system. Private eyes aren't supposed to have yellow phones, I thought sourly; pimps have yellow phones. But I went over and used it anyway, to put in a long-distance call to Ben Chadwick's office in Hollywood.

He was in, which was surprising because the time was only 9:30. "I had to come in early today," he said by way of explanation. "Heavy workload. I hate these early-bird hours, though."

"Yeah," I said.

"Listen," he said, "I tried to call you yesterday, but the operator said your phone had been disconnected. I thought maybe you'd gone out of business. Either that, or somebody blew you away."

"Yeah," I said. "What have you got, Ben?"

"*Evil by Gaslight*. You wanted poop, here's poop: Magnum bought the rights in 1950 from a guy named Frank Colodny. Nobody remembers anything about him; came in off the street to see Magnum's story editor, with an intro from some local flack he knew. Story editor liked what he saw, the moguls liked what they saw, and they paid him fifty grand for the property. Plus sweeteners. Pretty heavy sugar for those days."

"What did they buy? Story treatment?"

"Nope. Complete screenplay. Damn good screenplay too, from what I've been told. Only a few changes from original to shooting script."

"Did Colodny claim to have written it?"

"Yep. Under the Rose Tyler Crawford name."

"Was anyone else involved in the deal?"

"Not as far as Magnum knew."

"Who made the changes in the script?"

"Colodny did. They gave him an office and a typewriter on the lot. They also hauled him onto the set during shooting when they needed a few last minute changes."

"Those sweeteners you mentioned—what were they?"

"Two percent of the gross profit. Also not common in those days; Magnum must have really wanted that property Doesn't sound like much, but *Evil* grossed a bundle. Magnum paid Colodny another eighty grand or so over the years for that two percent."

"Were you able to dig up any local angles on Colodny?"

"Nope. He lived in Arizona, not down here; royalty checks were mailed to a P.O. box in a place called Wickstaff. But I don't know if the address is current. Last check went out some years back."

"Thanks, Ben. Let me know if I can do something for you up here."

"I will," he said. "Don't worry about that."

We hung up. And I sat down in my chair and put my feet up on the desk the way private eyes are supposed to do, new offices or not, and brooded out through the slats in the Venetian blinds. Things were beginning to come together. What I needed to do now was to shuffle all the pieces around and see if the full pattern emerged.

Okay. Meeker and Colodny are friends in New York in the forties; Meeker is a pulp artist and works for Action House, where Colodny is editor-in-chief. But Meeker has secret writing aspirations—secret because maybe he's not sure his work is any good, and he doesn't want to embarrass himself in front of the other Pulpeteers—and he writes . . . what? the short story or the screenplay? Come back to that later. He writes something called "Hoodwink" and decides to show it to Colodny. Colodny the editor recognizes its merit; and Colodny the bastard smells big money and plans to steal it for himself. He puts Meeker off, maybe tells him it's not very good but he'll see what he can do with it, and then a little while later he disappears. And where he goes is out to Holly-wood, where he sells the property to Magnum Pictures for fifty thousand dollars and a percentage of the profits. After which he buys a ghost town in Arizona, calls it Colodnyville, and settles in for the next thirty years.

Meeker, of course, doesn't know right away that he's been cheated. He only knows that Colodny has disappeared. He doesn't find out until the film is released—or maybe years afterward—and by then it's too late. He has no legal proof that Colodny stole or plagiarized his work since he obviously never copyrighted it; and Colodny's trail is long cold, so that even if Meeker tries to find him, he turns up empty-handed. So Meeker stays in New York drawing for the last of the pulps and the burgeoning paperback market, then later moves out to California to freelance. And all the while he grows more bitter and resentful toward Colodny.

Comes this year, the past several weeks. Lloyd Underwood and some others decide to put on a pulp convention, and somehow they manage to locate Colodny. Maybe the idea of a reunion with his Pulpeteer cronies amuses him after all the elapsed time, or maybe it's the prospect of seeing and bed-ding Cybil Wade again that amuses him. At any rate he agrees to come to the convention. The only thing that would have kept him away is the fact that Meeker would be pres-ent; but as far as Colodny knows, Meeker is among the miss-ing—Underwood, ironically, has had difficulty finding a man who all but lives in his own backyard. It isn't until after Colodny arrives at the hotel that he comes face to face with Meeker and his past crimes.

Meanwhile, Meeker is finally located by Underwood, who tells him that Colodny will be one of the guest panelists at the convention. This news has to have had a profound effect on Meeker. After thirty years he is at last going to confront the man who stole "Hoodwink" from him. So then—

So then *what*?

My speculations had been pretty solid so far, but now they

came to a skidding halt. If Meeker knew Colodny had stolen "Hoodwink," why had he sent copies of the short story to all the other Pulpeteers, along with the extortion letters? Unless it was some sort of mad purposeless game . . . but even at that, it didn't make sense. I had asked Cybil Wade a few more questions about Meeker during the ride back to the hotel last night, and she'd confirmed my impression of him as a flake, somebody who had always marched to the tune of a different drummer. It was likely that Colodny's betrayal had pushed him a little deeper into lunacy—anybody who would conceive that extortion gambit in the first place had to be at least half cracked—and yet he hadn't struck me as irrational. There had to have been some sort of method in it.

But there were other things, too, that wouldn't fit together: If Meeker had killed Colodny, if revenge in the form of a bullet was his primary intention, why bother to send the manuscripts and extortion letters? And if he hadn't killed Colodny, if murder wasn't his intention but someone else's, why had *he* been killed? And why had Colodny—apparently Colodny—stolen Cybil's gun? To threaten Meeker, as Cybil had threatened him, to lay off? But then why had Colodny turned up dead in the hotel and not Meeker?

Too many questions at once; they kept running around and bumping into each other, and they were giving me a headache. All right, then. Backtrack a little, take it from the original "Hoodwink" material. Was it the novelette or the screenplay? The short story seemed much more probable. Meeker was a Pulpeteer, he worked for a pulp magazine publisher, he was immersed in fiction as prose, not fiction as cinematic drama. Besides, if he'd written the screenplay, why would he bother to do a novelette version?

Next question: Then who wrote the screenplay? Not Colodny, in spite of what Ben Chadwick had told me. According to what I'd learned Colodny was not, and never had been, a writer. What he *was* was an editor, which explained how he was able to rewrite the script to Magnum's specifications and make last-minute changes on the film set; any good editor could do that much creative work without being a writer. But somebody else had to have written the initial screenplay, using Meeker's story as the basis.

Next question: Who did the actual plagiarism? One of the Pulpeteers? Could Colodny have taken one of the others in on the scam and then cheated him out of *his* share, just as he had cheated Meeker? And could Meeker, realizing that someone else was involved, suspecting it was a Pulpeteer—Cybil Wade, maybe, because of her affair with Colodny; that would explain the markings on the Arizona map—could he have sent the novelette and the extortion letters to each of them as part of his own screwball plan to find out which one was guilty?

I took my feet off the desk and got up and paced around a little. Now I was getting somewhere again. Colodny had had an accomplice, and the accomplice had killed him out of the same motive as Meeker had: revenge. And why murder Meeker later on? How about because Meeker had succeeded in his plan, had found out who the accomplice was—not Cybil after all, someone else—and threatened to go to the police; or maybe even because he tried a little blackmail of his own. The killer couldn't take the risk of being found out: exit Meeker. It made sense. There were still some small loose pieces, like who had really stolen Cybil Wade's gun and why, and still some big loose pieces, like how had the killer managed to pull off not one but two locked-room murders—but the skeleton of it was there, all the structural bones gleaming inside the dusty museum of my head. Figure out *who*, I told myself, and the rest of it, the "impossible" stuff, will follow. The solutions are there; you just haven't put them together yet.

Ivan Wade, I thought glumly. It's got to be Ivan Wade.

He was an amateur magician, and who better than an amateur magician to stage a pair of locked-room illusions? He was the cuckolded husband, and if he'd found that out, despite Cybil's protestations to the contrary, it doubled his motive for murder. It was Dancer who had been framed, and Wade had a long-standing hostility toward him. The Wades hadn't exactly been poor in 1950, by Cybil's testimony, but the prospect of a big Hollywood score was enough to corrupt anybody at any income level. Ivan had had experience in radio scripting at that time, and later did a number of TV scripts, so he understood the dramatic form; it was only a small step to the writing of a complete screenplay. And from what I'd learned about Colodny, he had been the kind of perverse bastard who'd have enjoyed working a scam with the husband of the woman he'd seduced and was then blackmailing.

Wade fit the bill, all right—and I hoped to God I was wrong about him. If I wasn't, and if I helped to put him in prison for murder, what would happen between Kerry and me? I had a pretty bad idea. Once before I had got involved with a woman and a murder case at the same time, and the killer turned out to be her brother, and I was the catalyst in his eventual suicide. The relationship had died along with him. It made me ache to think of the same thing happening with Kerry and me.

But I was in too deep to back out now, even for her sake, even for mine. I owed the truth to Dancer and I owed it to myself. The one hope I had was to turn up evidence that exonerated Wade by pointing conclusively to someone else. Innocent until proven guilty; give him the benefit of that and slog ahead, try to find proof either way.

And I had an idea where I ought to go slogging, too. If there was one place proof might exist, along with some other missing pieces, it—

The telephone rang.

I moved over and caught up the receiver. "Detective Agency."

"Hi, it's me," Kerry's voice said. "Are you busy?"

"Sort of. But not too busy for you."

"How are the new offices?"

"Terrific," I lied. "Where are you? At work?"

"Yes. I just spoke to Cybil; she said she saw you last night."

"I got back a little earlier than expected and we had a talk."

"So she said. She wouldn't tell me what about, though."

"You, for one thing."

"I'll bet. She approves of you, you know."

"Yes," I said, "I know."

"Well, I wish you'd have come and talked with me too. What you told me on the phone about Ozzie Meeker really had me upset. Are you positive he was murdered?"

"Pretty positive."

"Two murders," she said. "What if a third Pulpeteer dies?"

"I don't think that'll happen."

"Convince me in person. Will I see you tonight?"

"I wish you could. But no, not tonight."

"Are you trying to avoid me for some reason?"

"Honey," I said, "the last thing I want to do is avoid you. No, I'm going out of town."

"Out of town? Where?"

"Arizona."

"Why Arizona?"

"I want to talk to some people in Wickstaff, where Colodny lived. I also want to have a look at this ghost town he owned."

"But why?"

"Just a hunch, that's all. I'll have more to tell you when I get back."

"I hope so," she said. "And I hope it's good news."

"Me too," I said. "Me too."

I spent the rest of the morning at the Hall of Justice, filling Russ Dancer in on the latest developments, asking him questions about Ivan Wade and Colodny and Meeker. He didn't have anything new to tell me, except that Wade had begun experimenting with television scripting as early as 1949 and had also written an unsuccessful play. So there was no question that he had had the talent and the know-how to write the *Evil by Gaslight* screenplay.

Dancer was in better spirits than he had been on Sunday, even though I was careful not to build up his hopes. His faith in me was almost childlike. "You'll get me out of here," he said. "I know it; it's just a matter of time. You're the best there is."

Yeah.

Then I drove out to SFO, parked my car, took the overnight bag out of the trunk, and went in and bought myself a ticket. At 3:45 I was up in the friendly skies on my way to Tucson.

NINETEEN

The town of Wickstaff, Arizona, was one of those places plunked down in the middle of nowhere that make you wonder about their origins. There was nothing much surrounding it in any direction except rough terrain dominated by cacti, scrub brush, and eroded lava pinnacles—mile after mile of sun-blasted emptiness that stretched away to low, reddish foothills on three sides. Two roads cut through it north-south and east-west, both of them county-maintained and both two-lane blacktop; scattered here and there in its vicinity were a few hardscrabble ranches. And as far as I could tell, that was all there was. So why had it been created and nurtured in the first place? What had kept it alive when hundreds of others in the Southwest, including the fabled Tombstone, which was not all that far away and in a better geographical location, died natural deaths and became ghosts crumbling away into ruin or tourist bait?

On the outskirts was a sign that said, with evident civic pride, that the current population was the same as the date Wickstaff had been founded: 1897. I passed it, driving the cranky Duster I had rented in Tucson, a few minutes past noon on Wednesday. The temperature was in the nineties, but streaky clouds and heat haze gave the sky a whitish cast, made the sun look like a boiled egg, and kept the glare down outside. Inside, the air-conditioner whirred and clanked like an old Hoover vacuum cleaner and funneled dust along with cool air through the vents.

I felt somewhat relieved to finally get where I'd been

going. Twenty hours alone on an airplane, in a motel, driving back-country roads gives you too much time to think about things. Like Eberhardt and how marriages can go sour. And the murders, how they might have been committed. And Cybil Wade's affair with Colodny. And Ivan Wade's jealousy. And Kerry—mostly Kerry. I had lots of ideas, some of them good, some of them not so good, some of them unsettling; but on more than one level, it came right down to this: Was Ivan Wade guilty of murder or wasn't he? Without knowing the answer to that, I could not resolve my situation with Kerry or convince the San Francisco cops that Russ Dancer was innocent.

But now here I was, welcome to Wickstaff, and I could start doing things instead of brooding about them. The first thing I could do was to find out where Colodny had lived when he wasn't keeping house with a bunch of ghosts. The second thing after that was to find out how to get to Colodnyville.

Neither figured to be difficult, Wickstaff being as small as it was, and they weren't. The town had a three-block main street, with about a third of the buildings of grandfatherly vintage, made out of adobe brick and sporting Western-style false fronts. One of these in the second block housed something called the Elite Cafe. I parked in front and went in there, on the theory that if anybody knows everybody in a small town, it's the people who run a local eatery. It was a good theory in this case: a dour middle-aged waitress told me Colodny had boarded with a Mrs. Duncan on Quartz Street; turn right at the next corner, three blocks down, first house on your left. I also learned that word had found its way here from San Francisco about Colodny's death; the waitress asked me if I was kin or a friend of his, and when I said no she said, "He was a mean old bastard," and left it at that. Colodny, it seemed, had not been any better liked among the folks of Wickstaff than he had among the Pulpeteers.

I went out and got into the Duster and turned right at the

next corner, drove three blocks down, and stopped again in front of the first house on my left. It was a big frame house, somewhat weathered, with a wide front porch that was shaded by paloverde trees. A Conestoga wagon wheel, painted white, had been imbedded in the patchy front lawn, and against it was propped a sign that said: *Room for Rent.* On the porch, in the shade, a fat woman in a straw hat sat in a wicker chair and peered out at me with kindled interest.

The walk from the car to the porch was maybe thirty yards, but I felt wet when I got there. The Arizona heat was something; so was that starched-looking sky. And so was the fat woman. She must have weighed three hundred pounds, and she had an angelic face, a voice that came out of a whiskey keg, a pair of raisinlike eyes that picked my pocket and counted the money in my wallet. The most interesting thing about her, though, was the fact that she didn't sweat. She sat there in her chair, swaddled in heat, and her face was powder dry; she didn't even look uncomfortable. It seemed unnatural somehow, particularly when I could feel myself dripping and simmering in front of her, like an ice cube on a hot stove.

"Hot day," I said.

"Is it? Didn't notice."

"Are you Mrs. Duncan?"

"That's me. It's one-fifty per week, meals included."

"What is?"

"The room. That's why you're here, isn't it?"

"No, ma'am. Not exactly."

She lost interest in me. She didn't move, her expression didn't change, but the light of avarice went out of her raisin eyes and was replaced by a dull glow of boredom. If it had not required too much effort, she might have yawned in my face. Or told me to go away. As it was she just sat still and watched me sweat.

"I'm here about Frank Colodny," I said.

That didn't interest her much either. "Policeman?"

"Private investigator, from San Francisco."

"Is that a fact."

"Yes, ma'am. Would you mind answering a few questions?"

"About Frank?"

"Yes, about Frank."

"Don't see why I should, if you're not a cop."

"It might help save a man's life, Mrs. Duncan."

"Whose life?"

"The man in San Francisco charged with killing Colodny," I said. "I think he's innocent and I'm trying to prove it."

"If he's been charged he must be guilty."

"Not in this case. If you knew the facts—"

"I'm not interested," she said.

We looked at each other. She was not going to give an inch, you could see that; she was a sweet old bitch. I rubbed sweat off my forehead with the back of one hand, and that made her mouth twitch in what might have been a smile. Then I dragged out my wallet and opened it and took out a five-dollar bill. That put the smile away, made the avarice reappear in her eyes—not much of it, just about five dollars' worth.

"Answers," I said. "Okay?"

She held out one flabby arm. I gave her the five and she made it disappear into the folds of her housedress. The greed-light disappeared with it. She was bored again, now that she had the money.

I asked her, "How long did Colodny board with you?"

"Six years, give or take."

"Where did he live before that?"

"Place over on Cholla that burned down. Most of the time he lived out in the hills with his wife."

"Wife? I didn't know he was married."

It wasn't a question, so she didn't say anything.

I said, "Where can I find her?"

"Graveyard, I reckon. Been dead, those six years."

"What did she die of?"

"Suffocated in the fire, so they said."

"Accidental fire?"

"Smoking in bed. Her, not him."

"What was her name?"

"Lisa Horseman."

"That's an Indian name, isn't it?"

"Navajo. She was a half-breed," Mrs. Duncan said, and curled her lip to let me know what she thought of half-breeds and interracial marriages.

"Was she from Wickstaff?"

"Folks had a ranch nearby."

"How long were she and Colodny married?"

"Since he come here, back in the early fifties."

"Did they have any children?"

"Nope."

"Are her relatives still living?"

"Nope."

"Did Colodny still spend time in the ghost town after she died?"

"Ghost town. That's a laugh."

"How do you mean?"

"You fixing to go out there, are you?"

"I was, yes."

"Then you'll see what I mean when you get there."

"But he *did* go there regularly?"

"Sure he did. Two-three days a week."

Which meant that he maintained some sort of home in Colodnyville, probably the same one he'd shared with his wife when she was alive. I went on to ask her if the local police had stopped by to see her and to check through Colodny's belongings—a routine undertaking in homicide cases where the victim is killed in another area or state, and has no immediate next of kin.

She said, "They have, but wasn't much for them to go through."

"No? Why not?"

"He didn't keep much here," she said. A small bitterness

had crept into her voice, as if she begrudged that fact. The police were not the only ones who had checked through Colodny's belongings in this house. "Clothes, some books, not much else."

"Did the police go out to Colodnyville too?"

"I suppose. They didn't tell me."

"How do I get there?"

"Straight out of town to the east until you come to Ocotillo Road, winds up into the foothills. Old dirt track off there about a mile in. You'll see a sign. Crazy old fool put up a sign."

"One more question. Has anyone else been around asking about Colodny in the past few days?"

"Just you. Hyped-up dude named Lloyd Underwood called him three-four weeks ago, said he was a pulp magazine collector. Said he'd heard about Frank from some other collector passed through these parts on a book-buying trip. That's why Frank went off to San Francisco. Pulp magazines," she said, and curled her lip again. They were right up there with half-breeds and interracial marriages in her esteem.

"But nobody's called since?"

"No. Who'd call? He didn't have any friends."

"Why didn't he?"

"Mean and tetched, that's why. Married a half-breed, kept to himself like he had secrets, bit your head off when you spoke to him, lived out in that godforsaken place claiming he was a prospector." She made a piglike snorting sound. "Prospector. No gold out there anymore, not in fifty years; he didn't take a hundred dollars out of those hills in all the time he was there. But he always had plenty of money just the same."

"If you disliked him so much, why did you give him a room in your house?"

She looked at me as if I might be a little tetched myself. "He paid me one-fifty a week," she said. "Why do you think?"

I left her sitting there, not bothering to thank her or to say goodbye, and pushed back through the sweltering air to the street. The back of my shirt and most of the underarm areas were sopping wet, but not one drop of sweat had appeared anywhere on her face or arms and her dress was desert-dry. I disliked her for that as much as for anything else.

Back in the car, I let the dusty air conditioner dry me off as I drove to Main Street again, then turned east on the country road that cut through it in that direction. There was not much traffic and nothing much to look at except lava formations and tall saguaro cactus. The sky was so milky now that the sun looked like a cataracted eye. That and the heat glaze and the absence of movement anywhere beyond the road itself gave me an eerie feeling, as if I were driving in a place not of this world. My turn in the Twilight Zone.

I added what Mrs. Duncan had told me to what I already knew about Colodny, and it fit together nicely in the pattern I had evolved. He had come here thirty years ago with his boodle from Magnum Pictures, bought the ghost town, married, settled down to act out his fantasy of life as a gold prospector, and thumbed his nose at the world for a quarter of a century. The death of his wife, maybe coupled with creeping old age, had left him lonely; that had to be why he'd spent more time in Wickstaff over the past six years. It might also explain why he had consented to attend the pulp con and the Pulpeteer reunion. And why he had tried to force Cybil Wade to share a bed with him again after all those years.

The fact that he kept most of his possessions in Colodnyville might also be significant. If he had retained anything incriminating from his New York days, such as evidence of his partner's identity in the "Hoodwink" plagiarism—and that embarrassing photograph Cybil had told me about—it was likely to be there. Unless the local law had found it and confiscated it, of course. If I had no luck myself I would have to check with them right away. But I hoped that if they had found something, it was not the photograph; that was not for anybody to look at, including me. The first thing I'd do if I came across it myself would be to shut my eyes and burn it.

The road took me in a more or less straight line for better than five miles before an intersection loomed up. On the near side was a sign that indicated the narrow two-lane cutting off to the southeast was Ocotillo Road. The foothills loomed up here, too—more lava formations, huge rocks balanced on top of each other and strewn along slopes that also bore catclaw, cholla, organ-pipe cactus abloom with pink and white and lavender flowers. Higher up, crags and limestone walls stood dark red against the starchy sky.

Ocotillo Road zigzagged through this rough terrain, sometimes climbing, sometimes dropping into shallow vales—past a lonesome and not very prosperous-looking ranchhouse tucked behind one of the hills, past stretches of the thorny brush that had given the road its name. A little more than a mile along, by the Duster's odometer, an unpaved and badly rutted track appeared on my right, leading off onto higher ground. Tacked to the trunk of a paloverde growing alongside it was the sign, made out of weathered shingles and painted in faded black letters, that Mrs. Duncan had told me about. It said: *Colodnyville • Population 2 • No Trespassing.*

When I made the turn there I had to slow down to a crawl. A jeep was what you needed to navigate a trail like this, and the Duster was a long way from being jeeplike. It jounced and banged and kept scraping its undercarriage on jutting rocks; I thought that one would tear the pan or at least flatten one or two tires, and I had visions of being stranded out here in the middle of nowhere with snakes and gila monsters and Christ knew what else that inhabited these rocks. But none of that happened. All that happened was that I cracked my head against the door frame a couple of times and wound up with a headache.

The trail twisted upward for a time, slid sideways, and then hooked around and along the wall of a limestone cliff. There was a pretty steep drop-off on one side; I tried not to look down in that direction because I'm a coward when it comes to high places. Then the track began to descend in a series of sharp curves that were almost switchbacks. And pretty soon it straightened out again, and I was in another hollow, not large enough to be called a valley but large enough nonetheless to contain Colodnyville.

It was not what I had expected. When you think of ghost towns you think of open spaces, two or three blocks of crumbling false-front buildings, tumbleweeds everywhere, a saloon with one of its batwings canted at a rakish angle, hitchracks and horse troughs and broken signs flapping in the wind. But that was Hollywood stereotype, not Colodnyville. Now I knew why Mrs. Duncan had said, "Ghost town. That's a laugh." Because it wasn't even a town—not unless you can call four buildings huddled more or less together in a small sea of cactus and rocks a town.

All the buildings were plaster-faced adobe ruins, three of them with glassless windows, the other one with rusted iron bars like a jail and a crisscross of boards tacked up inside. The one with the window bars was the largest, maybe forty feet square, with a roof that had a little peak in front and slanted downward to the rear. There was nothing else to see except for a well dug off to one side, sporting a crooked windlass that looked about ready to collapse, and the remains of a crude wooden sluice box set up alongside it. In the crags above and beyond, there was evidence that mining had once been done here—tailings, the boarded-up entrances to at least two pocket mines. But it had never been a rich lode, judging from the ruins, nor had the miners who'd worked it stayed on for more than a few years.

I eased the Duster forward until the road began to peter out among the rocks and cacti, twenty yards or so from the nearest building and sixty yards from the nearest crag. When I got out it was like stepping into a vacuum: dead silence everywhere. Not a breathless hush, but a complete absence of sound, the way it was supposed to be on the moon. And the heat was thick, smothering, under that murky sky, acrid with the smell of dust. Sweat came popping out again and made me feel soiled and gritty.

Carefully I picked my way across to the largest building. Enough sunlight came through the haze to put a gleam on the cracked plaster facing; it looked like thin icing on a crumbled and petrified cake. There was a door cut off-center in that front wall, and when I got close enough I could see that it was made out of heavy timbers reinforced and bound with rusted iron straps. Above the latch was the hasp for a padlock, and set into the adobe was the ring that it fastened over. But it was not fastened now; the hasp stood out from the door at right angles. And lying in the dust to one side was the remains of a thick Yale lock.

I leaned down to pick up the padlock. It had been sawn through with what might have been a hacksaw, and recently: the cut ends were still shiny. Had the local police done it when they were here? Or had someone else been around?

I dropped the padlock where I'd found it, moved over to try the door. It opened, creaking a little like the door in the old *Inner Sanctum* radio show. At first I couldn't see anything except gloom streaked with thin shafts of light that came through gaps in the window boarding. I stepped inside, blinked several times to help my eyes adjust from the outside glare. Then the interior began to take shape—a low single room beneath a slanted beam ceiling—and I got my second surprise of the past few minutes. Or second and third, because this one was double-barreled.

The first thing was the way it was furnished. What I had expected to find was spartan prospector's digs: bunk beds, an old potbellied stove, a table and a few chairs—that sort of thing. What I found instead was something out of an 1890s whorehouse. The room was jammed with wine-red, velvet-covered settees and chairs, rococo tables, glassed-in cabinets, a four-poster bed with a lace canopy, a fancy nickel-plated, high-closet stove, even a hanging oil lamp with what looked to be a Tiffany shade. The wine-red carpeting on the floor was worn and coated with dust, but you could tell that it had once been expensive. Colodny may have moved out here into the middle of nowhere, but it was not to live in squalor; he had taken esoteric New York tastes with him. And created a kind of decadently elegant private world for himself and his wife.

The second part of the surprise was that the place was in a shambles—it had been turned upside-down by somebody looking for something. The bed and most of the cushions had been ripped open, the canopy was in tatters, the carpet was strewn with hundreds of hardcover and paperback books that had once occupied space inside the glass-fronted cabinets; drawers had been pulled out and emptied, the stove emptied of ash and charred wood fragments; wall cupboards stood open and their contents lay scattered everywhere. A four-foot stack of pulp magazines in one corner was about all that had been left undisturbed.

The Cochise County law would not have done anything like this. So who, then? The person who had killed Colodny and Meeker, the accomplice in the "Hoodwink" plagiarism? It added up that way. And what he'd been looking for figured to be the same thing I was here to look for: evidence that would ruin him as a plagiarist and establish his motive for murder. The big question was, had he found it?

Either way, I was here now and I was not going to leave without conducting my own search of the premises. Technically I was trespassing, but with Colodny and his wife both dead, and no next of kin, there was nobody to prosecute me. This was one time I could bend the rules a little with a clear conscience.

But even with the door open it was gloomy in there, full of shadows. I didn't have any matches, or any particular inclination to light the oil lamps, so I would need the flashlight clipped under the Duster's dash before I started in. I went back to the open door, through it into the hazy afternoon glare. I stood for a moment, squinting, rubbing wetness off my forehead, as my eyes readjusted to daylight. Then I took three steps toward the car.

On the fourth step something went whistling over my right shoulder, just under the ear, and made a chinking sound in the plaster facing behind me. At almost the same time, noise erupted from the rocks across the clearing, a small echoing clap of it like thunder from a long way off.

Gunshot.

Somebody's shooting at me!

And then I moved, on reflex and instinct—turned and dove headfirst back through the open doorway just as a second bullet slashed the air above me, rained chips of plaster down on my back, and another hollow explosion rolled out of the rocks like the Biblical crack of doom.

TWENTY

I landed on my forearms on the rough wood floor beyond the threshold, scrambled forward until I had my ass-end out of the doorway. A third bullet came winging inside, but it was well over my head; I heard it smack into something on the far side of the room. I rolled out of the wedge of light that slanted in through the open door, across the carpet, and into the shadows; came up on my knees. And caught the edge of the door and threw it shut so hard it rattled in its frame.

Shaky-legged, I got up and stumbled over to the wall beside it. There was no key latch or tumbler lock on the door, but what it did have was a pair of angle irons bolted to the wood, with another pair on the wall parallel; and down on the floor was a heavy two-by-six about four feet long. I caught up the bar and shoved it through the angle irons. Once it was wedged in tight, ten men wielding half a tree couldn't have battered the door down. Then I leaned hard against the wall, gripping it with my hands, and tried to get my breathing and my pulse rate under control.

A minute or two passed in silence. There had not been any more shots, and that made me wonder if he'd left his hiding place up in the rocks, come down onto open ground. If so, I wanted to know it. And I wanted a look at the son of a bitch in any case—Ivan Wade or whoever he was. He must have been here all along, searching the damn place, and he'd heard me coming down that winding road. He'd had enough time to get his wheels and himself out of sight before I appeared—and more than enough time to draw a bead on the front of this building. If he had been a marksman, I would not be alive to think about it right now.

A pair of narrow windows flanked the door; I went to the nearest one and peered through one of the chinks in the boards. The clearing—what I could see of it—looked as still as before, and nothing seemed to stir among the rocks beyond. But the sun had broken through the milky haze, and its glare off the Duster's hood was dazzling enough to create blind spots from this vantage point.

I moved across to the other window and found a gap to look through there. A little better; I had a wider range of vision and not so much reflected glare. As I looked, something glinted up above, between a pair of boulders that leaned toward each other at forty-five degree angles, like two drunks on a park bench, to form a cavelike open space at the bottom. Two or three seconds later, I heard the report of the rifle as he squeezed off, saw the pale muzzle flash. But he was not shooting at me or the building this time; he was shooting at the Duster. It was a stationary target and he had better luck with it than he'd had with me: he hit what he'd been aiming at, which was the right front tire. The faint hiss of escaping air was audible after the echoes of the shot faded.

His reason for flattening the tire was obvious enough, and it made me dig my nails into the palms of my hands. He did not want me opening the door and making a run for the car and driving the hell away from here. He wanted me right where I was, trapped inside, where he could finish me off one way or another, sooner or later.

He put a second shot into the right rear tire, just to make sure the Duster was crippled good and proper. When he did that I shoved away from the window and went groping through the dark room, looking for matches and some kind of weapon. The matches were no problem; I found a box on top of the stove's high closet. But a suitable weapon was a lot harder to find. There was a rifle lying half under the canopied bed, but the firing pin had been removed; I threw it into a corner. Over against the south wall, I found a wood hatchet with a rusted blade—and that was all I found. A hatchet against a rifle. Some odds.

I took it and the matches over to where the Tiffany-shaded lamp hung from the ceiling. But there was no oil in the fount, and the wick was dry as dust. The only other lamp in there lay shattered near the bed; it was matchlight or nothing.

I went back to the window, peered out again. Stillness. What was he up to now? Sit up there and watch and wait? If he had water, food, and enough time and patience, he could wait for days until thirst and starvation forced me out; there wasn't anything at all to eat or drink among the wreckage. There were other things he could do, too. He could come down and break through the boards over one of the windows and shoot me through the bars. Or toss in some sort of incendiary device, then sit outside and pick me off when the fire drove me out.

And how was I going to prevent him from doing any of those things? How was I going to get out of here alive, armed with a hatchet and with all the windows barred and the only exit this one door?

The irony of it was bitter. Both Colodny and Meeker had been killed in locked-room situations, and now the murderer had me trapped in similar circumstances—closed up inside a box, with no evident means of escape. He didn't need any gimmicks this time; the juxtaposition of events had done it all for him. All he needed was that frigging rifle of his and a little patience, and afterward he could bury my body up in the rocks somewhere or toss it into a ravine. Who would ever find out what had happened to me? Who would ever know I had become victim number three?

It seemed futile, hopeless, but I refused to let myself think that way. If I did, it would lead to panic, and as soon as you panicked in a crisis like this, you were a dead man. I leaned back against the rough adobe wall and shut my eyes and tried to concentrate on ways and means.

I managed the concentration part of it all right, and right away my mind began to throw up answers. Click, click, click, like tumblers falling one by one in the combination lock to a safe. The only problem was, my brain works in mysterious ways, and none of the answers had to do with a way out of here.

What they did have to do with was the deaths of Colodny and Meeker. Inside of five minutes I knew—Christ, I finally knew—how both of them had been killed, or seemed to have been killed, in locked rooms. *Both* of them, because the answer was the same in both cases. Not *who*, yet—I still wasn't sure if it was Ivan Wade or not. But *Who* was outside and I was in here, and how the hell could I tell Eberhardt or anybody else how Colodny and Meeker had died if I couldn't get myself out of *this* locked room?

I began to prowl again, chain-lighting matches. The furniture shapes reared up out of the gloom; the flickering match-light crowded shadows into corners and up against the ceiling beams. There was no window in the back wall, where the bed was, but one was cut into each of the left- and right-hand walls. Getting the boards off them would be no problem; could I get the iron bars off too? Maybe. The adobe was old and cracked and I might be able to chip the bars loose with the hatchet. But then what? Even if I could get out through the window, I still had a good sixty yards of open space to cross, no matter which direction I took, before reaching any kind of cover. He could sit up there with his rifle and pick me off when I—

The ceiling, I thought.

Not the windows—the ceiling, the roof.

I fired another match and followed it back to where the bed was. The downward slant of the ceiling's construction put it about seven feet from the floor where it joined the rear wall; the space between the last beam and the joining was a good three feet wide. I was getting old, not to mention fat and scruffy, but I still had some strength and dexterity of movement left. And I could still fit through a hole a couple of feet wide.

If I could make the hole in the first place . . .

When I climbed onto the bed, dust blossomed upward from the velvet coverlet, clogging in my sinuses, clinging grittily to my face and arms. The heat in there was stifling; sweat drenched me, and I had to pause to wipe it out of my eyes before I lit another match. I was half crouched, but I saw in the matchglow that I could stand all the way up. And when I did that, my head was a couple of inches below the ceiling, between the beam and the wall joining. Which made an awkward position to try doing demolition work. Even crouched again, it would not be easy to get any leverage into my swings.

I held the burning match up close to the ceiling and banged on the adobe with the hatchet's blunt end. Dust and small chips showered down on me, put out the flame, and set me off into a spasm of coughing for the next several seconds. Another match showed me gouges in the adobe, a seaming of small cracks that spread out from them. I could break through it all right for the first few inches, but what if it had been reinforced with wood or heavy wire? What if it was too damn solid for me to penetrate all the way to daylight?

The hell with that, I told myself. Get to work, for God's sake. You think too much.

The match had gone out; I scraped another one alight and started to bring it up. But I was looking past the gouges I'd made, toward the beam, and in the wobbly flame I saw something that caught and held my attention. It was a three-sided mark near the top of the beam, where it was set into the adobe; it shone up faintly and blackly in the matchlight, like a scar. When I moved the flame closer to it I realized that it wasn't a mark but three cutlines sanded smooth and painted over so that you had to be where I was to see them. From down on the floor and away from the bed, they would be invisible.

I switched the hatchet to my left hand and probed over the cutout area with my fingertips. And as soon as I pushed against the upper left-hand corner, the whole section popped out like a lid on a hinge. Inside was a space—a hidden cache—that had been hollowed out of the top of the beam and part of the ceiling. And inside the space was an iron strongbox about eight inches long and six inches wide.

With the aid of another match, I fumbled the box out of there and managed to get it open; it wasn't locked. It contained several papers, some of them yellowing, at least two photographs, three small gold nuggets, and a packet of ten- and twenty-dollar bills that looked as if they would add up to at least two thousand. I closed the box again, without looking at the photographs or any of the papers, and laid it down on the pillow end of the bed. Then I straightened back up and went to work on the ceiling.

It was slow, hard going. Pieces of adobe and clouds of powder poured down on me, forcing me to duck away after every swing, to stop every minute or two until the air cleared. The muscles in my arm and shoulder began to ache from the awkward strokes. My chest tightened up, the way it used to when I was still on cigarettes; I could feel each breath, little shoots of pain in the lungs. I made a lot of noise, too, but I did not care if the sounds carried up to where he was in the rocks. He wouldn't know what I was doing, and unless I kept it up too long and made him suspicious, I doubted he would come to investigate. The real worry I had was whether he could see the back part of the roof from his vantage point. Those two leaning boulders had not seemed that high up, but from ground level height angles can be deceiving. None of this would do me any good at all if he had vision of the roof from front to back.

But I was making progress with the hole, widening it out to better than two feet. I came across a layer of chicken wire, but it was so old and brittle that I had no trouble whacking through it with the hatchet. At the center of the hole, where I had penetrated farthest, it felt four or five inches deep. I told myself the roof couldn't be any more than six inches thick and kept on methodically slugging away at the adobe.

A long time later—what seemed like a long time—I made another weakening swing . . . and broke through.

Along with adobe chips and powder, a shaft of daylight came slanting down into my face this time. I blinked at it, coughing, for two or three seconds. Then fresh determination and a sense of rage buoyed up my strength, and I hammered and scraped at the edges of the hole until I could feel the sun hot against the upper part of my body, see a good foot-and-a-half's-worth of the hazy sky. But I was careful not to send any pieces of adobe up onto the roof, where they might be seen in the air or heard clattering. All of it fell down around me: the bed and the floor near it were half buried under shallow layers.

When I had the hole widened out to two feet I dropped the hatchet, came down off the bed, and leaned against one of the posts, dripping. I had known a guy once, in the Army, who had worked as a cowboy on a ranch in Wyoming, and his favorite expression was, "I feel like I been rode hard and turned loose wet." That was how I felt right now. My right arm tingled with fatigue, my neck and back were stiff, my head throbbed, my throat burned from the dust and heat. Even if I were ready to drag myself up through that hole, which I wasn't, my body was not yet ready to respond.

The room was full of light now, spilling in through the hole; I no longer needed matches to see where I was going. I dragged myself over to the right front window and squinted out through the boards. Absolute stillness, like looking at a slide picture on a screen. I went to each of the side windows in turn, and it was the same in those directions, too. If he had come down while I was working on the hole, he was somewhere around to the rear or behind one of the other buildings. But I did not think he'd come down; I couldn't think it, because if he had, I was finished. No, he was still up there under the leaning rocks, still waiting.

So all right. Maybe he had heard me banging through the roof and wondered what I was doing, but now he was going to hear and wonder plenty. Now I *wanted* him to get suspicious and come investigate.

I went back to where the hatchet lay on the bed. My right

arm was on the mend; I picked up the hatchet and started to beat on the nearest window boards with as much strength as I could muster. Then I moved to the front and beat on those boards for a while. Then I got some tin plates from the mess on the floor and pounded on them, yelling and screaming all the while like a lunatic. Then I used the hatchet to pry loose some of the boards on a side window and hurled them out through the bars. Every minute or so while I was doing all of this, I looked out toward the leaning rocks. But the son of a bitch didn't bite. Maybe he suspected it was a trick. Maybe he had steel nerves. Maybe he was as crazy as I was pretending to be.

Maybe it was just a matter of time before he *did* bite.

I tore off more side-window boards, flung them outside. I found several unbroken glasses, cups, plates, and hurled them against the walls and the window bars. I screamed like Tarzan on a jungle vine and imitated a cackling laugh at the top of my voice. I used the hatchet to beat some more on the remaining window boards. I looked out toward the rocks for the fiftieth or hundredth time—

Movement.

Just a shadow at first, moving among other shadows. But after a few seconds he came out into the open, a man-shape in dark clothes—too far away for me to see who he was. Not that I was particularly interested in his identity right now. I kept watching him, yelling and banging things with the hatchet, as he started down out of the rocks. He was coming, all right. He was coming.

I hurried across to the bed, shoved it out of the way, and dragged one of the tables over under the hole. Then I went back, breaking more crockery on the way, hooting and cackling, and looked out again. Still coming. I might have been able to recognize him if I'd stayed there a little longer, but all I wanted was to make sure he was going to come all the way to this building. And it looked like he was—warily, slowly, but on his way just the same.

I picked up two of the tin plates and hammered on them

as I went back to where I'd positioned the table. I found two more glasses, another cup, and laid them and the plates on the table. When I climbed up and poked my head out, the roof slant and front lip blocked my view in that direction; I could see part of the distant rocks but not the two where he had been hiding. I picked up the glasses and cup and plates and set them on the roof to one side, anchoring them in little potholes so they wouldn't slide off; laid the hatchet beside them. Standing on tiptoe, I got my arms through the hole and wedged down on the roof. And then heaved and squirmed upward, head down, angling toward the rear wall so I wouldn't reveal myself above the roof's peak.

Doing it silently was my main concern, and I seemed to manage that well enough. But a sharp edge of adobe or chicken wire put a gash in my leg as I came through. I tried not to pay any attention to it, except that it stung and burned like fire. The roof's surface was irregular, pocked with little holes, studded with bumps; I got my feet and hands braced and turned back to face the hole. Leaned down into it with the glasses and the cup and shattered them back under against the walls. Then I beat on the tin plates, down inside so the noise would come from in there. After ten seconds or so, I tossed the plates back against the wall, pushed out of and away from the hole, and began to crawl up the roof slant to the front, the hatchet in one hand, like an Indian in an old cavalry movie.

When I got to within a foot of the edge I lay still and listened. Silence. Have to chance a look, I thought; I've got to know where he is. I eased my head up, an inch at a time. And there he was, forty feet or so from the building, moving at an angle toward the left-hand corner—eyes fixed straight ahead, the rifle jutting out in front of him at belt level. I gawped at him a little as he cut past the corner and started around on that side.

It was clear enough what he had in mind. He could not see inside from the front, because I hadn't broken any of the boarding off those windows. But he could look in through one of the unboarded side windows. Which was just what I wanted him to do—come right up close and peer through the bars.

I eased my body around to the left, teeth clamped against the pain in my leg, and crawled toward where I judged the near window to be. I had to do it even more slowly than before, because of his nearness and the risk of making noise. He was not trying to be quiet, though; I could hear the faint shuffle of his steps on the rocky ground.

Close to the side edge, I stopped again and lifted my head for another look. Twenty feet away now, still angling toward the window. A few more steps and he would be near enough for me to make my move, even if he didn't go all the way up to the window.

I drew back onto my knees, got one foot down—the leg that wasn't gashed—and unfolded myself in sections until I was standing up. My shoe scraped a little on one of the pebbly bumps; I froze in place. I could see him, his head and shoulders, and I thought that if he looked up, I would have to take an immediate running jump. But he did not look up. He moved forward one more pace, until only his head was visible.

I took a limping step myself, closer to the edge. The building was built low to the ground, but anything above three feet was too high for me; standing up there, looking down, made my stomach queasy and more sweat roll out of my pores. I took a firmer grip on the hatchet. I was not breathing at all now.

He had stopped and I could see him crane his head forward as if startled: he was staring through the bars and I knew he had seen the hole in the ceiling. I took one more step—and as soon as I did, he jerked his body and his head back, looked up, started to bring the rifle up.

I swallowed my fear and jumped straight down at him.

He tried to dodge clear, but surprise made him slow and awkward; one of my bent knees hit him in the chest, the whole weight of my body drove him over backwards and flattened him into the ground. We broke apart when we hit, like something splitting in half, and he lost the rifle and I lost the hatchet. But I didn't need the hatchet. I dragged myself onto all fours, hurting and shaky; he didn't move at all.

I could have broken both legs, I thought fuzzily. If I hadn't hit him just right, coming off that damn roof, I could have broken a dozen bones.

Yeah, another part of me said. And he'd have shot you dead if you *hadn't* jumped off the damn roof.

It took me a minute or so to get up onto my feet again. After which I went over, checked to see if he was still alive— he was—and then stood looking down at him, gawping a little the way I had on the roof. Because he wasn't anyone I had expected to see. Because there were some holes in the deductive reasoning I had done back in San Francisco. Not only wasn't he Ivan Wade, he was not even one of the Pulpeteers.

The guy lying there on the ground was Lloyd Underwood.

TWENTY-ONE

At two o'clock on Thursday afternoon I was back in San Francisco, sitting in Eberhardt's office at the Hall of Justice, getting ready for story time. Eberhardt was there too, of course, and so was a police stenographer. And so was Russ Dancer; Eb had had him brought down from the detention cells at my request. Nobody else had been invited.

The one other person I'd have wanted there was Underwood, but he was being held in Arizona, in the Cochise County jail where I had delivered him late yesterday afternoon, on an attempted murder charge. There had been no way to have him brought back to California, not without going through extradition proceedings. But then, Underwood had been sullen and uncommunicative anyway; he hadn't said anything to me when he regained consciousness, all trussed up like a turkey, as I was changing the Duster's flat tires—one spare from the rental's trunk, one from Underwood's Dodge hidden in the rocks nearby—and he hadn't said anything during the long ride out of there. He'd opened his mouth pretty good after I hauled him into the county police offices in Bisbee, but only to yell for an attorney. He had not admitted anything.

Not that his presence was all that necessary at this little gathering. Its purpose was for me to explain the entire chain of events to Eberhardt and convince him I knew what I was talking about. Which would then bring about a dropping of charges against Dancer, his release, a reopening of the Colodny case, and a reevaluation of the Meeker homicide by the Sacramento authorities. The subsequent investigation would slap Underwood with a murder charge, or so I hoped. I had nothing conclusive against him except the attempted homicide in Arizona, but if the police were convinced of his guilt, they were bound to turn up some sort of substantive evidence. Either that, or the pressure would get to Underwood and he would crack wide open. He was an amateur at crime, and amateurs convict themselves a good percentage of the time.

I had had plenty of time to reshape my theories so that Underwood, not Ivan Wade or one of the other Pulpeteers, fit the role of murderer. It had been eight P.M. before the Arizona law and I were finished with each other—too late to drive back to Tucson, much less catch a flight to San Francisco. So I had made two telephone calls, one to Eberhardt and one to Kerry, and then spent the night in Bisbee. Early this morning I'd driven to Tucson, just as an eleven o'clock flight out was boarding. By the time we touched down at San Francisco, I had a complete progression worked out. It hadn't been all that difficult, really. Once I realized what my mistakes were, as I had pieced it together initially, Underwood fit in with no trouble at all.

The office was as blue with smoke as it had been the last time I was there: Eberhardt puffing away on a billiard briar, Dancer chain-smoking cigarettes. But at least the electric heater wasn't on, and the temperature was at a tolerable level. Dancer, who still appeared ludicrous in his orange jumpsuit, kept looking at me with big dog eyes full of gratitude, as if he wanted to come over and lick my hand. He made me a little uncomfortable. I liked him much better in his role as the cynical and seedy hack writer, because I could deal with that. Fawning admiration was something else again.

Eberhardt took the pipe out of his mouth and said gruffly, "All right, let's get this show on the road." He did not look at me as he said it. He hadn't given me a direct look since my arrival. That was easy enough to figure, too: he was embarrassed at having shown up at my place drunk on Tuesday morning to discuss his sexual problems. So he was dealing with it by not dealing with it, by reverting behind the mask of hard-edged authority. He seemed to be bearing up all right, though. His eyes were bloodshot, which may have meant another drinking bout or just that he wasn't sleeping much, and his face still had that blurred, grayish look. But he was tough, one of the boys from the old school; he was not going to fall apart.

"I'd better lay everything out chronologically," I said. "It's complicated, and it'll be easier to follow that way."

"Tell it whichever way you want. It's your party."

"The central factor is the 'Hoodwink' manuscript, so what happened to both Colodny and Meeker had origins more than thirty years ago." I went on to explain my theory about Colodny's theft of the novelette Meeker had written and entrusted to him, the bringing in of someone to plagiarize it into a screenplay, the eventual sale to Hollywood. And also how I had come to the fact that Meeker was the "Hoodwink" author.

Eberhardt said, "Who was this someone Colodny brought in? You're not going to tell me it was Underwood, are you?"

"No, not Underwood. He's not a writer, and he didn't know Colodny in those days."

"Ivan Wade?" Dancer asked, as if he were hopeful the answer would be yes.

"It wasn't Wade either," I said. "It was Waldo Ramsey."

"Waldo?"

"There was a strongbox inside Colodny's place in the ghost town. He'd kept a letter in it from Ramsey, written in 1950; it mentions the screenplay."

"Why would Frank keep an incriminating letter all these years?"

"I guess he was something of a packrat," I said, but that wasn't the truth. Colodny had kept the letter because it was the stuff of potential blackmail—the same reason he'd kept the photograph of Cybil Wade and a couple of other items I had found in the strongbox. Whether or not he had used it against Ramsey was a moot point; but I doubted it. The Hollywood score had ended Colodny's blackmailing pursuits, at least for the intervening three decades. I did not mention any of this because I didn't want to go into the blackmail angle. It was more or less irrelevant to the two homicides, and I wanted to protect Cybil's reputation. I had burned the photograph, sight unseen, back in Arizona.

Dancer was shaking his head. "I wouldn't have figured Waldo for a plagiarist," he said. "He was on his uppers in those days, sure, but we all were. He always seemed honest enough. And he never mentioned anything about writing screenplays."

"Well, he had the talent—he's adapted a couple of his own books for the screen, remember? But I'm not so sure he even knew he was a plagiarist. The wording of his letter indicates he believed Colodny had received permission from some anonymous author to have the novelette turned into a screenplay. He may have suspected there was funny business going on, but as you said, Russ, he was on his uppers back then. Colodny paid him pretty well for the job." With money he got from blackmailing Cybil Wade, I thought.

Eberhardt said, "Enough with the history lesson. Bring it forward thirty years, will you?"

"Sure." And I told them my speculations on Meeker: his discovery that he'd been cheated, the festering grudge, the invitation to the pulp convention and the chance to confront Colodny after all those years, and his half-cracked scheme to send out copies of the novelette, along with bogus extortion letters, in an effort to find out which of the Pulpeteers had been Colodny's accomplice in the plagiarism.

"*Did* he find out?" Dancer asked.

"I don't think so. Ramsey had to have realized right away what 'Hoodwink' was all about, and it must have scared him pretty good; his career is going great guns and something like this could hurt him if it went public."

"Which gave him a sweet motive for murder, no?"

"If he'd been inclined that way. That's how I figured it at first: whoever the plagiarist was was the murderer. It seemed to add up; I didn't consider that somebody else—Underwood—had got tossed by accident into the pot that was brewing. I doubt if Ramsey knows to this minute that Meeker was the true author of 'Hoodwink.' Or if Meeker learned that Ramsey was the unwitting plagiarist. The circumstances forced Ramsey to keep his mouth shut and bluff it out; there was no confrontation between them."

"How did Underwood get tossed into the pot?" Eberhardt asked.

"I'm coming to that. There are a couple of other things that need explaining first. The thirty-eight that killed Colodny, for one. Cybil Wade's gun. But it was stolen from her last Thursday night, while she was at the cocktail party."

"By whom?"

"By Colodny. He was the man I surprised in the Wades' room. He wanted the gun to threaten Meeker with; it was the only weapon he could have gotten on short notice. Maybe he even intended to kill Meeker with it—we'll never know."

Dancer said, "How did he know Cybil had the gun?"

"He knew because she'd threatened *him* with it. He made a pass at her, swatted her around when she refused, and she pulled the gun."

Dancer smiled sardonically. "I didn't think the old son of a bitch still had it in him. Even for Sweeteyes."

"He had it in him, all right. But he was running scared at the same time. He hadn't expected to find Meeker at the convention—that was the only reason he'd consented to come in the first place, because Meeker wasn't supposed to be there—and meeting him face to face had to have been a shock. Particularly when Meeker confronted him about the plagiarism, which is what must have happened; Meeker was having a high old time playing catalyst, shaking up the entire group—taking his own warped kind of revenge—and Colodny was his primary target. That had to be what caused the flare-up between the two of them at the cocktail party: Meeker goading Colodny, maybe trying to force a public confession."

"Is that what Meeker was after?" Eberhardt asked. "A public confession?"

"I'd say so. Maybe he wanted money, too, reparation, but after thirty years he wasn't likely to get it. He had to know that, screw loose or not. I doubt if he was really a blackmailer or an extortionist. The poor bastard's primary motive all along had to be revenge."

"Okay, go on."

"So Colodny got desperate after the cocktail-party incident; he went to the Wades' room, jimmied the lock, and swiped the gun. The fact that I caught him at it, almost ran him down, must have shaken him up even more: he couldn't be sure whether or not I'd seen him and could identify him. He decided to lay low, not go after Meeker right away—wait until he saw how things went down. He probably hid the gun somewhere, to be on the safe side. That way, if I had seen him and did identify him, he could bluff it out."

"So did he go after Meeker?"

"Yes, but not until Saturday. He found out on Friday that I hadn't got a clear look at him in the Wades' room, but there were other things going on then. You throwing your weight around in the bar, Russ, that was one."

"I was sure he'd put that second extortion note in my pocket," Dancer said. "Who did if he didn't? Meeker?"

"Meeker. He could have done it any time that morning; the shape you were in, you wouldn't have noticed. I think you were one of his top suspects for the plagiarist."

"Me?"

"That's why he kept palling around with you, feeding you drinks. He was setting you up, trying to get you to incriminate yourself."

"Jesus."

"He spent most of Friday with you, working on you, so he

must have left Colodny pretty much alone. And Colodny left him alone. But on Saturday it started again—Meeker goading him. That's what led to the shooting."

"Yeah, the locked-room trick. I've been going nuts trying to figure that out."

"It *wasn't* a locked-room trick," I said. "Which is why neither of us could figure it out. No gimmick, no illusion, nothing like that at all. Just a sort of freak accident, with you getting caught in the middle."

"Accident?"

"That's right—a juxtaposition of circumstances that combined to create a false impression."

"I don't get it. What juxtaposition?"

"Let me tell it chronologically," I said. "The first thing is that you came in drunk a few minutes before noon. You remember you told me you knocked on Meeker's door to see if he wanted to buy you a drink?"

"I remember."

"But there was no answer: he wasn't in. So you went down to your room, and after that everything is a blank in your memory. What you figure you did was to go straight in and collapse on the bed, but that isn't what you did at all."

"What did I do?"

"You bought yourself another drink."

"The bottle of rye that was on the couch? But I don't even remember it being in the room—"

"It wasn't in the room. You went and got it."

"Where?"

"Out of Meeker's room," I said. "He had plenty of liquor in there; you told me that yourself. You also told me that on Friday when I rang up your room, while you were in with Meeker having a drink, you'd heard the phone ring but you couldn't get through the door in time. You didn't mean the hall door, did you? You meant the connecting door."

"Ah Christ, that's right. The connecting door was unlocked; I remember Ozzie doing it."

"And he didn't relock it again. It was open on his side when you came into your room on Saturday. So you opened the connecting door, went into Meeker's room, got the bottle, took a drink or two when you came back, tossed the bottle on the couch, and *then* went in and passed out. You also did one other thing—the most important thing of all."

"What was that?"

"You left the connecting door open," I said. "Maybe not all the way open, but not latched either."

Eberhardt's expression altered slightly. He took the pipe out of his mouth and said, "I think I'm beginning to see it."

"Sure. After Dancer was back in his room, passed out, Meeker came into *his* room. He didn't notice that the connecting door was open, or maybe he did and didn't care. A little while after that Colodny showed up with the gun, either to threaten Meeker or to shoot him. They had an argument, they scuffled, and in the scuffle they bumped into the connecting door and went through it. They were actually struggling inside Dancer's room when the gun went off and Colodny, not Meeker, was shot."

"What happened with the gun?" Eberhardt said. "Did Meeker throw it down afterward?"

"Maybe. Or more likely it popped loose from his hand when it went off. Or from Colodny's hand—whoever had hold of it. It's easy enough to figure what happened next: Meeker, in surprise or fear or both, jumped back inside his own room. Colodny, on the other hand, was mortally wounded; but even somebody shot through the heart can live five or ten seconds afterward, that's a medical fact. So either he or Meeker threw the door shut—an instinctive reaction, born of fear. For that same reason, fear, Colodny managed to turn the bolt on Dancer's side, and Meeker did the same on *his* side of the door, double-locking it. The sound of the shot woke up Dancer; the other sounds he heard were the door shutting, the bolts being thrown, and Colodny falling to the floor. When Dancer staggered in from the bedroom, Colodny was already dead. He saw the body, picked up the gun. And that completed the false impression that confronted me when I let myself in a minute or so later."

"I'll buy it so far," Eberhardt said. Dancer didn't have anything to say; he just sat there looking relieved. "But now where does Underwood fit in?"

"He must have showed up at Meeker's room, for one reason or another—he was the convention chairman, remember—some time during the scuffle, probably just seconds before I got off the elevator. The hallway door must have been open or at least unlatched; he heard scuffling sounds, he went in just in time to see Colodny get shot and what happened afterward."

"And then what? Blackmail?"

"Either that, or Meeker offered him money to keep him quiet. Underwood needed money, evidently; he told me he was selling off part of his pulp collection, and no big-time collector like him would do that unless he was having financial problems. In any case Underwood became an accessory and the two of them beat it out of there the first chance they had—maybe right away, maybe later, while I was in talking to Dancer or after the security guy and the manager showed up. Meeker also figures to be the one who planted the typewriter—his own portable—in Colodny's room to make everyone think Colodny was the one behind the extortion."

Eberhardt nodded. "Now we come to why Underwood killed Meeker. And *how*."

"Well, I'm not sure on the why part," I said, "but I can make some guesses. Maybe he wanted more of a payoff than Meeker was willing to give. Or maybe Meeker had second thoughts about the killing and was making noises about confessing all, which would have put Underwood in the soup as an accessory. Or maybe it was another kind of greed: Meeker must have told him about 'Hoodwink' and the rest of it, including Colodny's big Hollywood score and the fact of an accomplice in the plagiarism, and it could be that Underwood had visions of a horde of money stashed down in

Arizona, or maybe of running his own blackmail scam against the surviving plagiarist."

"The locked-room business with the shed," Eberhardt said. "Was that just a freak accident too?"

"No, that was planned so that it would look like Meeker died accidentally. I think it must have been the way Colodny died that gave him the idea."

"Meaning?"

"It's the same solution in both cases, Eb," I said. "I realized that in the ghost town. When Underwood took his first shot at me I dove back inside the building, slammed the door, and barred it. See the parallel? It was the same sort of thing that happened when Colodny was shot."

"I don't see any parallel in the Meeker case."

"It's there. Colodny was mortally wounded when he locked the connecting door; in effect he was a dead man. And it was a dead man—Meeker—who locked the door of that shed."

"Oh, it was? Listen, I talked to the cops up there. Meeker's head was split open like a melon; the coroner says he died instantly. He didn't have time to run into the shed and lock the door after him."

"I don't mean it that way," I said. "I mean it literally: he was dead when he locked the door."

Dancer was sitting forward on the edge of his chair, squinting at me with rapt eyes through his cigarette smoke. Even the stenographer looked expectant. Eberhardt, though, just sat glaring at the front of my shirt—still avoiding my eyes. "Make some sense, will you? Spell it out."

"There was a length of fishing twine in the grass outside the shed," I said. "Underwood must have dropped it before he beat it out of there. I thought at first he'd used it to gimmick the key in the inside lock. You know, the old bit about running pieces of cord under the door and turning the key with slip knots. But one of the investigators up there, a guy named Loomis, told me that the shed key couldn't have been turned that way; it had to have been turned by hand. He was right on both counts: the fishing twine was used for something else and the key *was* turned by hand."

"Meeker's hand, I suppose?"

"Yes. Well, more precisely, Meeker's finger."

"His finger."

"Index finger, right hand. Loomis told me it was lacerated; that was what finally tipped me."

"Come on, don't keep drawing it out. What happened?"

"Meeker was lying in that shed with his head near the ax and the stepladder overturned. The assumption was supposed to be that he'd been standing on the ladder, lost his balance, and fallen down onto the ax. But he was killed somewhere else, with the ax, and then put into the shed. All right. What Underwood did was this: he set the stepladder close to the door, leaving just enough room to open the door so he could get out, and balanced Meeker's body over the ladder. Then he turned the key as far as he could without shooting the bolt—and wedged Meeker's finger through the hole in the key's top. All he had to do then was position the ax, loop the piece of cord around the leg of the ladder, run the cord ends out under the door, slip outside himself, shut the door, and then jerk the cord to jerk the ladder and make the body fall. Meeker's finger turned the key in the lock and slipped out of the hole as the body toppled; that's how the finger got lacerated. It might have been tricky to get all the elements—ladder, body, finger, key—balanced right in order to make it work; he might have had to do it more than once. But he had time. And he did do it."

Eberhardt gave it some thought. Then he shrugged and said, "It makes a screwy kind of sense, I suppose. Why did Underwood search Meeker's studio after he killed him?"

"Looking for money, probably. More or less the same reason he went down to Arizona to search Colodny's place. There are three reasons I should have tumbled to Underwood's involvement long before I saw him in Arizona with his rifle, and one of them has to do with those two searches. But I didn't tumble to any of them, not even the most obvious, until I went back over everything trying to fit Underwood in as the murderer."

"What was the thing about the searches?"

"In both Meeker's house and Colodny's place there were stacks of pulp magazines," I said. "And in both places the pulps were the only items that hadn't been scattered around or torn up. Who else but a pulp collector, somebody who understands what they're worth and reveres them, would spare a bunch of pulps when he's ransacking a room?"

"And the other two reasons?"

"One is a small slip he made when I talked to him on the phone on Tuesday. He must have just got back from Meeker's, and here I was, calling for Meeker's address so I could go up and see him; it had to have shaken Underwood a little and put him off his guard. He asked me if the reason I was going to see Meeker had anything to do with poor Colodny being shot through the heart. But how did he know Colodny had been shot through the heart? The newspapers didn't carry that information; all they said was that he'd died of a gunshot wound. And you or your men weren't likely to have mentioned a fact like that when you questioned him. The only other way he could have known was if he'd been there at the time of the shooting and *seen* where Colodny was shot.

"The third reason is the most obvious one. Meeker's alibi for the time of Colodny's death was that he was with Underwood, attending to his pulp art display. And Underwood must have corroborated that when you talked to him. But if Meeker was involved in the death of Colodny, as he obviously was, then Underwood had to be involved too; otherwise why would he lie on Meeker's behalf? I should have worked that out a hell of a lot sooner than I did. If I had, I might have saved myself some grief."

Eberhardt relit his pipe. "Is that it? Or have you got any other loose ends to tie off?"

"I think that's about it," I said. "After Underwood talked to me on Tuesday, he must have driven that Dodge of his straight down to Arizona. He got to Colodnyville before I did. but not by much. And that was another juxtaposition of events that almost ended in tragedy."

"Almost, yeah," Dancer said. "Christ, if he'd killed you down there, where would I be?"

"How about me?" I said. "Where would *I* be?"

Eberhardt made a couple of notes on a form sheet he drew over in front of him. Then he shooed the police stenographer out and said to me, "You pull some of the goddamnedest rabbits out of your hat. But okay, you got me convinced. I'll have the charges against Dancer dropped, and we'll see what we can do about building a case against Underwood."

He reached for the phone, punched out an inter-office number, and spoke to someone up in Detention. Dancer came out of his chair and headed straight for me. He got hold of my hand and levered it up and down as if it were a pump handle, breathing the odor of cigarettes and toothpaste into my face. "I'll never forget you for this," he said. "I mean that, never. You saved my life. I'll pay you back, just like I promised. And if I can ever do anything for you, anything at all—"

"How about letting go of my hand?"

"Oh . . . sure. Sorry. Listen, how soon do you think they'll let me out of here?"

"I don't know. Not long, I guess."

"I hope not. We've got some celebrating to do."

"What do you mean, celebrating?"

"What do you think I mean? Man, I'm going to tie one on tonight like you wouldn't believe!"

I sighed. He was never going to learn; never. And I was never going to get paid for my time on this rescue mission either, or reimbursed for expenses like gasoline, parking, air fare, car rental, and motel accommodations. Dancer may have been well-intentioned, but he was the kind who would always be living on the edge of poverty. Nobody was paying for my services except me.

No tengo dinero—goddammit to hell . . .

TWENTY-TWO

Kerry and I were sitting on the balcony of her apartment on Twin Peaks, sipping beer and looking out at a pretty spectacular view. The sun had just gone down—there had not been any fog today to blot it out—and the sky was still streaked in gold and red and dusky purple. There was a little wind, but it had not got cool enough yet to drive us inside. A nice night. A very nice night.

We hadn't said anything for a time, companionably. A three-quarter moon was starting to take on definition as night closed down; I had my eye on that, thinking moon thoughts, when she said, "You really believed it was my father? The killer, I mean?"

"Yeah," I said. "I really did."

"I ought to swat you one. Don't you know by now that the Wades are pure of heart and mind?"

"Sure," I said, and thought about Cybil's affair with Frank Colodny. "But a lot of circumstantial evidence pointed to him. You're not offended, are you?"

"Well, I ought to be."

I looked at her, but she wasn't serious. She looked terrific: coppery hair combed out fluffy, no lipstick—I don't like lipstick much—the last of the daylight highlighting her face, giving it a kind of delicate softness, making the chameleon eyes look black. She was wearing flare slacks, a peach-colored blouse, and a woolly vest that curved around her breasts. I liked that vest a lot; it made her look even more sensual than she was.

"I still can't get over it," she said.

"Over what?"

"Lloyd Underwood. Of all people!"

"Greed does funny things to people's heads," I said.

"I know. But I kept thinking it had to be one of the Pulpeteers. Not my father or Cybil, but one of the others."

"Me, too. That's the way it looked all along."

"I guess you were surprised when you saw Underwood in that ghost town."

"Not as much as I might have been in less tense circumstances."

Her face clouded abruptly and she was silent for a time.

I said, "What's the matter?"

"I was just thinking about him shooting at you—about you being locked up in that old building. God, he might have killed you."

"But he didn't."

"But he might have."

"Would it have bothered you much if he had?"

She gave me a look. "Don't ask dumb questions."

"Okay."

"You've almost been killed before, haven't you."

"A couple of times. No more than most public cops."

"I don't like that part of your job at all."

"Neither do I. But pulp private eyes get shot at all the time, and bashed on the head all the time too. I've only been shot at a couple of times and never bashed on the head." I paused. "And I've only been seduced once."

"Oh?"

"By you."

"Phooey," she said. "I'm going in to use the loo. Do you want another beer?"

"You bet."

She got up, wrinkled her nose at me, and went inside. I sat there and looked at the dark waters of the Bay, the lights of the city, the lopsided moon. And my mind was full of all sorts of things.

Eberhardt, for one. He was looking a little better, starting to cope with the breakup of his marriage, but I would have preferred it if he were less of an introvert. Like me, he tended to brood too much about things, and brooding never did you any good in the long run. Would Dana come back? It did not seem that way; it seemed she was gone for good. He'd live with it if she was. But he wouldn't be the same. I knew him well enough to understand that and to feel the sense of loss: he would not be the same man.

I had the Wades on my mind too. Cybil because of the way she had opened up to me, what she had told me about her past; Ivan because in his eyes I was nothing but a fat, scruffy private detective. I'd wanted to talk to both of them again—to tell Cybil I had found and destroyed the photograph without looking at it, and to see if I couldn't make peace with Ivan—but they had left for Los Angeles last night. Cybil had wanted to stay a while longer, Kerry said, but Ivan had book commitments. So off they went.

And of course I had Kerry on my mind. All over my mind, in fact. All of the thoughts were pleasant, but some of them—the same ones that had been there when I first started running around Arizona—were also unsettling. *Very* unsettling because they kept intruding and would not be pushed away

I told myself that you had to take time, lots of time, to weigh the pros and cons. On the one hand there was Eberhardt and Dana, Cybil and Colodny, infidelity and divorce; you could not overlook things like that, especially now, when they hit so close to home. But on the other hand there were other things like moonlight, perfume, woolly vests, warm hands, soft lips, a spicy sense of humor, compatibility, gentleness—togetherness. Two by two, wasn't that the way it was supposed to be on this earth? No man is an island, no man should live his life alone.

I'm fifty-three years old, I thought. I've been alone most of my life. What the hell do I want to think about togetherness for?

But the answer to that was obvious, even to a slow type

like me. It was that which made the world go round, the many-splendored thing, the thing that created babies and dreams and happiness—and lots of heartaches too. Fifty-three years old and in love again, in love for real. Well, if that wasn't the damnedest thing. If that wasn't the *silliest* damn thing for an old lone wolf.

Right, Mr. Marlowe?

You bet, Mr. Spade.

When Kerry came back, I had a funny feeling I was going to ask her to marry me. . . .